A *Good* White Woman

Michael Massey

PAGE PUBLISHING, INC.
Conneaut Lake, PA

First originally published by Page Publishing 2020

ISBN 978-1-6624-1014-7 (pbk)
ISBN 978-1-6624-1016-1 (hc)
ISBN 978-1-6624-1015-4 (digital)

Printed in the United States of America

THE SWORD

For those in the know, this beautiful stretch of hidden land was most valuable to their dolorous way of living. For others, this same secret valley was completely nonexistent, a myth only spoken about in drollery. Horseshoe Valley, as it was perceptually dubbed by a multitude of frequent visitors, was a covertly located hollowed cavity of fertile earth. Spaced seven acres around and, in most places, sank more than twelve feet below the surrounding land level, Horseshoe Valley's structural makeup left all in awe.

To its habitual guests, the indented vacancy was like a small piece of paradise—a place where they could let loose, relax their minds, and allow primal cultivated nature to shine free without fear of correction. Horseshoe Valley was resplendent, blanketed by an evenly ingrained carpet of soft green grass, which, for reasons then unknown, seemed to stay trimmed to the perfect length. Nearly weed-free, this plush grassy field was completely void of any naturally grown furniture, save the one tall would-be-great oak, which inhabited the exact center of the lot. This old oak tree appeared almost lifeless with only a niggard amount of multicolored leaves sprinkled about its branches.

The single thirty-plus-foot tree in the center of the valley was the one sore spot in an otherwise flawless setting. The unsightly wood was a vile creation. It was a cursed omen—undoubtedly one of the Lord's least revered plants. Monstrous, bloodthirsty, death inducer—all attributes were dully bestowed onto the single Horseshoe Valley tree. But for most, the murderous wood was simply deemed the Dead Man's Swing.

For many colored folks in and around the small state of Connecticut, Horseshoe Valley was an absolute last destination. The beautiful lot was no friend to the minority. In hushed jargon among the secret society of valley faithfuls, it was said that no colored person—black, red, yellow, or brown—had ever laid eyes on the seclusive field and lived to tell about it.

Since as far back as white men had been busying this part of the world, nonwhites had been brought to this field to die. Dead Man's Swing was puissant to the Caucasian race. Rumor had it that in one record-setting event, twenty-seven blacks swung the tree on a single evening. The branches were remembered to have resembled decorative ornaments on a December bush.

The location and drudge integrity of Horseshoe Valley was protected religiously by earnest keepers. There would be no paltry junctures occurring in their sacred park. Horseshoe Valley was a place exercised for one reason and one reason alone: the extermination of colored folks.

In the spirit of tradition, this day spore no exception. The moderate gathering inside the bowl-shaped sub-rosa park was tantamount to any other. The group of a little over twenty was about the customary assembly collected around such a prominent employment. Several men (grown twenty years and older) busied themselves firing heavy shotgun rounds into the hanging body that was strung up by its neck. This happened while others threw dry wood, fallen leaves, and handmade liquid-filled combustible objects into the fire set at the heels of the quickly kindling man.

With every cocktail tossed, the flames would roar with exaggerated vigor, exciting folks brought out to witness the sacrificial abbreviated purge. Eleven men, four women, and a number of mid-aged to suckling children loitered the infamous field, hooting and howling in celebration as the merciless firepit clawed and ripped at the lower region of the overly charred black corpse.

For this group of undesirables, the impromptu festival of flames was a complete and utter blissful orgy—a family concourse complete with food, drink, and live entertainment. The evening was a special one, the actual born day of one of the older kids in attendance. Jesse Longfelt, son of the organizer of the event, was turning nine; and his father, Rollen, wanted to do something extra special for his eldest boy. This human barbecue was the benefaction.

It never took much to provoke such a get-together. Every thirty days or so, one of the valley's secret societal groups would make sure to find some unlucky colored fellow to string up for one reason or another. The crime in which to merit such an outcome varied. The misfortunate individual dangling this evening was charged with recklessly peering after the wrong white woman.

Picnic baskets, feathered pillows, and an assortment or redneck china were spread over colorful sheets; as men, women, and children enjoyed the fireworks exhibit. For most in attendance, this roasting was nothing unfamiliar. Still, for some of the less experienced, the imagery was a difficult bit to digest.

As the liquor poured freely, the said adults tossed to their elitist heritage and natural-born right to rule. Sizable cups of quickly vanishing hooch emptied and just as fast were refilled. Happily they drank and partied in defiance of the new union-constituted laws.

Blissful laughter and raunchy cheer filled the night as the once-vibrant young black stud, now a blistering fire-crisp dead body, smelled a half-mile out. The human remains cooked with a fragrance that resembled nothing remotely appetizing.

How could they stand it? a masked stranger standing beneath an oversize black hood questioned of the devil-spun swarm as he watched the horrific proceeding from atop the twelve-foot bank.

CHAPTER 1

This was her first time formally on the job working beyond the confines of Thelma's Motel and Bar. Courageously challenged, Darla, the longtime veteran harlot, didn't trust the ideal of being alone with strange men in secluded locations unfamiliar to her. Women in this young lady's profession were exposed to all sorts of potential dangers. In the absence of a stable environment, there was always the risk of some sort of abuse, the apex being unsustainable.

For today's outing, Darla Arlington was making an exception to her normally steadfast position. This evening, she was on her way to make her first home visit in nearly forever. Fortunately, the gentleman purchasing her time and effort was a preferred customer of hers.

Over the past year or so, affluent young Mr. Michael Townsman's presence at Thelma's had become constant. Always a willing spender, the man had energetically sampled all the white women in the noteworthy whorehouse and most of the black ones as well. Throughout his illustrious tenure, Darla had dealt with him maybe ten times; and to her recollection, he gave her not the slightest indication that he was anything less than sterling.

An entire weekend of her services was required for this assignment. As for compensation, she was poised to receive thirty dollars.

Thirty dollars in the state of Georgia at that moment in time was an excessive amount of money for a romp in the sack. Darla knew she was good, but thirty dollars' worth of good was pushing it. Darla couldn't turn down such an offer.

Darla was a semi-slim yet sturdily framed working girl who took great pride in her ability to please. At five foot six and 110 lb., she was considered an average-sized whore. What set her negatively apart from the other girls was her not-so-average frontal cushioning.

When fully clothed, Darla could usually hide her less-than-relished deformity; but once the towel fell, the handsomely chiseled blonde's upper body was a glaring deterrent. Her protruding candy-red nipples sat motionlessly atop little more than a finger pinch of soft breast meat. For occupational reasons, concealing this embarrassing flaw was essential. Nonetheless, Darla was not without her own set of tangibles. This being her plenty alluring but usually less desired wide hips and generously proportioned derriere. This was not the build of a prototypical brothel gal. Big boobs ruled the arena, and Darla's lack thereof put her at a distinct disadvantage. As a result, her sexual services were frequently passed over by the motel's male patrons.

Most of the other women working at Thelma's would accentuate their ample busts by wearing tops that pushed their breasts together, causing the fleshly advertisement to leak out over their blouses. Darla envied this quality in her felicitous colleagues.

Self-conscious about her unfairly deprived upper body, Darla homed in on her ability to please. She needed to be wilder and nastier than her competition. She wanted to outperform every whore in the building to offset her lack of frontal showmanship. Two men at once, swallowing, and even anal access were on the table.

Darla always tried to keep her hygiene superb, and she was certainly worth a second glance. But by competitive standards, she wasn't overly attractive. For this reason, she was surprised when Michael offered her the job.

The previous days leading up to her decision to accompany him to his home had been very uneventful. In the last forty-eight hours, she had only managed to wrangle up two paying customers.

Darla had been seeing too many days of shortcomings as of late. The motel's Madam Thelma warned her on three separate occasions to start producing or else.

Thelma's Motel was the most popular motel in town. Darla could hardly afford to be thrown out of such an exclusive establishment. Michael Townsman's offer came right on time. The rich, well-dressed young Yankee-bred patron had given Darla fifteen dollars up front; ten of which she immediately gave to Thelma. She would receive the last fifteen upon the completion of her two-day obligation.

The wagon ride from Thelma's to the Townsman Plantation took only a little over two hours, but it took another nearly thirty minutes to get from the property entrance to the main house. The grounds within the plantation were a delight to the young woman's eyes. At 6:00 p.m., the sun was still shining brightly over the open green plane. The big area was cleverly divided by perfectly trimmed bushes that looked to be strategically placed.

As they neared, amazingly the grounds around the gigantic house got even nicer. There were livestock fields divided by painted wooden fences. There were large vegetable gardens and beds of flowers, and running along in a pattern were a variety of fruit trees. The place was a paradise. Even the slaves working the grounds seemed to appreciate the ambience.

The seemingly upbeat blacks were sprinkled throughout the landscape. Some were working in groups; others were tending to individual assignments. *What a lovely place to reside if one had to be cursed with the task of being a slave*, Darla reasoned.

As their carriage pulled up the road, a group of small black children—all running shirtless through the beefy brush—began to angle into their path. Darla grabbed a tight hold of Michael's arm as the young field children approached.

"Eh!" Michael yelled, halting their progress. The tallest of the five smiled a wide rotten-toothed grin before grabbing a rough handful of shoulder, calming one of his associates. The children waved their small hands as the carriage passed. Then they were off once again, galloping barefooted through the leveled brush.

Giving the reins a good snap to speed up their progress, Michael looked down at Darla, who was still securely snuggled beneath his arm, and whispered, "Niggers—too much damn energy." With manufactured concern in her teasing eyes, Darla nodded.

The main house was huge—biggest home Darla ever saw. The place was all white with cream trimming, and it had large bay windows and a full porch that wrapped halfway around the side of the house. A large flower garden was planted right outside the home. The colors of the flowers were also cream and white, matching the windowsills and porch.

The two-horse wagon pulled to a stop in front of an old very dark-skinned slave, who was dressed in a surprisingly clean light-gray suit. The old slave put out a hand in an attempt to offer Darla assistance out the wagon. Startled, Darla pulled back. A Southern belle at heart, she wasn't accustomed to being in such close proximity to so-dark-a-male slave. Michael caught her apprehension and hopped out the carriage to help her down.

In the South, male slaves and white women seldom ever made physical contact. Michael's parents were a lot less sensitive to this constrictive custom. Marcus, their stableman, would often help Mrs. Townsman out the carriage with no thought of it being inappropriate. The slaves on the Townsman Plantation were more or less treated as round-the-clock help. The more they worked, the more freedom they were awarded.

Michael held Darla's hand as he guided her up the steps to the porch. When they reached the landing, the front door swung open. With a bright smile, Meissa, a light-brown slave girl dressed in a lime-green sundress, held the door for the couple.

"Good evening, Master Michael sir," Meissa greeted Michael with a curtsy. In the same motion, she gave Darla a respectful nod. "Ma'am."

The young Negro woman's plump chest meat hung out over her well-worn top, teasing Darla psychologically as she passed. The dress Meissa was wearing was very well-threaded, and the fabric looked expensive, too expensive for a slave girl. Darla instantly took a dislike to Meissa. The dress she had on looked better than the one Darla was wearing, and for the occasion, Darla was wearing her best.

"Meissa," Michael began addressing the young woman in green, "put on a pot of tea and tell your mother to get dinner ready."

"Yes, sir Master sir," Meissa answered enthusiastically. "Right away, sir." She scurried away.

CHAPTER 2

Darla's visual perception was on high alert as she was led through the large home. Everything looked so expensive and well-placed that she made a concerted effort to take small steps in order to avoid bumping into something she could ill afford to replace.

Their winding voyage through the house ended with them in a dining room area still on the first floor. The room was brightly decorated, culminated by a light-brown eight-seat dining table that had custom-designed carvings trimmed into the wood. Overly manicured, the table's artwork was preserved beneath a thick sheet of clear glass. The six-sided high-ceiling dining room was surrounded by a number of well-crafted white vases that sat in the corners of the wall, like romantic gargoyles. Each of these containers was cratering fistfuls of a variety of sweet-smelling flowers that provided the room with a wondrous fragrance. This faint but pronounced aroma put Darla in a good mental space. Her comfort level was right where it needed to be on this, her first business trip.

Michael sat her down at the opposite end of the table. "Are you hungry, miss?" he asked with a noticeable tenderness in his voice. He was being really polite and gentle. Darla was taken aback. She wasn't used to being treated with such consideration. She was a whore. This was supposed to be a hard couple of days of intense sex, sore throats, and some definite rear-end activity. This was what she had been expecting. This was what she had been paid for. But as the evening wore on, the experience began to feel more and more like a first date. Darla had never been on a formal date. She hadn't had much experience being treated like a lady. For as long as she could remember, she was considered to be nothing more than a physical release.

Darla was shoved into the business of whoring the year her mother died, when her father started making drunken visits into her bedroom. Too young to fight him off and too naive to try, Darla was forced to learn how to ease his aggressions with her body. It didn't take long for her old man to start inviting his friends over to join him. After a while, her room became a way for him to make a few extra drinking dollars.

When her father disappeared a little after her fifteenth birthday, her childhood home was repossessed by the bank. Beyond the cutoff age for an orphanage, Darla was left hungry and homeless, lost to the cruel world. With no tangible skills other than the obvious, she began drifting from man to man in order to keep herself fed.

One bright spring day, her fortune was changed when she wandered into the right motel. Now at the mature age of twenty-two, Darla was a certified lifer. Eating, sleeping, and fucking were her world.

Michael's politeness was unusual to her. She liked it. Her undergarments began to moist as she thought of the extra attention she would give him for his courtesy. Darla smiled over her teacup at the thought.

Michael caught her fleeting eye. "Miss?" he inquired.

Darla shook her head. "Nothing. It's just…this is nice. Thank you."

"The pleasure is all mine. I'm going to try and make this weekend as comfortable and as pleasurable for you as possible."

"Well, when you're ready, I'm going to try my damnedest to do the same for you." The message behind her words was confirmed by the seductive look in her eyes.

Smothered baked chicken, mashed potatoes, sweet peas, corn on the cob, fluffy buttered bread, and thick mushroom gravy were enjoyed by the couple. A large bottle of white wine was served as a thirst quencher. The two finished the entire bottle before cracking open another. Successfully inebriated, Darla was more than ready to fulfill her end of the bargain and flushed with anticipation. Michael was ready to let her.

His parents were out of town this weekend, and his brother, Blake, was back at the other house almost five hundred yards away entertaining guests of his own. So besides the presence of the indoor slaves, Michael had the entire place to himself.

CHAPTER 3

Taking the party upstairs, Michael's bedroom was just as Darla expected—brightly colored with a pleasant fragrance that had her pulling out of her clothing several steps into the door. Walking over to the bed, she hopped out of her shoes and seductively shook off her dress.

Without looking back, Darla then wiggled free of her underwear bottoms. Climbing onto the bed, she was wearing only a thin slip, which was so short Michael could see the parted promise she had cradled between her thighs. When she finally did look back, her counterpart was already birthday-suit clean. His urgency amused her.

Michael's eyes were lust-filled as he glided over and pushed her onto her back, covering her petite body with his own. Darla was so turned on and wet; her insides spoke as she came only two minutes into the experience. Fighting for control, Darla finessed Michael onto his back and climbed aboard his loaded weapon. This pistol was going to empty in dramatic fashion; this she would make certain of.

Vigorously Darla began working her hips with an intensity that caught the young man off guard. She was determined to pay back his favor with her intense and oftentimes breathless work ethic. She bounced all over him, shifting speeds at random. From cowgirl to reverse cowgirl, Darla creatively altered, each time stopping briefly to take him in her mouth.

They were at least a half-hour in when Michael, who at this point had been pumping into her from behind, grabbed both her ankles. From their many encounters at Thelma's, Darla knew this was one of the ways he liked to get off. Locking her fingers in the sheets, she drove her ample rear backward, matching his aggression with her own. His deep-penetrating thrust left little possibility of an alternative motive.

Darla felt a profound shift in his situation a split second before he pulled back to release his seed all over her exposed bottom. She let her torso fall to the bed as she felt the warm gel cover her backside. Michael's orgasm was strong. Darla felt like half a cup of warm milk had been poured onto her back by the finish. Michael wiped the tip of his penis on Darla's behind before climbing off the bed.

"Is there somewhere I can clean up?" she asked while looking up at Michael then back at the mess he had left on her.

Pulling on his undershorts, he nodded toward the door to her right. Michael left the room wearing only his bottoms.

Darla lay on her stomach for a while before she went to clean herself in the washroom. There was a large metal barrel that sat over a small fireplace on the wall. Not many homes had hot water in their young town. Darla was impressed. *What a nice home.* For a brief moment, Darla fantasized about how different her life would be if she lived the life of a woman Michael would have considered for a wife. Feeling the itch of the dried semen left on her rear curbed that thinking. She was a boy toy and would remain so until she was too old to be considered such.

Not bothering to try and get the fireplace working, she used a cloth rinsed in room-temperature water to clean herself. She was wrapped in a towel when she heard a light tap on the door.

"Excuse me, ma'am. Would you like me to help you warm the water?"

"No!" Darla barked across the door at Meissa, the pretty, big-breasted young woman whom she met at the front door. "I'll manage. Thank you."

Darla stood silently until she heard the woman's departure. When the outer door shut, Darla stuck her head out from behind her wooden screen. There was a thinly woven yellow gown hanging over the armrest of the chair by the bed. A pair of house shoes was by the foot. Darla dressed without bothering to put back on her undergarments; she was planning to come out of everything again at any moment.

Lying across the silky-soft comforter staring out the large oval window off into the night, she waited patiently for Michael to return. It had been the better part of an hour before she pushed off the bed and went to the door. *What type of host leaves his guest alone for so long? Even a guest whore deserves better*, Darla mentally griped.

Pulling the door open, she peeked out into the hall before stepping forward. The hallway was dark, with only a few oil lamps to light her path. Half-naked, Darla pushed past three closed doors on her way to the staircase she had come up earlier. By the last door to her right, she heard a familiar chorus of squeals. The sound of a woman navigating her way through a mixer of pleasure and pain stalled her campaign.

The door was a quarter of the way open, and the dimly lit light within spilled out into the corridor, where Darla stood muddled. Drawn nearer by curiosity, she took two measured steps toward the light. Nosy, she had to take a peek. *Surely the slaves aren't permitted to engage in such lurid behavior inside the house.* Looking into the room, Darla's hands flew up to her mouth. She couldn't be seeing what she was seeing. If her observation proved true, Michael was lying on a thick carpet at the foot of the bed stark naked being ridden by Meissa—and ridden well. The image was appalling, but this wasn't the height of her disgust. On the large king-size bed above them was a black guy lying between two dark legs of a black woman, while another woman was lying on the bed next to them waiting for her turn or recovering thus from, and this woman…this woman was white. The image was unreal. Both the women on the bed were a bit overweight with large flopping breasts that danced in the candlelit glare.

Oh my God! Darla wordlessly cursed as the black man pulled out of the black woman. Between his legs, he was wielding the biggest, thickest, and blackest penis she had ever seen. The unbending object sticking out of his pelvis cut through the air and was then swung around to the heavyset white woman. Darla gritted her teeth as it plowed down into her. *My!* Darla silently gasped. She could practically feel the pressure in her own stomach.

Darla had seen enough. Turning to leave, she mistakenly bumped into the small desk table sitting by the door, knocking down a vase full of flowers. The vase hit the hardwood floor loudly and broke into a thousand pieces.

"Shit," Darla cried, looking back and forth between the open door and the smashed glass on the floor. Michael came out of the room first, followed shortly by the tall brown-skinned fellow. Both the men were totally naked and still fully erect. Darla was in shock as she stared wide-eyed down at the massive tree branch sticking out from between the black stud's legs.

Michael followed her line of sight and gave a light chuckle. "Um, this is Blake. Blake, Darla," Michael introduced.

"Hi," Blake greeted her with a smug grin, aware of the attention being paid to his unmentionables.

Darla gave a quick glance up at his face then turned back to his lower region. Still she said nothing.

"If you don't go put that away. You're scaring her," Michael insisted, playfully pushing Blake back into the doorway.

Darla was confused, embarrassed, and horrified as she stared blankly into Michael's face.

"Sorry about that," Michael said before looking back into the room. "Can you come clean this up, please?" he called to Meissa, who was just stepping into her shoes.

Darla looked down at the shattered vase. Snapping to, she took a step back and stuttered an apology, "Oh, I...um...s-sorry." Then with a gloss forming in her eyes, she turned and trotted back to the room from which she came.

Her face was full of tears when she reached the bedroom where she had worked her best stuff. Apparently that wasn't enough, being that Michael was just within the confines of another woman.

Entering with his hands raised above his head, Michael began, "Let me again say how sorry I am that you had to see that. I guess—"

Darla cut him off mid-explanation, "She...she...he...he was black."

"Yeah, Blake is definitely black. A big black pain in the ass."

"He...he was having sex with a white woman."

"Yeah, Beth. Well, she likes them big. Don't worry," Michael said, holding up a reassuring hand, "he's never going to touch you with that thing."

Darla was insulted, her sad eyes instantly switching to angry beads. "I would never. Okay, I would now like to leave your home."

"Darla."

"Now, Michael, please. I want you to take me home."

Michael turned his face to the ground as he contemplated his next words carefully. If Blake hadn't come over with his two sex-crazed women friends, he wouldn't be going through this messy conversation. Calmly he walked over and took a seat on the bed. Darla moved away from him and folded her arms across her chest. She had shifted all her weight to one side, poking her hip out while trying her best attempt to keep a determined look on her face.

Michael was butterball naked. He began, "Darla, Blake is my brother."

"He's black."

"Yes, but he's my father's son."

"He's a slave."

"No!" Michael snapped with more anger than he intended. "He's not a slave. He's a free man. He's a free black man, and he's my brother. And in this house, you will treat him accordingly. And you're not leaving until Monday evening, just as you agreed."

"Michael—"

"If you want, you can get dressed, return my money, and try your luck making it back to town on foot. But I'm not taking you anywhere until Monday."

Darla was at a loss for words. She just stared down at him for a long brief moment. Then doing what came natural to her, in one smooth motion, she pulled her gown over her head. Succumbing, she said, "Fine, but you…you…go wash that slave's stink off you."

Michael smiled graciously and stood to go do as the high-handed woman mandated.

CHAPTER 4

The next morning was met by a hefty smell—the delicious aroma of a freshly prepared breakfast. Drinking it in, Darla was anxiously anticipating the introduction between her mouth and what was permeating from somewhere in the house. Darla kept Michael up half the night trying to make sure to satisfy his complete sexual appetite. A nice breakfast would be well-received in counteracting her fatigue.

Michael's actions that previous night were mortifying to Darla's sexual self-esteem. As a result, she made sure to go all out. She left little on the table—front, back, mouth then mouth, back, front. There was no way she was letting him return to the bed of a slave, not while she was brought to the house for that very reason. The morning meal was soul-touching. Darla was in heaven, and she made no attempt to eat like a lady. She and Michael were midway through the meal when Blake walked into the room followed by the well-cushioned white woman and her equally plump black female companion. Darla gave all three of them an evil look but said nothing as she turned back down to finish her meal.

"Good morning," Blake opened, giving Darla a polite smile. The pretty blonde just nodded. He was exuding an infectious confidence. "These are Beth and Julia," Blake continued, introducing his female friends.

"How do you do?" Darla said, standing to her feet and extending a hand to Beth. Julia, the black woman, reading the temperature of the moment, chose not to offer her hand.

Three more plates were set at the table, and though already full, Darla stayed seated out of curiosity. Blacks and whites eating at the same table was forbidden in her rendering. Still, knowing it was wrong, she had to see how it would play out.

Folding a napkin over his lap, Blake looked over at Michael, who was sitting across from him. "You going out this morning?"

"No, I and Darla are going to stay in and get more acquainted."

"You get that pool drained yet?"

"Yeah, that reminds me. I have to go in the shack and make a new handle for the crank on the well. Brownie said that ever since you and Meissa were—"

"No, no, no, don't you try and blame that on me," Blake cut him off. Michael laughed.

"No, finish. What were they caught doing at the well?" Beth inquired.

"No. You better not," Blake warned.

"Oh," Michael started, "he didn't tell you?"

"No," Blake fired back, picking up a saltshaker. "I'll bang you in the eye with this."

Michael put up a defensive arm. "All right, all right." He laughed.

"No," Beth said, grabbing Blake's arm. "What happened?" she demanded as she tried to wrestle the saltshaker free of Blake's outreached arm.

The scene was foreign to Darla. At this table, in this house, on this plantation, it was like race rules didn't apply. The place was like something out of a bad joke, but in a way, she was kind of amused. The love being shown around her had a gravitational pull that sucked her right in.

The breakfast party ran over long. At the end, everyone—including Darla—was talking to one another as if old friends. Beth and Julia were comical to her. They were from the Northeast, and it showed in their mannerism. Formally, Julia was Beth's slave, but they behaved and carried on as if they were just a couple of girlfriends who were simply having fun with a couple young men. Darla couldn't help but get pulled into the friendly atmosphere of the moment.

The air around the room was befittingly pleasant; that was until the acquisition of Meissa muddied the equation. Cute as a button, the pretty light-skinned young woman walked into the room wearing a beautiful white ruffled dress, which Darla thought had to cost more than most of her wardrobe combined.

With the exception of Darla, everyone at the table greeted Meissa enthusiastically. To her, Meissa was a dick-stealing, overprivileged half-breed black slave shit who was being uncharacteristically pampered.

Contempt soiled the vibe in the room. Noticed by all was the animosity held by Darla toward Meissa. This conflict unnerved Michael most of all. He was sitting right next to Darla as she stared a hole in the side of Meissa's face.

"Meissa," Michael began, "we were just finishing up. Could you be a dear and clean off the table, please?" He then leaned over and kissed Darla on the cheek.

Darla's exterior brightened right up. She was glad that the sex-stealing slave girl was being forced to work while everyone else was having a good time. Watching after the girl, Darla noticed that Meissa's waist and ass were almost exactly shaped as hers was. Still, Meissa had a set of breasts that brought most men to their knees. Darla rationalized, however, that Meissa was black with thick curly hair. This made her raunchy accessibles less than adequate.

The slave whores were indeed popular at Thelma's, but Darla knew that was because they were cheap. For the most part, if a white man had his choice and enough money, he would choose a white woman over a black one ten times out of ten. This line of thinking was brought into question last night when Michael left to be with Meissa.

Snapping to, Darla looked over at Julia whom she had begun speaking to as an equal. Julia and Beth were going out to fly kites and were now asking if she would like to join them. Darla had never actually flown a kite. She had seen it done as a child, but never had she participated in the process herself. Looking over at Michael, her eyes asked if it was okay.

"Go ahead. Have fun. I'll be out there in a few. Meissa, go and tell Brownie to get four kites out the shed."

It took Darla five tries before she was able to get her airborne toy to the sky. She hadn't run in quite some time, so gathering the proper momentum it took to lift the kite was a chore. Once she had it stable in the air, her heart thumped with the joy she hadn't enjoyed as a kid. The adolescent freedom stolen from her by her monstrous father was now glaring in her big blue eyes.

In the midst of having so much fun, Darla lost track of Meissa, who had been out with the other two women in the open field. Looking around, Darla stopped to search the area for Michael, who apparently hadn't come out to join them. An urgent chill ripped up Darla's spine. Letting go of the kite's string, Darla began to walk back toward the house with a terrible thought on her mind. Slowly her pace began to quicken until she was running full-on toward the house.

In through the front door and up the stairs, she burst into the room where the interracial orgy had taken place—empty. Backing out of the room, she slowly, as if walking the plank, pushed down the hall toward the bedroom she shared with Michael that previous night. *He wouldn't*, she thought. Not in the room where she gave him her beautiful white insides. Not in the bed where she lent him her precious white mouth. He couldn't think to have that slave in the same space where she had let him part her beautiful, tight white booty for an uncomfortable twenty minutes or so.

When she made it to the bedroom door, Darla paused. Trembling with negative anticipation, she placed her hand on the door handle. Stopping briefly to catch her fleeting breath, she put her ear to the door. Darla could hear the wailing of the young woman's pleasure-filled groans as the bed creaked in the background. Darla pushed the door open forcefully and saw what she hoped she would not. Meissa was on all fours in front of Michael, who had worked up a substantial lather. With the outrage from yesterday's imagery heightened, the tears returned in multiplicity to Darla's reddening face as she stood in the doorway.

"Darla!" Michael gasped as he pulled out of Meissa. The petite black woman was embarrassed. Quickly she rolled her naked body from the side of the bed and grabbed her clothes off the floor. Her eyes were apologetic when she looked into Darla's sad face.

"How could you?" Darla began. "Why would you when you brought me here?"

"Darla, please," Michael appealed, beginning to aggravate with the presumptuous whore's perceived relevance.

"No, Michael. If you are going to be with her, then bring me home."

"Darla."

"Now, Michael. I want to leave!"

"Come in and close the door."

"No."

"Now!" Michael said with a forcefulness that caught Darla off guard. Darla, all too familiar with being at the mercy of an angry man, was frozen with fear.

"Did you hear me?" Michael questioned with heavy accusation in his tone.

Sliding off the bed, he stood his full six-foot-three frame as he glared menacingly down at Darla. His eyes were dangerous, and his demeanor said he meant business.

Taking tempered steps, Darla made her way into the large room, pulling the door shut behind her. Not exactly scared but cautious, she stood with her back to the wall far away from the hard-faced bedroom commander. At this time, Meissa was fully dressed, holding her black hard-bottom shoes in her hand.

"What are you doing?" Michael scolded her. "Did I tell you to get dressed?"

"No, Master sir, I—"

"Take your fucking clothes off and come get on your knees."

Meissa's face held a joyless void as she dragged the straps of her dress down her arms. Looking back and forth between Darla and the floor, she stripped down.

Michael was standing by the foot of the bed when Meissa came over and dropped to her knees in front of him. She had a cloth in her hand, which she used to wipe the remnants of her rectum juices off his penis. Darla looked on quietly as the pretty black girl began to steadily massage him between her soft lips.

"Come here," Michael called to Darla. "Sit on the bed and watch."

With hesitation in her steps, Darla did as she was told. Meissa had her eyes straight ahead as she kept a steady rhythm on Michael's penis.

"Stop this nonsense and get going," Michael instructed the woman at his pelvis.

Meissa adjusted her position and started to suck Michael in hard and deep.

"Faster," he insisted. Meissa proceeded to work him in and out with an expertise that made Michael brace his legs against the foot of the bed. Strong and deep, Meissa's practiced jaws labored. Then speeding up, she began hitting the back of her throat only every third stroke. Michael had his hand on her shoulder, not restricting or adjusting but politely urging her on.

After a few minutes, he pulled away. "Damn," Michael said before looking back at Darla with a you-see-what-I-mean look on his face. Darla could now sympathize. Meissa had handled him better than she ever saw it done. Darla began looking at Meissa's face as if she was witnessing the birth of a child. Darla was intrigued, jealous, and surprised all at once. She wanted to say something to her but knew not what to say.

Taking a seat beside Darla, Michael pulled Meissa onto his lap. She climbed on to his seated position with her legs on top of his forearms and locked her feet behind him. Michael had her ass clasped securely between his two hands. Meissa began riding him slowly, her titties dragging against his chest. Then she quickened her pace, allowing her chest to jump around like elegant beanbags. Relentlessly she bucked and bounced.

Darla figured she must had interrupted a very intense sexual moment when she burst in because after only a minute or two, Meissa began to sound, "Oh. Oh. Master sir, oh, it—it's coming. You—oh." Meissa sighed. "You feel it?" the young slave asked in a seductive tongue.

The way Meissa's body jerked, Darla knew that, that was an orgasm that had been building for a while. Meissa's pace dragged as she ground through the piercing feeling, which seemed to last longer than usual.

Darla's lower region was dripping from the erotic showing. Before she was even aware, she had begun undressing; her hands were pulling off her final piece of clothing. Michael smiled as Darla ushered Meissa off him. His privates were slimy with Meissa's inner succulence. Darla grabbed his penis and slid her hand up the length of it. She then wiped her wet palm on the bedspread. Curious, she licked the remaining liquid off her hand. Darla did this a lot when she was with a client who paid for two girls, but she never tasted a black girl's insides. But this wasn't a regular job she was on. She was beginning to understand why Michael had chosen her. There wasn't too much Darla would complain about when it came to the art of nasty, and this set her apart from most. Mentally adjusting, this weekend would get downright disgusting between her and his favorite slave.

Smiling a full spread, Darla climbed on to Michael just as Meissa had. Enviously driven, the blonde seven-year vet wanted to eclipse the feeling that the black girl had given him. This was a competition for her. Michael had intentionally set the two women at sexual odds. Anything the slave could do, she could do ten times as well. *Or at least I could learn to*, Darla reasoned.

CHAPTER 5

By the end of the intense sex-off, the three of them were spent. Darla had a newfound respect for Meissa. Her three holes were worn rare, and Meissa had taken more of a pounding than she had, so she knew the woman was just as sore. Michael had stamina; she had to give him that. The man was a professional hammer. Darla was sure if the shoe were on the other foot, there would be women lining around the barn to purchase his services.

Meissa was lying on the bed to his right, moving her hand up and down his chest, as Darla occupied his left flank, his penis being kept warm in her active hands.

"The reason I asked you here," Michael began, looking into Darla's eyes, "is I like the way you fuck. Not only that but you also have a strong motivational aggression that I admire in a whore. You never complain no matter how hard I push you, and your threshold for pain is impressive."

Darla was quiet as he spoke, her eyes locked intently on his. She loved to hear her sexual praises. Michael continued, "I am opening my own brothel, and I want you to head up my white whores, and Meissa here will head up the blacks."

This news hit Darla with mixed emotions. While what he proposed was a great honor in itself, in the back of her mind, she was hoping he was working up momentum to ask her to be his wife or at least his live-in recreation.

"Um, why me?" Darla hesitantly asked as she sat up.

"Well, you... I like you. And I am going to need someone to train my girls to fuck at a really high level. I want my brothel to set a new precedent. Besides, you look to me like you weren't too happy with your present position at Thelma's."

"Why her?" Darla said, gesturing over at Meissa, who immediately rolled her eyes to the ceiling.

"You know why," Michael answered matter-of-factly. "You saw how good she is. You stuck your fingers inside her. When it comes to sex, she is by far the best." This made Darla frown. "But you are good too," Michael corrected. "You just need a little practice using your mouth."

Darla gave an acknowledging shrug. She had no argument there. Meissa was certainly better orally. The way she had Michael on edge was like nothing she had ever seen before, and she thought she had seen it all. Meissa had an extra door built in the back of her throat. Darla mentally saluted her. The girl's oral tolerance was incredible.

Michael got up from between the two and scooted off the bed. All eyes were lazily trained on him as he walked into the washroom. Darla could smell the furnace burning in the room as he warmed the water.

"Tell me when the water gets ready," he told Meissa before walking out the room barefoot and shirtless.

When Meissa went to sit forward, Darla stopped her. The black girl was startled stiff. Looking into Darla's face, she felt her legs being spread. Darla stuck two fingers into the young woman's slit. She was tighter than most women she knew.

"How do you get it all the way down your throat without gagging?" Darla inquired.

CHAPTER 6

On Monday evening, a midsize white cloth-covered double-horse-led wagon carried Michael and Darla into town. Darla, now open-minded, saw the world differently. It wasn't as black and white as she had previously thought. This past weekend had served as a sobering experience for her—a hard-flung educational gut punch.

Darla was through with Thelma's; she was all in with the concept of becoming the town's new leading madam.

Everything had changed for her. She couldn't look at the vast multitude of subservient blacks in the same dim light anymore. She now knew that they were a lot smarter than modern society made them out. Blake, Julia, and even Meissa were very well-spoken compared to the blacks she had come in contact with previously.

On the east end of town, far away from where Thelma's was presently operating, Loner's Hotel, Bar, and Grill was being constructed. Out an acre and a half away, one could begin to smell the freshly laid wood in the air. The foreman had white and black laborers working hand over fist, rushing to assemble the place. Loner's rose three-stories high in the front part of the doughnut-shaped building. The hotel was being built around an open courtyard where outhouses sat to one side and tables and chairs occupied the other. Paying customers could either sit inside and enjoy their purchase or go out to one of the many picnic tables. The hourly rooms were stacked three floors up, while the regular hotel rooms were spread out across the circular bend.

Loner's was supposed to resemble nothing in recent history. It was to be a beautiful fortress of solitude—pleasure-inducing, alcoholic, as well as femininely stimulating. The dream was to construct a place that not only conformed to the physical needs but also to visual fantasy as well. Loner's was envisioned to be the ultimate vacation destination.

Michael and Blake wanted to create a sin-filled wonderland—a place that brought the average John and Sally out their everyday shell. Walking into Loner's was to be like walking into an alternate universe. Leave your problems at the entrance; all that is required inside are your wallets.

This hotel was huge—a virtual giant in comparison to the other buildings around town. Michael explained to Darla that he needed her on her A game. He and Blake meant to draw settlers into their growing town with this venture. Darla just nodded and smiled. She would continue this practice most of the day, starstruck at the life Michael had exposed her to. It was as if opening her eyes for the first time. Everything was foreign to her. Thelma's was her entire life for so long, the shock of the illustrious environment had her shaken. Being outside her comfort zone was scary, but the fear was exuberating.

Until this week, Darla never bothered to stray too far away from Thelma's Motel. Confined to a few acres of movement, she was unaware of all the new businesses that had sprung up around town.

What a Monday, beginning of the workweek, beginning of the rest of my life, Darla mused as she floated through the early day's events on cloud delight. Her pretty blue peepers were on full display as Michael guided her to and fro. The muscles in her seldom-used authentic smile ached from all the atypical activity.

The two made appearances at three different clothing shops—the one a few roads over from Thelma's, where Darla usually purchased her attire, and two others she didn't even know existed.

Michael bought her a half-dozen dresses, three pairs of shoes, several scarves, and a bunch of sexy underwear.

To her surprise, Darla was informed that Julia and Beth were responsible for making all Meissa's pretty dresses. Also a shocker was finding out that Michael was with Beth prior to Blake. It was by mere chance that Michael and Beth crossed paths. A month before his mother's thirty-seventh birthday, Michael was already out searching for the perfect gift. Blake had already gotten her a dandy, and Michael wanted to really blow Blake's gift out of the water. While casually walking through a fabric shop, Michael bumped into Beth. Being polite, he complimented her on the dress she had on. One thing led to another. Blake walked in on them, and Beth was receptive—it was a rippling effect.

In other news, Beth explained that she and her slave and best friend, Julia, had done the sewing on all her outfits and that she was actually looking to open herself a shop here in town. Impressed with her work, Michael contracted her to make his mother a few things. Beth and Julia began stopping by the plantation so often that Michael had them put together a closet full of things for Meissa. This, in turn, moved to her designing the wardrobe for several of the blacks on their workforce.

Michael and Blake's parents were raised in New Haven, Connecticut, where the mistreatment of Negro workers were frowned upon. This line of thinking stuck with Mr. Townsman. He taught his children to treat their slaves with a degree of humanity. Besides taking pride in being a fair slave master, Mr. Townsman was a consonant perfectionist. He insisted that every black who worked in or in close proximity to the house be properly clothed.

Mr. Townsman was brought up around free blacks. His family did business with them, and he even served alongside a colored platoon in the Mexican War. The plight of the black men in this country was a hot topic for him. Mr. Townsman felt strongly that if free, a black man should be allowed every opportunity a white man enjoys. This was his reasoning for raising Blake as his own.

When the problem arose where it seemed as if Mrs. Townsman was unable to have children of her own, Mr. Townsman began taking one of his servants into the barn. Blake was not a mistake. Mr. Townsman plotted the child's existence.

As fate would have it, Mrs. Townsman began processing his seed just as Mr. Townsman embarked on a chemical pilgrimage with Lizzy, Blake's biological mother. Michael was born a month before Blake. Though he finally had a son sought from his wife, Mr. Townsman wasn't about to turn his back on the son he planned with Lizzy. He loved Lizzy, and her child was just as special to him as the one who came out of his wife. Forced to come clean, newborn Blake nearly ruined his marriage. No matter his wife's reserve, Mr. Townsman insisted that his biracial sons be raised under the same roof together.

The embarrassment of raising a black son as her own was too great for Mrs. Townsman to endure while living in her hometown. Within a few months of the boys' birth, the decision was made. Mr. and Mrs. Townsman took the then three-month-old Michael and two-month-old Blake down to Atlanta, Georgia, to start over. The deal was Blake would remain a family secret and his biological mother was to be sold off, discharged as if simple livestock to the highest bidder. Mrs. Townsman handled the transaction herself. Her husband, though it cut him deep, had not a leg to stand on in this matter. Any protest he had was disregarded; Mrs. Townsman's terms were nonnegotiable.

As the ever-revolving hands of time ticked along and the now family of four got settled into their new habitat, baby Blake's light-brown behind eventually started to win her over. Little by little and brick by brick, Mrs. Townsman's defenses came tumbling to the earth. After long, her love for her two boys was without bias.

As for the boys themselves, they were inseparable from day one. Michael, being a month older, would rub his seniority in his younger sibling's face, but that simple thirty days also made him naturally protective over his little brother.

Regardless of how close they were, boys will be boys, and these boys' fights were epic. Blake was definitely the better athlete, but by no means was Michael decadent. Mr. Townsman was often the instigator of their scrimmages. He encouraged his sons to go at each other. He wanted to install a toughness in them that would prepare them to overcome the obstacles that the world would hurl their way. Black eyes and busted lips were commonplace for the kids growing up. Though Blake was naturally stronger, Michael offset this encumbrance by being twice as relentless. It was only so far Blake would take his aggression, whereas Michael was balls to the wall from start to finish all the time.

Mr. Townsman thought the world of his boys. He made it a point to teach his heirs everything he knew. Being in the gun business, his sons practically grew up with rifles in their hands. By the time they were allowed to go off unsupervised, the two were just about expert marksmen. Hunting and target practice were two of their more treasured activities. Raised on two hundred acres of land, there was plenty of room to practice.

Mr. Townsman struck it rich in the firearms retail market after being pulled into a partnership with a savvy old war buddy—a free black man named Sylvester Blackwell. Born into slavery, Mr. Blackwell earned his freedom papers by exhibiting exceptional acts of bravery while serving his country in the Mexican War.

One of Sylvester's more notable moments was when he lost a large chunk out of his shoulder saving an all-white unit's hide in a vicious exchange with the opposition. Sylvester and five other blacks rescued a dozen white soldiers who were pinned down in a makeshift bunker, taking enemy fire. The Mexican soldiers had them outnumbered and flanked. To make a long story short, Blackwell and his five raised so much hell that they were able to back the enemy down enough for every one of the white officers to escape. Mr. Townsman was among the select.

When the war ended, Sylvester Blackwell made a return trip to Mexico a free man, but this was no social visit. Blackwell had an epiphany. Though the rifle was the weapon of choice during the war, the production of handheld pistols were quietly gaining ground among the civilian population. Blackwell figured since the fighting had concluded, there'd be a shitload of military-styled weapons floating around the battered country.

Mr. Blackwell began buying as many weapons as he could accumulate at a bargain price. He cleaned them up and resold them to the civilian public here in the states at an inflated rate. Being a blacksmith by trade, he easily made the transition to gunsmith. His first attempts at purchasing a license to sell firearms were blocked by the local magistrate. Undeterred, Blackwell continued to move his arms via black market. Free or not, the country wasn't ready to accept a black man's acclimation into its high society. His fortune was forever altered when he walked into a small gun store in Connecticut.

Mr. Townsman immediately recognized his brave savior, and inviting him over for dinner that night was one of the smartest things he ever did. The partnership was forged. Blackwell had the connections, and Townsman was a seasoned gunsmith who just happened to be the correct color. When Townsman landed the contract with an overseas company that sold a special metal stronger than anything being used here in America, their business really flourished. Sylvester's Pistols was a hit.

The company's success put the Townsmans in a class that was without financial worries. Michael and Blake grew up privileged children. Still, Mr. and Mrs. Townsman encouraged their sons to find their own niche in life. They wanted them to blaze their own trails. Never in a million years did they suspect that when the boys started experimenting with the opposite sex, they would follow their dicks into the brothel business. But a deal was a deal.

Loner's Hotel, Bar, and Grill was rounding into form. The final touches were being applied to the building, and the whores were vigorously being recruited.

Back at the Townsman Plantation, now only a few weeks away from the doors opening, Michael and Darla, each on their individual horses, rode past the main house to the smaller but still sizable house toward the rear of the plantation. This was where the two young men spent majority of their time when their parents were home. The house was built for this very purpose. Mr. and Mrs. Townsman wanted Michael and Blake to have their own space. Beth and Julia pretty much lived here also. Four out of seven days, they were at the plantation playing house. Sex was not only Michael and Blake's hobby but it also was their addiction. It was only natural that they make it their profession.

There was a total of twenty-four slaves who worked in the plantation: Meissa, her mother (the cook), Marcus (their stableman), nine semi-attractive slave women who were responsible for everything from gardening to cotton picking. Seven of the nine were often used as fill-ins in Michael and Blake's untamed orgies. Excluded were four not-too-desirable bondwomen; these women were either too old or too broken to warrant the boys' advance. Then there were eight male multipurpose field slaves. These men looked up to Blake. In their eyes, he was somewhat of a hero.

Also on the property, wards of married parents were seven kids (five boys and two girls); one of which was a newborn. The children on the plantation were free to be children; that until they were age-appropriate to contribute.

Mr. Townsman made it a point to purchase his slaves from the worst slave owners he knew. He considered this his way of rescuing them. He loved that the slaves on his plantation appreciated his hospitality. His property was like wonderland in comparison to what they were accustomed to. Whips and chains were unnecessary. The mere threat of returning them to their previous situation was enough to straighten them out.

For the last past week, Darla had been staying at the main house with Michael and Meissa, learning how to avoid losing her lunch while orally pleasing a man on Meissa's level of notability. Darla was an exceptional student in Michael the guinea pig's opinion. There were some long days and late nights. It was definitely a process. Darla had to build up her tolerance for thrust absorption. A professional's professional, Darla worked her rump off to rectify this problem. Within days, she had begun to take it all the way down to the hairs in rapid consecutive succession. Keeping steady when she really focused, she was able to go a good while (five to ten minutes) without gagging. "Love your craft" was her mantra. If practice makes perfect, Darla was on her way.

CHAPTER 7

Mr. and Mrs. Townsman returned home that Friday afternoon. Their arrival was a welcomed surprise for Michael who missed his parents terribly. Even more enthusiastic was his brother, Blake, who couldn't stop gushing about the new rifle his father had given him.

Before the invention of the pump action, shotguns were mostly limited to one or two shots before the need to reload. This revolutionary fashioned weapon worked like a revolver. Framed with a dense new metal, the six-chambered shotgun that they were calling the Townswell was supposed to take Sylvester's Pistols to a new plateau. Working out the schematics was why Mr. Townsman was forced to visit their main factory in Connecticut. The crafting of the Townswell had to be perfect before the decision would be made to put it into production. This new shotgun weighed around twenty pounds when fully loaded, but for the amount of punching power it was capable of, the extra weight was a welcomed addition.

Upon introduction, Darla was greeted with open hospitality from Mr. Townsman. Mrs. Townsman was a bit more reserved. It only took for Darla to be caught drinking the last of Mrs. Townsman's freshly squeezed lemonade for her to be relocated to the back house with the others. Mrs. Townsman insisted it was only because she was thinking of having company over and didn't want one of Darla's potential customers to equate her with their plantation. It didn't matter; in less than a week, Darla, Meissa, and two of the other slave women would be moving into the hotel. Their rooms there were already set up and modernly furnished.

Michael was skeptical about Blake working with him at the hotel. These were fragile times, and Blake was a proud man. One of his favorite things to do was correcting people about his liberal status. "No, excuse me, but I'm not a slave. I am a free man." This got him and Michael into a half-dozen near altercations growing up. Though he had no misconceptions about the state of the black men in America, Blake was not about to allow anyone to treat him like a slave.

Mr. Townsman had become a very important figure in the community. His gun store brought in a lot of revenue to the city, and his charitable donations were well-documented. This brought his cocky biracial son some much-needed leeway. Though he often had to endure plenty of evil looks and at times some unsavory words, the young man was pretty much off-limits with the locals. Still, the South was in a weird moral place as a whole, and Michael worried about his smooth-talking brother.

The rumors of civil war were floating around. The North had begun campaigning about freeing the slaves. This type of talk had most slave owners up in arms. The lazy Southern whites needed their slaves. Just the sight of an unchained black boiled their skin. These emancipation rumors made some of the more unsavory folks that much more unreceptive to an already free black man, especially one who spoke and dressed better than most of them did.

Try as he might, Michael could not talk Blake out of working opening day. He had been the one who suggested the barbecue pit. There was no way he was going to allow someone else to christen his grill.

CHAPTER 8

The April 17 opening day was a smash hit on every level. So many free-agent whores showed up for the event that the place looked like the setting of a spring-break concert (not to get out-of-date). The food was delicious, the liquor was strong, and the women were beautiful. What more could a horny customer ask for?

The one blemish on the otherwise perfect day was when Lanson Bell, better known as Bell the Fighter or simply the Fighter, showed up to the hotel already drunk as a skunk. To his detriment, an unsuspecting older gentleman made the terrible mistake of knocking over Bell's mug of beer. For this incursion, the Fighter knocked three teeth out of the man's mouth. It took two good Samaritans along with Michael and Blake to wrestle the man free. The Fighter was well-known for his brutality in that part of the city. His antics were practically folklore. No one in the room was willing to provide too much assistance in fear of the man's wrath. Fortunately, Michael was able to turn a bad situation into a positive.

After they managed to settle the Fighter down, Michael pulled him to the side and offered him the job of head of security. In the midst of so much running around, Michael and Blake somehow forgot to address the issue of crowd control. The two were definitely way too prestigious to get their hands dirty every time a situation occurred.

The Fighter was a middle-aged underprivileged knucklehead who, at the age of thirty-four, was still living with his parents. The man was three hundred-plus pounds of mean, but even he recognized a good opportunity when it presented itself.

Later on that night, after the crowd had withered some, Michael, Blake, and Bell took a carriage ride out to the countryside. There in the dusty field under the glimmer of moonlight, Michael put a much-needed beating on the slower drunken Fighter. Michael and Blake practiced hand-to-hand combat under the tutelage of their father for so long that there was no way Michael was going to let a falling-down drunk get the better of him—especially when he had so much room to maneuver.

The lesson was taken in stride. The Fighter agreed to stay sober during working hours, and all parties involved promised never to speak of the incident in public.

Three months into the venture, Loner's had overshot everyone's expectations. People from all over were coming to visit their grand hotel. Recruitment of the Fighter turned out to be one of their most important hires. He only had to put his hands on a few troublesome folks before his message spread throughout the masses. For the most part, his prestige alone kept most customers in line.

A few times, Michael did have to take Bell to the side and speak to him about his drinking, but this was more run-of-the-mill rather than incident-based. These were the happiest times in the Fighter's life. He had his own place. He was bringing in decent money. He was even popular with the girls, being that the very mention of his name prompted the would-be hagglers to straighten up and pay the necessary toll.

Life was grand for Michael and Blake. They had the ideal occupation, owners of a high-end brothel. Michael would sample all the new white prospects who showed up looking for work, and Blake was knocking down the blacks. They had to make sure the newbies met the hotel's usual high standard of performance.

Again life was grand, but under the surface, something was eating at Blake—jealousy! Michael was pushing into as many blacks as he was with whites. This was his fetish. On the other side of the coin, Blake had a thing for white women, an unfed hunger that was driving him mad. The delicate glow of their skin, the distinct sound of their moan, the silky hair on their privates—everything about them turned him on. Working at Loner's was eating him alive, and Beth wasn't satisfying that craving.

One white woman wasn't enough. He needed to have at least one more. He knew laying with a white woman could get him killed, but he felt the risk was very well justified—just one more.

Michael and Blake had had numerous discussions about this issue. These debates usually ended in a loud screaming match; at times they even got physical.

CHAPTER 9

The dusky country terrain was beautiful this evening. Blake and his brother had been working tirelessly night and day. Drained in more ways than one, he needed a couple of days off—a few sunsets in his own bed, just to refresh his mental.

Stopping by the big house, Blake was welcomed with a big dinner with his parents. Mrs. Townsman was so proud of her boys. They were the talk of the town. And although she wasn't a big fan of their career choice, they were productive men. Her sons did not simply choose to mooch off the family money. Her children were stand-ups.

"Blake, baby, I'm so glad you finally decided to stop by and visit your old folks. We were beginning to think you were avoiding us," Mrs. Townsman began. She and Blake were sitting alone at the dinner table. Mr. Townsman had gone off to the shed to finish up on a few work-related projects. This left Mrs. Townsman time to get into her son's brain. When her husband was around, he would always insist that she not prowl. Michael was too bold-headed for her to get anything from, but Blake; Blake was putty in her hands.

"Come on, Mom. You know we're working hard in town, trying to keep this hotel afloat."

"You mean your upscale whorehouse?"

"Oh boy, here we go."

"Here we go nothing. I'm not being negative. I'm just stating the facts."

"Mom, every hotel in the country has women who work the lobby."

"Yeah, work, not selling their ass."

Blake let out a healthy snicker. His mother was impossible, but she was funny as hell. "So what?" he asked. "You rather us have a business that struggles rather than allow women who are totally free to do as they please with their behinds to work at our hotel?"

"Blake, I am not judging you. No, you are allowed to make your money the way you see fit. However…"

"Here we go," Blake whispered while rolling his eyes to the ceiling.

"However," Mrs. Townsman reinterrupted, "I'm going to be needing some grandchildren out of you soon, and I want your children to be brought into this world within a traditional Christian union."

"Mom, we're nineteen years old. We're not ready to… I know I'm not ready to settle down."

"Do not dillydally around with every slave girl who shakes her tail in your face. And that Beth woman is no better. She might as well carry her fat ass down to the hotel and get on the job."

"Mom!"

"Mom my foot. You need to go find yourself a nice colored woman and settle your black ass down."

Holding in a good laugh, Blake could do nothing but shake his head. Something told him to run out when his father did.

Mrs. Townsman went on, "And that Michael is no better, bringing that whore to my home. And Meissa—you got Meissa down there selling her little rear!" She playfully began hitting Blake with the towel she had resting on the arm of her chair. "I always hoped you and her were going to end up together."

"Mom, you know Michael isn't going to let that happen. And to be clear, Meissa takes no clients. Your son will kill everyone in that hotel." Blake smiled. "No one's going to lay a finger on his Meissa."

"Michael—that boy is going to be the cause of my demise. He likes the blacks, and you like the whites."

"I have to go, Mom."

"No, don't run out on me now."

"I'm going, Ma."

"Boy, you better…" Mrs. Townsman went to get up, but Blake was quicker.

"Love you," Blake said, rushing over and grabbing her in a bear hug in an attempt to keep her seated. With an onslaught of kisses, he began, "Love you." Kiss. "Love you." Kiss. "Love you." Kiss.

"Unhand me."

"Love you." Kiss.

"Boy, get your strong ass out of here."

"Love you." Kiss.

"Boy, let me loose. I can't breathe." Mrs. Townsman was laughing so hard she felt a tingle in her bladder.

Blake left the house through the back door. He stretched the air out of his full tummy.

"Why does your mother hate me?" a voice said, catching him by surprise.

Spinning to his left, he said, "Darla? Girl, you scared me." Blake let out a breath, unballing his fist.

"Why?" she asked again. Her small voice was cracking as if emotionally compromised.

"What?" Blake asked as if he didn't understand the question.

"It's because I'm a whore, isn't it? But she loves Meissa. She's a whore too. But she's a slave whore, so it's okay?"

Blake smiled. "Darla, stop," he said, putting his arm around her as he walked her away from his parents' house. "She doesn't hate you."

"I heard her. I heard the whole conversation."

"Sneaky woman," Blake teased.

"No, I was coming to find you, and I guess I just wandered by… It's not the point. The point is, she doesn't want me with Michael because I'm a whore, but she wants you to be with Meissa."

"Darla—"

"And why doesn't Michael want you with Meissa?"

"He had her first."

"So you have no problem sharing Beth and Julia but not Meissa. Little princess is off-limits."

"He doesn't want me to stretch her little hole." Blake gave a small chuckle.

"So what about what happened at the well?"

"How do you know about that?"

"Michael. Remember during breakfast at your parents' house?"

"What?"

"Blake!" Darla said with a stop-playing look on her face.

"Okay, we were both a little… No, we were a lot drunk. One thing led to another, and to make a long story short, she was pulling the handle on the well so hard that she bent it stuck." Blake smiled. "She can't take too much. The girl is built for white guys."

Darla was glad to hear that Meissa wasn't perfect after all. She couldn't even satisfy her own race. *By far the best my ass.* Darla and Meissa were now civil, but Darla still had a competitiveness about her—a rivalry that Michael had installed between the two.

As they neared the back house, Darla stopped Blake in the road.

"What?" Blake said, looking around. "What? You saw something? A coyote?" Blake grabbed his concealed pistol.

"No, I want to see it."

"What?"

Darla's eyes confirmed her request.

"No. Michael will kill me."

"I've seen it before. I just want to touch it. I'm just curious."

"Right here?"

"I don't want Beth to catch me. I think she already thinks I want you."

"Darla…"

"Hurry up."

Blake pulled his trousers down to his ankles. Darla's hands instantly went to his penis—tentatively at first, then she held it firmly. Asserting herself, she began stroking it back and forth to wake it up. It didn't take much convincing.

"You satisfied?"

"Wow," Darla said, gasping at his size. She'd handled some good-size dicks in her day, but this was an entirely different monster. Darla's mouth hung open as she massaged him with both hands. "Wow," she said again. Allowing a sneaky smile to slowly distend, she spoke, mostly to herself, "I can do it. Yeah, come on." Darla slid out of her underpants before taking a knee, dragging Blake down to accompany her on a fluffy sheet of well-kept vegetation.

Blake knew this wasn't smart, but he couldn't resist. This was maybe a once-in-a-lifetime offer. Carefully he slid his thick head up against the crease of her inner thigh. She was so wet, but still it took a healthy shove to get the tip inside. Darla took a deep breath and held on to Blake's neck as he widened her forever.

"You all right?" he asked.

"Yes. Come on. I can take it."

Blake pushed inch by inch as he rocked back and forth, bird-feeding her a little more with each thrust until she began to hold his hips out of her. She was at her limit. Now he had a measurement of how much she could take.

"Uh," Darla cried as she screamed. "Uh God. God. Oh." Blake was giving her a feeling she reasoned only the royal should be privy to.

It took a while, but after a few, she was able to loosen her pelvis as Big Blake began to familiarize her unfamiliar walls. Working her hips, Darla was beginning to own his size.

"Let me get on top," she ordered. Obediently Blake rolled her over without ever pulling out of her. It took literally seconds on top for her to explode down on his thickness. This was her third orgasm, but still she worked, never missing a beat. She was going to make this big black dick erupt like it had never before.

"Am I doing it right?" she asked seductively.

"Yeah, Darla. You feel amazing."

"Am I better than Meissa?"

"Hell yeah. Ten times."

The more she spoke, the more aggressive she became. Darla was now almost taking his full length. Blake was in heaven. "Get up. I'm about—"

"Uh-uh, come inside me."

"No, woman, are you crazy? Get off me."

"No!" she said as she fought to keep her place, grinding him into her hard and fast.

Blake's orgasm was what dreams were made of. He never came inside Beth or even Julia. He tried to pull out of all the women he laid with. He knew this was a mistake, and by the amount of power he released into her, he knew right away that the chances of her being pregnant were likely.

Lying in the grass side-by-side under the stars, Blake opened, his voice carrying a ghostly tone, "We should not have done that."

"Why? Because of your mother?" Darla teased.

"No, because white women don't have babies from black men."

"Why? Black women have plenty of babies from white men."

"It's not the same, and you know it. I can get in a lot of trouble for this. You can get in a lot of trouble for having sex with me too."

"I'm not worried."

"Darla, this is serious."

"Blake, calm down. I have been a whore my whole life, and I never once got pregnant. I can't have children. But if I could, I would love to see the look on your mother's face."

"Your bad."

"Hell yeah." Darla laughed. "Same time next week?"

Blake shook his head vigorously, and together they both burst into a sounding laughter.

*****

The Sword

How could they stand it? a masked stranger standing beneath an oversize black hood questioned of the devil-spun swarm as he watched over the horrific proceeding from atop the twelve-foot bank. Under the cover of a bantam-lit night escorted by a very slim crescent moon, this vengeful caramel-complexioned gunman stood witness to the hatred-inspired, culture-driven flock as they actively pillaged. The sadness he should have felt for his fellow black brother was handicapped by the burning hate he now harbored for the evil, sanguine pale lot responsible.

He was positioned just beyond the shadows of the watchful trees, looking down over the perimeter of the smooth valley grounds. The darkly dressed, masked would-be vigilante stood arms at the ready, clutching two large custom-designed smoke-black revolvers. Encased in unforgiving black fabric from skull to heel, the self-proclaimed heaven's sword remained unmoved, patiently assessing the enigma below.

How could I, one black, triumph over so many ironhearted whites? he questioned.

On most nights, the male patrons in host of such events would conceal their identities by draping white makeshift mask over their faces. So in contrast to their hue preference, the Sword chose to mask himself in opposition (black).

Though the product of both races (black and white), the Sword, by all accounts, was undoubtedly a Negro—through and through. In his thinking, the hanging man above the flames could easily have been him. The brave heavily armed observer wore a large overhung hood that looked as if it could have been a coat stolen from the closet of the Grim Reaper—Death himself. The black hooded shirtsleeves were cut short so not to get caught on a protruding object or snag on the ridge of his belt. After this night, gunfighting was likely to be his life. Planning his attire for the unseen was essential.

His awkwardly assembled hero outfit had taken quite a bit of thought. His boots were light but firm; his socks warm and thick. The pants he wore, though ripped and ragged, held sentimental value. They were pants he found laying on the ground yards from the very first black man he found dead in that very valley. His assailants didn't even bother to string him up. They just stripped him nude and let multiple shotgun rounds course through his exposed body. Then like an animal, they left him lying there, dead on the ground.

The dead man's pants were baggy around the Sword's legs. If not for his murdered father's leather belt, his britches would surely have fallen from his hind side. The Sword spent many days running long and hard within the confines of the dark fabric, preparing his body for battle. The pants themselves gave him a riotous sense of duty.

The morning he found the infamous trousers, he buried its previous owner in the field he lay. Afterward, he took the dead man's pants, blood-soaked and torn, to the local sheriff as evidence. Still his complaint was said to be unfounded. Nothing was done, and any further persistence would only serve to bring him trouble. To him, the pants were a reminder that the black man would receive no quarter. If there were any chance of equity to be won, the blacks would have to seek it themselves.

If he followed through with the nefarious plot his subconscious was cooking up, everything would change. His actions this evening would set a new standard for self-defense. Murder was a simplistic act. For this night, the Sword was poised to tread beyond murder. Tonight he would make a statement. As for the valley dwellers, death was a certainty. In addition to mere physical pilferage, the Sword wanted to take with him their evil souls. And not only those within the party below. With this act, he meant to punish the evil collective as a whole. With this blow, he needed to rip at the core of the culture that spurred such activity.

The bunch before him was evil-incarnated. Their kind only respected one thing—violence. They couldn't be reasoned with. They weren't even human. Not a folk song, God's prayer, or civil rights law would deter them. "Pray not to the heavens," the Sword spoke inaudibly. "I will be the hand of God tonight. I, thy heavenly sword, will smite thine enemy."

CHAPTER 10

The popularity of the Loner's Hotel was spreading faster than the small town could adequately handle. From mid- to early evening, the place was like a tourist attraction. It was often the first place out-of-towners visited when they rode through and an essential destination for sectarian men come payday.

Young men, old men, even some of the more liberal women—they were all captivated by the hotel's allure. Prostitutes came from across states to find a spot on the hotel's roster. Michael and Blake were thinking about expanding the already-capacious hotel; it was so packed at times.

No matter the skin color, once a woman started working at Loner's, she was required to be runway-stunning at all times. Top fashion clothing and theme-inspired outfits were provided. Monthly shopping sprees along with round-the-clock overindulging kept the feminine products looking phenomenal and edible-fresh. Slave masters often came in to sell their most attractive slave women, only to return when they began to miss their familiar warmth.

As the days and months peeled from the calendar, Blake's smooth personality started to win over even some of his more racially charged critics. His family's relevance in the community was unquestioned, and no matter who was looking, all could see that he was every bit as intelligent as any white man in the room. Most simply chose to equate his acumen as the black blood in his body not being as profound as his father's dominant white blood.

Spending a couple of days in his father's gun shop was how Blake chopped up his workweek. Sylvester's Pistols Inc. sat only four lots over from Loner's, and though it was a very lucrative traffic, the physical and mental demand was a lot less strenuous. Moving firearms was child's play compared to managing women or even working the barbecue grill. Still, Blake became so accustomed with his easy-rider role that he now instituted the practice of keeping two hotel women with him at all times.

There was a back room in the gun shop that he offered to preferred customers if they were making a sizable purchase. Every time his father saw someone coming out of that room, his heart swelled. His sons had savvy business minds. Sex was an intangible cog in modern society. His youngest knew this, as his biological mother had. Mr. Townsman could see the woman in his son's demeanor. Proud, strong, and sure of herself was Lizzy—his son's slave mother. Selling her off was one of the hardest things he ever had to endure, but the woman was a dark shadow over his marriage. There was no way his wife would have agreed to raise the boy as her own with his slave mother hanging around.

"Dad," Blake called, breaking Mr. Townsman's active muse, "we're running out of .45 shells."

"Yeah, I'm aware. We should have enough to hold us. There's a shipment coming next month."

"We're also going to need some more revolvers. It seems the pistol is becoming even more sought-after than the rifle."

"Yeah, you're definitely right about that."

"If you need me to, I can take a day or so and press up a few cases."

"No, I think we'll be okay. Besides, I don't predict this ammo grab will last that much longer. Fortunately, people seem to be coming down off that Nat Turner scare."

Blake nodded. "Yeah, I think you may be right. I haven't been getting as many frightful stares as of late," he joked, flashing an infectious smile.

His father returned the expression. "Oh, before I forget, which one of you boys is going to go with your mother this weekend?"

"Michael!" Blake announced emphatically. "It's definitely Michael's turn."

This got a raunchy cackle out of Mr. Townsman. "You better stop dodging your mother. I know you don't want her to start showing up at the hotel."

The look on Blake's face said just an inkling of how such a possibility struck fear.

CHAPTER 11

Mrs. Townsman loved going shooting with her sons. Although it was Michael's turn to bite the bullet, Blake was the one out with his mother, making it interesting but ultimately letting her win the target-shooting competition. Mrs. Townsman was a good shot by modern 1800's female standards, but Blake and Michael were phenomenal. The two were practically born with a rifle on their shoulders. Be that as it may, to actually beat Mom at anything was sure to warrant some sort of repercussion. The last time Michael made the mistake of outshooting his mother, she tricked him into getting out of the wagon. While he was checking on the wheel she insisted had been pulling to one side, she launched the horses into a gallop, leaving Michael to walk homes seven miles out.

"You did good, Blake. You almost had this old gal. Too bad you missed your last four shots."

"Yeah, I don't know what happened," Blake said, trying to sound sincere.

"I'll tell you what happened," Mrs. Townsman assured. "The pressure got to you. Happens to the best of us, kiddo."

"Next time," Blake told her snidely but confidently.

"Yes, son. There's always next time."

Mrs. Townsman let the silence take then for a half-minute before saying, "So how's the wife search going?"

"Aw, here we go."

"Don't you here we go me. I'm not getting any younger, am I? Do you see me dropping any years off this old body?"

"You're looking younger every year," Blake said, putting his arm around her shoulders.

"Flattery will get you nowhere," Mrs. Townsman promised. Continuing, she said, "Blake, you and that Caucasian son of mine are going to stop this nonsense and find me some grandchildren."

"Mom."

"Mom, mom, mom," she mimicked. "Mom me some grandchildren."

"I was thinking about letting Beth…"

The carriage was pulled to a dead stop. Yanking the reins abruptly, she said, "Don't even joke."

Blake was laughing so hard that no sound was coming out.

"Boy, don't even joke. That ain't funny," his mother squawked. Her frustration was heightened when she realized how much fun her son was having at her expense.

"Okay, okay, maybe," Blake said, fighting to catch his breath. "You know I know better."

"Boy, not only will that bring us all sorts of trouble…that Beth… Don't even joke. You better not bring no yellow baby to my house. In fact, I don't even want you to be with anyone brighter than your sandy-brown behind."

Blake had another light chuckle.

"I'm thinking of buying you someone fresh off the boat."

"Ma, you better not!"

It was his mother's turn to laugh.

CHAPTER 12

Beth and Julia were out of town on a trip that spurred them across the state. The purpose of this trip was to see about this new fabric that had been making a buzz around the city. The two women were supposed to be gone a week. With an empty residence and alone for the first time in a long time, Blake opened a bottle of wine and started early.

There was nothing like peace and quiet. He had been running his body ragged. Between the grill, the gun store, and the women, Blake had no time to kick back and unwind. Combing his fingers through his short curly hair, he tried to remember the last time he allowed himself to get roaring drunk. Sure, he had a few drinks while working at the hotel, but that was essentially uniform—just to take the edge off.

Today Blake wanted to get falling-down wasted. He deserved it. Sometimes he wondered if life would be less stressful as a slave. Taking a long swig of his alcoholic beverage, he snickered at the thought.

The murky country sky had just begun to gray. With unburdened time on his hands, the intoxicated hotel chef spent a good portion of the day grilling up a magnificent rack of barbecue ribs, glazed with sweet-and-spicy honey sauce, and a couple of ears of freshly ripped corn on the cob, with all made whole by two giant butter-soaked baked potatoes.

He usually nibbled as he cooked, but for this meal, he kept his fingers out of his mouth. He allowed his taste buds to build in anticipation of this personalized impending feast.

Blake was at the dining room table on the second floor, staring dreamy eyes at the massive platter before him. No fork, no spoon, no silverware whatsoever—he was going Neanderthal on this one.

Blake tore into his flavor-abundant conquest with bare hands. The thick assembly of beef and pork was so soft and greasy. *Damn!* It was just like he liked it. Mercilessly he attacked the savory carcass with tentacles drawn—sloppy fistfuls, taking no prisoners. Every bite was like a new adventure. In his intoxicated state, the vast assortment of spices meant more to his taste glands than normal. Blake was only a quarter of the way through his meal when he was interrupted by a creak in the stairs. *Who in the hell?* Blake mentally cursed his intruder.

"There you are," Darla said, announcing her presence. Standing at the doorway, noticeably under the influence, the second starlet was wearing a tight red dress that was designed to grab attention.

"Hey, um…when did… What are you doing here?" Blake stuttered, obviously surprised to see her—but pleasantly.

Darla looked around the room with a devious eye. "Where is everyone?"

"Beth and Julia went to… They went to check on a… What are you doing here? Today's… Aren't you supposed to be at work tonight?"

"Yeah, I cut out. I needed a day to myself. Plus Meissa told me that Beth and Julia were out of town," she admitted with a wide insidious grin. "You are all alone, aren't you?" The question was rhetorical, and her intent was anything but veneer.

"Yeah, I just wanted Ted…" Blake's statement was cut short when Darla began to unstrap her flowing gown.

Shaking his head, a feeble attempt at playing coy, Blake stayed seated. He could feel the alcohol in his blood slowly start to head south. This wasn't going to be a quick gentle encounter—not an experiment of guilty pleasure on the side of the road. No, tonight Darla would receive the full treatment. He had fantasized about getting a second taste of Darla's sweet apple pie.

Reading the lust in his eyes, Darla played to her femininity. Indecent intentions were written all over her face as she allowed the dress to fall to the floor. Keeping her eyes locked on her adversary, she stepped over the clump of fabric around her ankles. With her high-heels shoes as her only costume accessory, she stood seductively, steaming up the narrow doorway. Exercising a very alluring dominatrix expression, hips cocked to one side, and her thighs slightly spread, Darla allowed Blake's brain to mentally foretaste.

"You...," he began. "We shouldn't," Blake vocally attempted one last half-hearted thwart.

"Come on." Darla turned and walked out of the room. All the buck had left the young man. Blake's swelling penis took complete control, ushering him out of his seat. Like a homing device, it led the way as Darla's magnetic booty switched into the bedroom he frequently shared with Beth.

From Thursday night to early Friday afternoon, Blake and Darla were engaged in an off-and-on marathon of moans and groans. Darla had to accumulate at least two to three ounces of his seed in that time. This was all Blake thought about as he rubbed his fingers over Darla's naked sweaty stomach. "Are you positive you can't have children?"

"Positive. Don't worry, your sperm is safe with me." Darla laughed, but this statement was not in compliance with verifiable reality. Because two months later, while navigating through a sea of mixed emotions, Darla was forced to stop disregarding her mixed periods. She was pregnant, and by everything she held holy, Blake was the father—this she was certain of.

Being the madam at the hotel, Darla had begun refusing to take on clients herself. She was only tending to the girls and collecting the money. With a dark new yearning ever since the overnight romp with Blake, she was ruined for all others. With that fuse properly burning in her spine, Darla was finding herself making any and every excuse to sneak away to find her chocolate lover. The hotheaded young woman was hooked. Blake had her totally on his wire. But a baby! This was a complication—a potentially fatal complication.

On one hand, Darla feared for Blake's safety—and her own at that. The punishment for a black man sleeping with a white woman (in the South no less) and the ramification was already death from above. A white woman having a black man's child—this would be hell on earth. On the flip side, this was maybe her one and only chance at motherhood. For all these years, she thought herself sterile. *This is a miracle, isn't it?* It was her miracle child, and she knew that no matter what, she would love it more than life itself.

Laying a gentle hand across her belly, she thought, *This is Blake's child.* She smiled. Surely her baby was worth the risk. She never got pregnant before; this was God's plan. Blake Townsman's heir—of course, his family would help to conceal the child from any harm. They could easily move Blake and her away to a secluded place to live. His mother had raised him as her own; she should be sympathetic to her situation. The world was changing; he wasn't twenty years old. Why couldn't she have a black child?

Darla cradled her hardening stomach as she pondered Blake's reaction. He was a good man; he would do whatever it'd take to make this work. Though it started out as an experimental act then evolved into a pleasure chase, Darla was now positive that she was wholeheartedly in love with a black man. And as sure as the sky was blue, she was certain that he felt the same way about her.

Darla waited two long weeks. She felt that for what she had to share, precise timing was essential. She and Blake were both off this night, and he had already left for the plantation. After a long painstaking carriage ride, complete with adverse thoughts of mournful regrets, Darla pulled up the dirt road headed to the back house.

Gingerly, as if the child's conception depended on it, she climbed down out of the single-ponied wagon. Walking up the dark path, Darla saw that Beth was sitting on the wooden bench on the front porch. *Damn,* Darla cursed her luck. Beth was reading a book under the light of an oil lamp. Slightly rocking back and forth, the heavyset woman seemed to be in her own world. While she read, her free hand held a long thin cigarette, which she lifted to her lips with a gluttonous frequency.

"Hey, Darla!" Beth spoke with an animated gasp.

Darla could tell that the woman was startled by the way the breathy words came out of her thick cheeks. *This cow doesn't deserve my Blake*, Darla thought. Darla had been trying to avoid Beth when she could. Her most recent sexual occurrences with Blake would usually take place at the gun shop after hours or on the back of wagons or sometimes in his parents' home in one of the rooms downstairs when Blake was able to sneak her in.

"Haven't seen you in a while," Beth continued in that same out-of-breath voice.

Darla smiled politely. "How's your sewing been going? I've been waiting to see your new stuff."

"Oh, everything's coming together quite well. Michael has actually found a wonderful little lot that would be perfect for a clothing store."

"That's great," Darla said, trying to sound excited for her. "When do you think you're going to start the construction?"

"Soon hopefully. You know Julia has been sewing up a storm. We have like fifty dresses, all ready for sale."

"Wow, that is wonderful. Um, is Julia inside?"

"Yes, she is sewing as we speak. She's inside the room to your left. I'll be in, in a few," Beth said, holding up her cigarette as if to say when she finishes her smoke.

Blake was waiting in the front room. He heard the entire conversation. "Hey, Darla," he said, greeting her as she walked in.

"Blake, I didn't know you were off today." Darla returned a subtle shift in her eyes, and the meeting was set. Still the two spoke on.

"Yeah, I just wanted to sleep in my own bed tonight. I was just heading out to the other house. What brings you by?" Blake asked loud enough for Beth to hear.

"I was just… I needed a break from the hotel. You know, a night in a real bed. I hope I'm not intruding."

"No, no. It's fine. In fact, I am going to ask my mother if it is okay for you to sleep over in one of the guest rooms."

"Oh, that would be wonderful," Darla said excitedly.

"No problem. I was just about to see what Linda cooked for dinner."

"Thank you, Blake. A nice homecooked meal would do me good."

With that, Blake was out the door. Darla played it cool, asking Julia about the new dresses she had hung up around the room. But procrastination wasn't a quality that Darla was accustomed to. Within minutes, she was pushing out the door after Blake.

Darla was so aggressive yet attentive that at the finish, Blake was mentally prepared for the heart-to-heart he knew was coming. They were sitting on a bench in the back of the barn. Darla had him straddled, and though softening, he was still inside her.

With her hands on both sides of his face, she gently gazed into his eyes. "Blake, I want you to know that I have absolutely fallen for you."

The cocky black stud smiled arrogantly. "Darla   "

"No, Blake, I'm serious. I love you, and I want you to understand this. I truly love you."

Blake shook his head as he fought to restrain himself from laughing in her face. He couldn't believe she was really trying him like this. His hotel's head whore thinking she was even an option for him—it was comical. Still, it was his own fault. He had this kind of effect on every woman he had sex with more than a few times.

"I like you too, Darla," he finally managed to say.

"No, Blake. I love you, and I want to be with you. I... I love you, Blake," she said before passionately kissing him.

Blake's mother told him to never tell a woman that he loved her unless he was ready to dedicate his life to her. Darla was out of her mind if she thought she fit the build, and he wasn't about to patronize her.

Darla began again, "Blake, do you hear what I'm telling you?"

"Yes, Darla, and I appreciate your kind words."

"I don't want to be a whore anymore. I want to be your woman, your wife, or at least the racially compromised version of a wife." The look in her eyes suggested that she actually thought that he might be thinking on this absurd proposal. *This bitch is crazy*, Blake silently concluded, but still he said nothing.

"Blake, I know this is highly unusual, but it can work. We can find a place down in—"

"Darla, I like my life the way it is. You are a wonderful person, but we aren't running away together. I like you. You know this…but I like Beth. Hell, I like Julia. I like Betty," Blake said, referring to one of the slave whores at the hotel.

The mention of the popular black whore infuriated Darla. "Is her sex better than mine? Do I not take you deep into my body? Is my mouth not good enough for you?"

"Darla—"

"Blake, I'm pregnant." The words hit the man like a left hook. A numbing sound inside his ear carried down his spine to the bone in his behind. Darla spoke a few more lines, but the icy shock had clogged his hearing. After a long adjustment period, Blake's body began to shake off the haze.

"How is… Maybe… How do you suppose it's mine?"

"It is!" Darla snapped. Then stilling her tone, she said, "Darling, I stopped whoring months ago. You are the only man who's been inside of me for…since the night we made love at your house—the night we slept in each other's arms."

Darla was caressing Blake's bare arms as she spoke, but Blake had stopped listening. He was going over the details in his head. He had heard that Darla was refusing customers. At the time, her reluctance to accept another man into her was an ego boost. Now! "Can we get rid of it?"

The question shot Darla through the heart. "I would never!" the naked blonde barked. "I'm a Christian woman."

"You're a Christian whore," Blake corrected.

"How dare you!" Darla screamed as she raised her hand to swing. Blake caught her by the wrist. "Unhand me, nigger," she hollered. "You dirty slave. How dare you? I am a white woman."

Blake held her arms down as he contemplated his next move. He couldn't let this woman have his child. His mother would kill him. His family would disown him. If the public got wind of this, that was his neck in a noose. This was bad—all-the-way bad. Maybe he could send her away. Maybe it wasn't his. Maybe he should just break her neck right here and be done with the whole matter. He could leave her corpse for the coyotes to enjoy.

"I gave you my body, and this is how you repay me? My mouth, my pussy. I swallowed your seed, and now I can't have your nigger child… I hate you, you son of a bitch. You will unhand me, nigger."

"Darla."

"Get off me."

"Darla."

"I'll scream."

"I love you too."

"You… I…" Darla stopped struggling but tried to keep up her hate-filled scowl.

"I…you're right. This can work. I want to try and make this work with you. Our child is worth it."

"Yes, Blake. I know we can do this. Your family has money. We can buy fifty acres and raise our child on a beautiful plantation, just like this one. We can have twenty slaves. We won't have to do anything but love each other. We deserve this."

This bitch is crazy, Blake silently confirmed to himself, but he said, "Yes, Darla, we will. Um…we should probably get dressed."

Darla realized that Blake was still inside her. She climbed her naked rear off the side of his lap. With a big smile, she leaned over and took him in her mouth.

"No," Blake protested, pulling her up, but Darla fought her way back down to him. The girl would not be denied.

Blake couldn't concentrate, as both heads were being pulled in different directions. Darla was sucking like a mad woman, and Blake's brain was processing a thousand things at once.

First things first, he had to keep this woman quiet. Leaning back on the bench, he took in the moment. His black dick was in a pretty white girl's throat, and he had a very levelheaded brother who would know how to handle this. Starting to mellow out, he allowed his muscles to relax as he watched Darla go. Michael would know exactly what to do. He would rescue him from this demon woman.

After all, he was the one who brought her into the equation. This was half his fault.

Darla was excited at the prospect of the life being presented to her. She was using the extra ounce of energy as she tried her damnedest to eat Blake's entire length. This was her man, her dick. She and she alone knew how to make it happy. Blake grabbed a handful of Darla's hair and shoved her deeper onto his thick love stick. Darla struggled to contain it, but she didn't complain. She was going to die choking to death pleasing her man. Blake was amazed. *This bitch is crazy.*

CHAPTER 13

Michael wanted to crawl away and disappear. This wasn't happening to him. How stupid could he be? "Blake, you fool."

"I know. I know."

"You don't know, or you wouldn't have done such a thing."

"I do know. That's why I'm coming to you."

"Why did you... Brother, NO! This is the worst thing in the world. This...this is the fear of all white men—your big black dick in our precious lily-white angels. How dare you?"

"She came for me. I swear. Every time. I couldn't resist. She said she couldn't get pregnant. She lied, Michael. She lied," Blake choked out his slurred words between sniffles.

Michael's hands were in a tight-knotted fist. Blake's were up over his head in a submissive defense. Michael wanted to beat his brother to a pulp. He had ruined everything. His mother would blame him for this. *Her precious Blake.* Michael could hear her now. Of course, he had to be the bad influence. *Her brown baby boy.* Well, he wasn't a baby anymore; he was a stupid brown man.

"Help me, brother." *Look at this fool, eyes watering with synthetic tears. Poor Blake. No, Blake will be all right. Blake is untouchable, the chosen nigger. Moral laws be damned. Mr. Blake Townsend is above the law.*

"Michael, brother, please."

"Shut up, Blake, and wipe your damn face. You make me ill. Don't worry, little brother," Michael spoke sarcastically. "We'll figure something out."

"I don't want the baby," Blake began, burning distress tearing at his vocals. "But she won't get rid of it."

"Of course, she won't. You're her golden calf, her black knight. This child is her ticket out of a life of pain and despair. Me, I could just say that I want nothing to do with her or the child. But you, no, we have to coddle to her every whim. Just to keep her quiet. I bet she is going to want a great big house somewhere off the reservation."

Blake was shaking his head like the words were killing him.

Michael went on, "I bet she fucked you good after she told you about the pregnancy. Took in the whole pickle, didn't she?"

Blake was sniffling like a girl as he again agreed.

"You're a fool."

"We can kill her."

"Shut your mouth, brother. Do you think it's that simple? Have you ever killed anyone? Nevertheless a woman—a white woman. That is a one-way ticket to hell. With your nigger blood. Blake… black hell is ten times worse than white hell, a thousand times."

"Michael, don't tell Mom."

"I'm not telling her a damn thing. You're going to tell her."

"No, no, no," Blake cried through quivering lips.

"I haven't seeded the whore. You did. The only way she was having my child was if it was coming out of her mouth."

This comment broke Blake. He was crying audibly now, realizing that he may be stuck with a woman his brother had had in every possible way—every man in the county had, a professional penis eater. His child's mother, his fake white wife, was a bona fide whore.

"Let's just kill her, Michael."

"Shut your blasphemous mouth, Blake. You thought with your penis. Now you have to live with your decisions. Maybe I should get a black whore pregnant to even things out. We could build a home right next to you and Darla."

"No."

"Maybe Meissa. She's a treat, isn't she?"

"No."

"No? You had her, remember? Even though I told you she was mine and mine alone. You stuck your giant cock in her anyway, didn't you?"

"Michael."

"In fact, I'm going to go lay with her right now. I miss my tender African beauty."

"Michael, please don't leave. We have to find a way to—"

"Go home, Blake. I'll meet you there tonight. And, brother, don't say anything to Mother until I get there. I need to be able to defend myself. I'm sure this will somehow end up being my doing." Michael left Blake to soak in his own heartache.

What am I going to do? Blake thought as the world was crumbling down around him. And now his own flesh and blood was turning his back on him. He had let everybody down. He should have just killed Darla when she first told him. He should have buried her right there behind the barn.

CHAPTER 14

After a grindingly slow ride back to the plantation, Blake climbed off his horse and dragged his uncooperative feet up the dirt path. The air around the countryside felt dryer than normal, and the night air had a scent to it, a dreadful scent.

Moping around the house, Blake was in a dream state. Beth and Julia were there, but he felt all alone. His mind was running on empty, yet a hundred different scenarios kept jabbing at his subconscious.

"Blake. Blake. Blake!"

"What, woman?"

"I've been calling you for five minutes," Beth spoke angrily. "Michael is outside in a wagon with Darla. He wants you to come out."

Blake's face went lifeless. Slowly he rose to his feet. His knees were noodles, but he endured. There was nowhere else to go. One foot in front of the other, he concentrated as he marched to his reckoning.

In the wagon on their way to the big house, there were long speeches worth of word unsaid. Michael's face was bent in an angry scowl, Blake's presented a worried sulk, but Darla had on a cool, apprehensive sneer mixed with a hint of a triumphant glow.

As they pulled within a couple hundred yards of their childhood home, Blake called out in a panic, "No. Not yet."

"We have to do this, Blake," Michael insisted.

"No, not yet."

"Blake, let's just—"

"Shut up, woman," Michael scolded Darla, who tried her hand.

"Just stop at the barn," Blake suggested with a sense of urgency in his manner.

In the back of the large hay barn where Blake had defiled Darla on the night that more or less spurred this meeting, the three adults placed all their cards on the table. Voices amplified then hushed, tears were spilled and wiped, threats were distributed and taken back; but in the end, a conclusion was met. Darla and Blake would have a house built at the end of the town where they could raise their son or daughter in secret. Money would be funneled from the hotel to a small bank where both Darla and Blake would hold separate accounts. In the backwash of all this planning, Blake was able to convince everyone to wait until things were already set before they brought the news to their parents. Until then, everything was to go on as if nothing had changed.

CHAPTER 15

Three months roared by faster than a pack of wild stallions. The awkwardness of the situation had subsided some, and Blake's passion for white girls had all but fizzled. Darla was showing nicely. There was no hiding that perfectly round six-month-old midsection. Congratulations were scornfully doled out by passersby. No one really liked seeing a whore with child. The predicament was seen as a mournful one for all involved.

Unplanned pregnancies were an occupational hazard in Darla's line of work. For most whores, to be carrying was to be out of a job. With that in mind, prostitutes who were expecting didn't carry themselves like Darla did. But most prostitutes hadn't just received a blueprint on the home being built for her.

Loner's was anything but lonely this evening. It was a Friday night, and the joint was jam-packed. Blake had calmed down his sex-crazed behavior tenfold. Beth and Julia were now a thing of the past. This breakup was a nasty one, but Michael was the one who stepped in and made the final decision. So besides Darla, every once and again, one of his slave whores who hung around his father's shop was the extent of his sexual prowess.

All was well when…in walked Colonel David Olms—the one-armed veteran war hero who, for all applicable purposes, was maybe the most well-respected man in town. Colonel Olms's political as well as public influence over the community was unrivaled. Dressed in a creaseless steam-pressed dark-gray military uniform, Colonel Davis drew much attention. Keeping plenty busy was his lone limb, cuffing and shaking the hands of every male fortunate enough to be standing within speaking distance. Unaccompanied, the colonel was already a very polarizing figure; but in the hotel, on this night, the person standing next to him was the reason for all the extra attention.

Hellen was the most jaw-dropping high-yellow, thick-thighed, and long-haired slave woman most of the men in the building had ever laid eyes on. And for this undertaking, Colonel Davis had her dressed to kill. The slim-cut sultry red dress she had on hugged her gracefully formed curves like few were capable. Blake was practically on his feet. She was better than a white woman in his opinion. She was a black woman with all the white woman's characteristics—thin nose, good hair, light skin—but she still had the perfectly thick frame of a slave whore.

Blake swelled to a margin he hadn't in a long time. With tunnel vision, he walked right over to Michael who had been discussing the woman's price with the colonel and pulled him over for a sidebar. "Michael, we got to have her."

"No, Blake," Michael said, shaking his head. "This man is out of his mind. He's asking three times as much as we paid for any other slave whore."

"I don't care. Just get her." Michael saw the thirst in his brother's face. He hadn't seen Blake this upbeat in months. Shaking his head, he agreed to purchase Hellen. Before the money had changed hands, Blake had Hellen up on the top floor trying to fuck a bone out her ass. There was no clemency being shown to the newly acquired hotel employee. Blake proceeded to pound Hellen's thick ass through the mattress. This modern-day 1800s' pretty woman had no time to get adjusted to his size. She was receiving a crash course on how to work with advanced equipment.

Unfortunately for everyone, Darla spotted the whole occurrence. Since the day she told him about the pregnancy, Blake had been neglecting her womanly urges—only laying with her when she had him trapped off, and even then, she was forced to beg for it. *Oh no,* she grumbled mentally. *As soon as Ms. Big-tits Nigger Whore walked through the door, he acted as if she was the second coming.*

Darla paced the lobby floor furiously. Periodically, she looked up at the door that encased her unborn child's father. After waiting more than two hours, she was fed up and beside herself with jealousy.

Climbing the stairs to the third floor, half the lobby watched the scorned woman on her way up. Darla's emotions had been written on her face for hours now. Her feelings were so apparent that many of the girls working the rooms had asked her if she was okay. Now ascending the staircase, a feat she hadn't attempted since she had begun to show, an entire crowd watched to see where the hard-faced woman's evil sentiment was directed. The scene played out like a fistfight taking place in a crowded cathedral. First there were only a few eyes on her, then the others turned to see what they were looking at. Next thing you know, the whole place was paying attention. Again, Darla hadn't taken the steps in months. She had become a real diva. The round-stomached woman made it very clear that she was in no condition to be walking nobody's stairs, and she would pitch a fit when asked to do so.

On the third floor, with the entire world watching, Darla barged in on Blake and Hellen without so much as a knock. Her animated voice was so voluminous, it easily carried through the gaunt wooden door.

Blake jumped to his feet, and dressing frantically, he spoke in a whispered tone, trying to calm her. Darla was beyond mitigation.

"You've been up her for hours!" she screamed at the top of her voice. "Her pussy isn't that great."

Hellen's swollen breasts bounced up and down, to and fro, as she rushed to clothe herself. Her large global playthings seemed to be purposely belittling the flat-cupped mother-to-be.

"There are customers downstairs you are supposed to be cooking for. Instead you are up here for hours making love to this dirty slave whore." Darla's words weren't incriminating per se. She was trying to make a conscious effort to suppress the true reason for her blowup.

When Bell notified Michael, who was stuck behind one of his favorite employees, the hotel owner rushed up to the scene of the commotion. When he got there, Darla was being restrained from going after Hellen. The audio in the room was missed by no one. By the time Michael walked Darla out of the room, every eye in the building was suspiciously set on the two. Michael knew right away that no matter the explanation, Blake's perception at Loner's had been forever altered.

"I never said we were having relations. All I said was that he was up there too long and that he needed to get back to work," Darla feebly defended herself as she, Michael, and Blake—once again—found themselves face-to-face in a verbal standoff inside the now-infamous hay barn.

"You know exactly what I mean, Darla." Michael ferociously tore into her. "You saw the looks as well as I. Everyone in that place is thinking the same thing—that you and Blake are into something secretly immoral."

"Who cares what they think," Darla shot back.

"Everyone. That is the point. Perception is everything, woman," Michael responded.

"I made a mistake."

"Your mistake could get my brother killed."

"No one would ever think to—"

"Shut up, Darla. You're stupid."

"Blake, I'm sorry. It's just…"

Blake was silent, thinking over the ramifications of the night's events. Everything was spiraling out of control. *To think the year started off so well.*

"Blake!" Darla again called, trying to get his attention. "I don't know what came over me. If anyone asks, I'll make sure they know that we are just friends."

Blake's tongue remained still.

"Blake!"

"What, Darla?" The large black man finally reacted. "What do you want me to say? Haven't you said it all? Haven't you done enough? Have you not caused an adequate amount of trouble? Are you now here just to rip the scab off the wound?"

"I just want you to know that I'm sorry."

"I heard you. I heard you ten times, but it doesn't change anything, Darla. I'll be lucky if they don't string me up by the end of the week."

"They would never. Your family is too respected in this town."

"Shut up, Darla," Michael stopped her. "You're sleeping at the big house tonight. We'll see what tomorrow brings. And, Blake, you keep your penis behind the grill tomorrow. Don't move."

CHAPTER 16

With subtle and whispered voices, Blake and Darla remained the topic of rumors the next day. But as the drinks flowed and the women moaned, the conversations began to dissolve. There was nothing more capable of altering one's perception than providing sexual fruition.

The next few weeks passed by without incident. Michael played diffuser, shooting any and all talk about his brother and Darla. Blake was an exemplary employee—cooking, smiling, and basically just keeping his nose clean. Things were getting back to normal; however, Darla was still pregnant, aka she was like a stick of dynamite waiting for a light. And Wednesday night, just as Loner's was winding down, Hellen gave her the fire she needed.

Hellen had become a major attraction in the hotel. Her looks combined with the controversy of that dramatic night, and she was charging white-whore prices. With no dip in clientele, the woman had them lined up. After servicing her final customer for the night, she spotted Blake putting away the food from the grill. Many of the other women at Loner's, black and white, had expressed to her how nice Blake was and how much he had changed since that episode with her and Darla. Feeling guilty, Hellen just wanted to apologize for her part in the matter. The conversation took only minutes, but from where Darla was standing, it seemed like a lot longer. When Hellen walked off, Darla followed the woman with her eyes to her room. Ten minutes later, Darla was opening the door behind her.

Hellen didn't even have time for a greeting. Darla opened, "Look here, Ms. Uppity Slave-whore Bitch. Maybe I wasn't clear before. That black man down there is off-limits."

"I was just—" Hellen tried to explain before being cut short.

"I know what you were just trying to do, and it isn't going to happen. If he doesn't come looking for you, you make damn sure you don't go trying to find him."

"Why? Is y'all two?"

"Don't worry about what we are. You keep your nasty black ass away from him. He isn't your concern. Are we clear?" Hellen stared at her blankly. "Do you understand me?" Darla rephrased.

"Yes, Ms Darla ma'am. I's sorry. I's not sex your man no mo," Hellen said sarcastically.

Darla snatched open the door and left the room satisfied. In her own world, she was not aware of the crowd of concerned eyes trained on her. From the moment Hellen went over to speak with Blake, certain onlookers were watching to gauge Darla's reaction; and to no avail, her behavior gave them the confirmation they sought.

The very next day, the place was once again abuzz with rumors of Blake and Darla. This time, the banter coming from the alcohol-charged crowd was a lot more violently charged. Many of the prostitutes, white and black, really liked Darla; and to nearly all, Blake was considered a sweetheart. The thought of him having her pregnant was too far-fetched for any of them to swallow. Not even Hellen was willing to go as far as to insinuate such an outrageous claim. In spite of everyone's starch denials, the girls were swamped with these revolving questions by every other man they serviced.

Scheduled to work with his father at the gun store, Blake's absence at Loner's served only to fan the flames. Unable to defend his position, Darla was left to be the lone refuter. Disclaiming any physical interest in Blake, she used slurs that were more than a little racially insensitive; but to most, her performance came off as over-the-top and rehearsed.

Livid with the threat aimed at his brother, Michael, Bell, and two other hired security personnel brandishing pistols cleared the hotel of all unsavory customers. Anyone caught whispering about his brother in relation to Darla was instantly shown the door. Still, this didn't curb the frenzy.

The situation had got so out of control that it eventually showed up at Mr. Townsman's gun shop. Mr. Townsman was a no-nonsense type of guy. The five drunken accusers were quickly ushered out of his store at gunpoint.

Mr. Townsman had actually heard the grumbles before but brushed it off as hogwash. Now after such a scene, he was forced to look at his son and ask. Blake could only drop his head in shame. With confirmation from his own child, the gravity of the situation had him numb with anger.

At closing time, Blake helped his father load up the wagon with the store contents. With the controversy circulating, he was taking no chances. It would only take the wrong group to stumble upon this news, and his gun store would be picked clean.

The conversation was nothing more than a few short questions followed by abbreviated answers as they traveled that long awkwardly rode trail back to the plantation. Mr. Townsman had his Townswell shotgun at his side as they navigated the dark country path.

A black man sleeping with a white whore was bad, but he was confident that he could have found a way to muddle through the controversy. For him to get her pregnant—this was beyond political posturing. Blake had messed up. An error like this had the making of a night ride all over it.

After enduring the uncomfortable silent journey, Mr. Townsman instructed Marcus, who had met them in front of the house, to unload his supplies in the weapons shack. Walking into the house, Blake carried his father's Townswell in behind him.

Mrs. Townsman was in the kitchen. Blake kissed his mother on the cheek and gave her a big hug. Mr. Townsman headed straight for the liquor cabinet. Scanning the handwritten labels on the assorted bottles with an outstretched finger, he chose a good strong brand. Hungrily, he popped the cork and took a long swig. Blake was telling his mother about how he planned to kick her butt at target practice the following week when his father walked into the kitchen and threw him all the way under the stagecoach.

"Your brown baby has gotten the head whore, Darla, pregnant."

Blake's eyes widened twice it's normal size.

"What!" Mrs. Townsman screeched. "Don't even joke like that," she added, looking from her husband to her stupefied son. "That isn't my son's child."

"Do you think I would come in here—"

"Shut up!" Mrs. Townsman silenced her significant other. "Blake, tell me this is some kind of sick joke."

"Mom, I... I made a mistake. I—"

Smack! She cut him off with an openhanded swat to the face. *Smack, smack, smack.* She attacked her son. "You stupid, horny black son of a slave. How could you?" She continued to beat the submissive young man. She battered him until her hands hurt. Then she began throwing at him whatever she could reach. Mr. Townsman stood calmly in the corner sipping out of a bottle as his wife did what everyone knew she would.

When her strength left and her voice became hoarse, she scratched out what naturally came next. "Where the hell is Michael? How could he let this happen?"

On cue, Michael came running in the house. No soon as he made it into the kitchen was he ducking objects that were being hurled at him by a foul-mouthed woman he called mom.

"What have you got your brother into? I knew your sinful ways would come back to hurt your brother."

"Mom."

"You stupid—"

"Mom."

"Unclean, only good for—"

"Mom, we don't have time for this. Some men are on their way here to get Blake."

"What?" his mother gasped.

"They already grabbed Darla."

"Not my baby."

"Blake, we have to go."

"Nobody is coming on this property to do anything," Mr. Townsman assured.

"Go? Go where? My boys aren't going anywhere. That woman's a whore. Her word means nothing. Until that child is born… Boy, please go grab your Townswell. You are a Townsman. We aren't going anywhere. Running isn't in your blood."

"Dad?" Michael pleaded.

"Boy, did you hear what I said?"

"Mom?"

"Shut up, Michael, and go get your guns," Mrs. Townsman said as she turned to walk out the door. She had to go get her rifle from the shed. Michael was right on her heels.

"Mom, we don't need to do this. If Blake leaves now, in a few months, this whole thing will blow over. There's no way of telling who's on their way up here or how many." Michael's pleas fell on deaf ears as his mother stomped around the side of the house. The shed was fifty yards outside of the main house. While his mother loaded up, Michael packed his and Blake's Townswells in a dirty-brown duffel bag along with two rifles and a bunch of ammo. Mrs. Townsman had her rifle loaded and ready when she walked out the cabin door.

"Uh." Michael heard her grunt before her body hit the dirt. Michael dropped his bag and ran to his mother's aid. He was met by the long thick barrel of a .44-caliber pistol. "Mom," he cried right before he felt the thud of the metal butt of a gun smash against his skull. The impact instantly sent him to slumberland.

The moment seemed as if Michael were only out for a couple seconds, but when he came to, Blake was being hauled off on the back of his father's wagon followed by three horseman. And his father was in his mother's arms, bleeding on the porch. Michael staggered to the front of his house. His head was wet from the gash left behind by his assailant, and the blood kept running down into his eye.

He heard himself say, "Dad." "Dad," he called again. As he approached, his strength began to come back, but his vision was still blurred. His father wasn't moving, and from ten yards away, he feared the worst.

Falling to his knees, he let his emotions have its moment. The tears in his eyes fell with a stream down his face. "Is he…is he…is he—"

"He's dead, Michael," his mother said with an anger in her voice that he never witnessed. Her voice wasn't cracking, but it wasn't exactly clear either. Those bastards took my husband."

"Oh, Ma. I'm so sorry. I should have… I… I…"

Mrs. Townsman turned to her son. Her eyes were dead. "They have your brother. Go get him."

"What!" Michael said incredulously.

"I said grab your goddamned gun and go get my boy. You and he are all I have left."

"Mom," Michael said, reaching his hand out to touch her shoulder.

"Get your gun and get your ass up. Go get your brother. Now!" she screamed. Her forceful tone scared Michael to his feet. "Don't bring your ass back here without your brother." Michael still stood stuck. "Go. They're getting away." Slowly he began to back away. "Hurry!" she screamed. Her unfamiliar voice made him jump, but then he ran back to the shack and grabbed his Townswell.

CHAPTER 17

The road to their house was a winding one, but Michael and Blake had developed a shortcut over the years. If he hurried, he could catch them at the fork in the road. He was outnumbered but, with his Townswell, not outgunned. Plus he had the element of surprise on his side.

The bulky shotgun was heavy as it bounced up and down on his leg, but he had nowhere else to hold it. His two six-shot .45 pistols were loaded with twelve death rock ready to go.

"Lord, forgive me for what I am about to do," he prayed while running his horse full speed across the stubble terrain. They had killed his father, struck his mother, did who knows what with his unborn nephew's mother; and now they had his brother tied up on the back of a wagon. If God didn't forgive him for this, then he wasn't God. *Not one of those bastards is going to make it home tonight—not one.* If this was going to buy him a seat in hell, then he was riding front row. There would be no mercy tonight.

At the cuff, the road where the path split, Michael lay in a shallow hole in the ground by a thick tree trunk. He had been sitting in the ditch for only a couple minutes, but in that time, his mind had begun to play tricks with his psyche. Had he missed them? Did they have an alternative route in and out of the plantation? They had snuck up on him and his mother. Maybe they had been planning this for a while, and Darla was just the excuse they needed. *How did they get Pop? He was a wonderful shot. Oh my God, what if they already stopped and was burning and hanging Blake's body already?* Michael stopped to see if he could hear gunshots. Rednecks always shot the body a few times while it hung. He had to double back or ride up ahead. Had he missed them, or were they busy killing his brother?

Michael rose to his feet with his heavy Townswell in tow. Just then, he heard the hooves of their horses. Slowly he lay back down. His heart was beating so fast his lungs raced to keep up with the demand. His hands were sweating like he had been out working the cotton fields. He had fired his weapon a hundred thousand times but never at a human target that could move, dodge, think, and more importantly, fire back. His father trained him to hit moving targets, but this was a whole different ball game.

What if I fail? What if I miss the first shot and do nothing but put the men on guard? Is this hole really that hidden? Too many questions dawned his subconscious as the quickly approaching murdering kidnappers neared. These were experienced killers. They had gunned down his father—the most capable gunman he had ever known. Did he even have a chance?

The first glimpse of the horses was visible now. At this angle, they would ride right up into his line of fire. His first five shots had to be precise. He had to wait until the perfect time to fire. They were closer and closer as the seconds passed.

I can't do this. Murder is the worst sin in the world, but suicide is just as bad, and if I backed out now, at this angle, that would be exactly what I'll be doing, committing suicide.

A hundred yards, eighty, fifty, twenty, fifteen—*boom!* He hit the driver of the wagon in the neck to his lower face. *Boom, boom!* Two shots caught one of the horsemen in the high chest. Several horses screamed, and the cart took off with its captain bobbing lifelessly in the saddle.

With a controlled panic, Michael bounced to his feet. The last two horsemen went for their guns. *Boom!* The closer of the two went tumbling to the earth, as Michael shot his horse in the face. Dropping his Townswell, Michael pulled one of his revolvers. For whatever reason, the remaining driver hesitated to squeeze. Mistake! Five quick shots from Michael's powerful handgun took half the man's shirt off.

The horseman who fell from his dead steed had lost his pistol in the process. Quickly, as if his life depended on it (and it did), he scurried around the black ground on hands and knees searching for his fallen weapon.

The country night was dark as hell, but Michael was familiar with this gloomy climate, and he had the man on all fours. Counting back in his head—one hit the wagon, two hit the first dead rider, and one for the unlucky horse lying to his left—yeah, he had one shot left. Backing up a step while keeping his eye on the still-frantic man crawling in the dirt, Michael retrieved his Townswell. With a hot surge of energy in his veins, he eased toward the man as he scraped around still looking for what he could not find.

Michael was right above him five feet away, and the man's weapon was at the rifle holder's feet. The Townswell was no longer heavy. The weapon felt like Zeus's lightning bolt in his hands.

Giving up his pursuit of his lost property, the man looked up sadly and eyed the now-bastard child, pleading, "Who… I didn't do anything. It wasn't me."

"My name is Michael Townsman," Michael spoke. "My father's name was Michael Townsman Sr."

"I didn't want to come. The girl said he raped her."

This infuriated Michael. "Where is she?"

"We let her go. I swear we didn't hurt her."

"Where is she?"

"She's back at the hotel."

Michael fell silent for a long time. "My father was a good man."

"I didn't pull the trigger. Please, for God's sake, I didn't pull the trigger." The man was begging for his life.

This was no longer a justified shooting. His brother was safe in the wagon, and the man was unarmed and nonthreatening. Michael lowered his weapon.

"Thank you. Thank you, son," the submissive man said, dropping his pleading hands.

"Stand up," Michael ordered. "Who else was in on this?"

"No one else."

"Who else knew you were coming out here?"

"No one else. It was just the four of us. They were just going to come for the nigger, but Larry shot Mr. Townsman."

"The nigger? The nigger is my brother," Michael said, raising his Townswell.

"Please, son."

"I'm not your son, and you're not my father." *Boom!* The Townswell sounded, hitting the man in the face, taking off the entire top of his head from the upper lip back. "I have no father," Michael said, lowering his empty weapon.

It took half an hour to find the runaway cart. The horses had run until they had felt the safety of a silent area. Blake's pleading screams lured Michael to him. Blake was bonded like a pig, his face beaten and bruised.

Michael brought his brother home to his mother before heading back out to clean up the bloody evidence. The bodies were dragged on the back of the wagon and buried one on top of the other. The headless horse was too heavy to drag, so Michael gathered a pile of wood and a can of lamp oil. He set the pony ablaze and sat for hours feeding the flames as the horse's flesh burned away enough for him to handle the animal's corpse. The horse's final resting place was dug and refilled just in time for the sun to kiss the morning sky. Michael dragged into the house at dusk. His mother was sitting in the front living room looking out the window with her rifle laying across her lap.

"Where's Blake?"

"I sent him to the back house. He was exhausted," his mother answered in a calm, even voice. She was in her own world, speaking without ever looking back at her son.

"You all right, Ma?"

"Yes, baby. Your father is in the shed. I am going to need you to bury him sometime today."

Michael nodded, though his mother couldn't see his answer.

"Did you clean up the bodies?"

"Yes, Mother."

"Good boy. Go upstairs and get some rest."

"I have to be at the hotel in a few hours."

"Go get some rest, son. I'm sure someone will cover for you. You can be a few hours late today. Now go upstairs and get some rest."

"Yes, Mother." Michael conceded but stood and watched his mother for a silent moment. She was so relaxed, too relaxed really. "Are you sure you're okay?"

"Michael, I'm fine. Come give your mother a kiss and run off to bed."

Michael hugged and kissed his mother. Her embrace was weak but filled with a weighty significance. "Everything is going to be okay."

"I know, son," she said, still staring out the window.

"I love you, Mom."

"I love you too, son. You did well. Now run along."

Michael hit the bed like a log. His body began to ache all over. He could even feel his muscles throbbing in his sleep. He was so tired, but for some reason, he was wide awake two hours after shutting his eyes. Rising to his feet, he began to ready himself for work. If he and Blake both took the day off, they'd have some explaining to do. He had a chance if he acted like nothing had happened. The missing men, if they had acted alone, would be just that—missing. After checking on Blake, Michael rode into town with a large satchel hanging from his horse. If things got ugly, he would be ready.

CHAPTER 18

Michael had the weight of the world on his shoulders walking into the hotel that evening. He just killed four men, lost his father, and spent majority of the night discarding evidence that would surely noose his neck if discovered. Still, exhausted to the point of apathetic, with his Townswell slung across his back and his six-shooter on his hip, Michael put on a brave face as he pushed nonchalantly into the brothel where he was somewhat looked off by the crowd of fornicators.

It was business as usual. The women greeted him in their typical flirt-with-the-boss normality. Bell sat at the back of the lobby looking over the midday crowd—same I-hate-everyone expression on his face. Drinks were served; whores were used and then reused. The barbecue pit was lit and fit, greasy slabs of swine teasing the nostrils absent of Blake's expertise. If anyone in the room knew about the raid at his home last night, they were definitely hiding it well.

In his private room in the back of the first floor, Michael set his open satchel on the floor along the side of the bed. A second pistol was placed on the pillow next to him as he lay back to rest his weary body. Though he was relieved to have had such an uneventful entrance, his head was spinning with the potential ramifications of last night's events.

The rap on the door disturbed his blank dream. With his hand on his sidearm, Michael walked over to the locked door. "Who's there?"

"It's me, Darla."

Michael didn't see the pregnant woman when he walked in and was grateful he hadn't. Reticent, Darla stared worried eyes at Michael, searching for any sign of something amiss, but his face was nongiving.

"Hey, um, good evening. I, um—"

"What happened last night?" Michael said, cutting her off.

Darla's hands went to her face as the tears instantly swelled in her eyes. "They said they were going to ride out to your place and kill Blake. I'm so sorry. I tried to tell them that it was all a lie, but they were so determined. I... I..."

"Who was it?"

"I don't know. They were wearing white clothes over their heads."

"Did they hurt you?"

"No, not really, but they pulled me into the back of a stagecoach and held me down. They put their guns in my face. They promised the most dreadful things would happen to me if my child turned out to be a nigger baby." Darla had her hands protectively over her stomach. "They said Blake had been bragging about having me pregnant. I knew they were lying. Blake wouldn't do such a thing. I knew it."

"What did you tell them?"

"I... I told them that it was all lies. I'm a whore. I told them the baby could be anyone's. I told them I would never lay down with a nigger. But they didn't believe me. They said I smell of dishonesty."

"What else did you tell them?"

"Nothing. I promise. I denied it all. I swear!"

"Okay, okay, calm down. So what happened after they let you go?"

"They only rode me around for a short while. Then they told me to keep my mouth shut, or they would do to me what they were going to do to Blake. Michael, I swear I wanted to come warn you, but I was so frightened. I… I… I didn't know what to do or… I just…"

"Don't worry, Darla. Everything is going to be okay. I think they wanted to scare you into saying something. Blake's fine. He rode out with my father this morning. They should be back in a few weeks."

"So they didn't… But they sounded so determined."

"That is what cowardly men do."

"I wanted to go to the sheriff but decided to wait. Michael, I am so relieved nothing happened."

"Darla, everything is fine."

"But—"

"Darla, everything is fine."

"Okay. You said Blake left this morning?"

"Yes, he should be back in a few weeks. Now stop worrying," Michael insisted with as much of a smile as he could muster. He held a hand that Darla grabbed, allowing him to usher her to the door.

"I'm so relieved," she said again as he opened the door.

"Do me a favor. Tell Meissa to come here."

Darla gave Michael a nasty look, but she said nothing as she walked out. When Meissa knocked on his door, Michael's heart sped up. Her face wore a worried look on her way into the room.

"Is everything okay, Master sir?"

"Yes, I'm just a little fatigued. I just wanted you to lay with me." A slow smile crept across Meissa's soft face as she walked over and began undressing. Michael watched the pretty brown slave disrobe before he locked the door and walked over to join her. He was not in the mood for sex. He pulled Meissa into him over his clothes. Meissa's soft body felt good in his arms. He needed this moment. Though the devastation of last night's events weighed heavily on his mind, the woman's mere presence was soothing to his body.

Meissa was only sixteen, but Michael had been intimate with her for nearly five years now. She was, in a way, his longest relationship. He loved Meissa, and though the law prohibited him from teaching her to read or write, Michael made sure that Meissa learned to speak proper Northeast English. He taught her to be clean and to wash herself the way a white woman would.

Meissa's mother had worked with the Townsmans since he was a young boy. From the day she was born, the young Meissa was pampered—treated better than any slave on the plantation. Mrs. Townsman always wanted a daughter, so she would have Meissa at the big house most of the day, coddling and caring for the young girl as if she were her own. Meissa was as free a slave as there was in Georgia at the time.

The first time Mrs. Townsman found out that Michael was having relations with her, he was reprimanded something serious. His mother said that Meissa was far too young to be engaging in such activity. But as the behavior continued, Mrs. Townsman began to take it in stride. She started to accept that it was just a coming-of-age process for her son—a rite of passage. Meissa was a slave, and he was free to do with her as he pleased.

Michael slept the entire day away. Meissa lay in his arms. She was glad to have a day where she was not required to comfort the young black women who bore the burden of having strangers forced between their legs. Slave whores were not treated gently in this business. The redneck men chose to go with slave women because they could do whatever they wanted to them. Though beating the women, black or white, was not permitted at Loner's, sodomy and savagely jamming their privates down their throats thrilled the racist fiends. At the end of the night, the black whores' girl parts would be battered and bruised from the severe pounding in which they were subjected.

Michael stayed in his room with Meissa until midnight. The two had eaten together and lay cuddled up in each other's arms for the whole day. That night, Meissa rode home with Michael on his wagon. He wasn't ready to let the young woman out of his presence just yet. There was something about her that settled his nerves, and though he never allowed her to entertain a client, he decided right then and there that he was done allowing her to be seen as a whore.

He would appoint a new Negro madam to his hotel. No more sharing her with the world. Meissa was his and his alone.

*****

The Sword

"Pray not to the heavens," the Sword spoke inaudibly. "I will be the hand of God tonight. Thy heaven's sword will smite thy enemy."

More than an hour had come and gone without so much as a shiver from the Sword. Stuck still, gargoyle-like, he allowed only his active pupils the freedom to roam as he absorbed the crowd's scorn and disgust, permitting the much-needed hate to fester in his blackening heart.

No one is leaving this field alive, he promised. This was the fourth hanging he had witnessed from this very spot. *Four is my limit,* he reasoned. He could no longer stand privy to such aggression against his people. He was no slave, never had been a slave. The war was over; the North had won. The black man was not only free to fight for his liberty but also encouraged thusly.

Two of the Sword's four custom-made seven-shot revolver pistols were being choked in a tight clasp within his own warm palms. The other pair of guns sat uncomfortably in the holster on the small of his back. His four bulky constructed pistols held a total of twenty-eight rounds between them, and there were another thirty-some odd shells entombed in the ammunition strap fastened around his waist.

He was convinced the crowd muddled below represented the devil's secretary. Every being in the pit—man, woman, and child—was beyond extrication in his assessment. The Sword only saw evil before him. To eradicate such vile creatures was to be doing the world a service.

This was not about color. The Sword held no ill feelings toward whites as a whole. He had been raised with whites and loved by them. He knew very well the difference between good and bad whites. The evil flock ahead weren't just bad whites; they were something else—demons perhaps, demons shrouded in Caucasian wrapping.

The Bible taught that the Lord puts the riotous in place to do his bidding. It was left up to the man to recognize his employment and have the courage to follow it through. He was the sword of God. There was no way he could turn his back on that. The Sword had been preparing his entire life for this assignment, strengthening his body with choice exercises and sharpening his mind with books and studies. He didn't realize he was training back then, but all the personal losses he had taken, all the hurtful racist banter he had been subjected—all these experiences worked to push him to this point.

The Sword thought back to how his family urged him to master his firearms. He was drilled with "You are a Townsman." Townsmans' deal in guns, target practice, hand-to-hand combat literacy—they literally turned him into a sharpened weapon. The two pistols tightened in his fist as he inhaled the searing fumes of the burning black man. The crooked veins in the Sword's rock-solid forearm bulged from him choking so tightly the metal handles. An unexpected breeze blew up from the confines of the valley floor, cooling the spotted beads of sweat that had accumulated on his forehead. Enjoying the icy draft, the Sword tilted his head to the sky, allowing his mental to ease. Closing his eyes, he attempted to align his abstract thoughts with the reality of the moment.

The Sword's two reserve pistols felt sturdy against the small of his back. The cold steel touching his exposed skin gave him an extra boost of much-needed energy. His right pant leg was torn shorter than the left. There he stuck a foot-long hunting knife in a holster he had strapped there.

No one was lining up to help them; he urged his procrastinating feet. President Lincoln was in his grave, assassinated in cold blood by a fiend tantamount to those standing before him. The North had won his people their freedom, but here in the back farmlands of Connecticut, there were still some who were hanging on to their imperialistic ideologies.

Blacks weren't safe. It wasn't enough to live riotous. Keeping one's head down only served to hide you for a time. The night riders would eventually find you, racism sought you out, and bigotry was the bloodhound running one through the orchids. Evil had to be met head-on. Blood was going to be his gift to the ungodly—fear, hurt, bullets, and death.

There were too many for him to charge down at head-on. The Sword counted seven firearms among the twenty, all rifles and shotguns. The Sword had to get a quick start. All twenty or so would dine with Satan this night. It didn't matter their age. Size, shape, and gender were to be glossed over. These were children of hell—demons in training. They were women, wives, mothers, and sisters of perdition. *From the tallest man to the smallest child, all would fail at the hand of heaven's sword,* he emboldened himself.

The bonfire set beneath the burning corpse lit a good portion of the field with flickering grace. The fluctuating glimmer contorted the pale-face crowd's images, further authenticating the Sword's notion that these were no ordinary beings but creatures of foul creation.

Gunshots stirred through the darkness, hitting the hanging body, jerking it to a steady sway. Laughter and cheer followed every cruel assault, egging on the callous attack. So many shells surged through the dark crisp corpse that the Sword was sure they were trying to cut him in two.

Round after round, weapons were emptied, broke open, restocked, and unloaded again. Thunderous relentless fire reared through the swinging man, exciting the onlookers and infuriating the Sword, until his rage rose to a point where he could no longer stand it.

Twelve single-saddled horses along with two multipassenger wagons were parked at the far end of the park where a sloping hill was arched in a fashion suitable for the horses to climb. Surveying the best course of attack, the Sword figured to start by taking away their transportation.

Shaking free of his stone-like trance, he slowly began to animate. The balls of his feet all the way to his calf ached from standing nonmovement for so long. Working stiff limbs, he pushed around the elevated hilltop, keeping low and moving at an exaggerated pace to not allow anyone a glimpse of his stealthy descent. As his adrenaline picked up, so did his velocity. It was a long way around, and anticipation began to gain precedence over caution. Still wary of the danger of being seen, he kept low, sprinting around the valley just as fast as he dared. The two long black pistols remained at his side, dragging so low they brushed across the foot-high weed grown atop the elevated fold.

The drumming of his heart was thumping so loud that it involuntarily propelled the man's tempo. He was moving so fast at this point, one would have thought he was in fear of being too late to save the young man above the raging flames.

Finally sucking in a gust of air, he reached the opening to the field. With the slim sliver of moon at his back, a slight hint of apprehension began to prickle up his spine. Suddenly he was wary of casting a shadow or silhouette that could be caught by the group across the valley. Dropping to his stomach, the Sword held his pistols parallel above his head and rolled down the steep slope. The incline was a lot more abrupt than he anticipated. His body banged violently against the hard sloping ground as he sped down. When he reached the bottom, his momentum carried him several yards across the even plain. Finally letting his body pull to a stop, the Sword was only twenty or so yards behind the stable of horses.

Easily, so not to elicit a startled reaction from the four-legged animals, the Sword pushed up to a knee. Enthralled in the moment, he again went motionless, listening to the medium around him. The twenty bonfire participants were still hooting and howling across the way. Inhaling deep, the smell of the burning man was a lot less pronounced on this side of the field; and outside of the fire's illumination, the world seemed to be completely clothed in blackness.

Suddenly, out of the darkness, the vague sound of activity caught his attention. Concentrating his senses, the Sword zeroed in on the disturbance. To his left, a bit off from where he was sitting, he heard the faint but unmistakable sound of a couple joyfully engaged.

Damn, the Sword cursed his clumsy approach. Moronically, he failed to factor in the possibility of there being persons in the hard-covered carriages. If not for him luckily stopping to tumble down the hill, he would have been discovered, caught in the act, and killed before he had even began.

Mistakes were a concession a man martially ordained could ill afford. *Stupid,* he reflected. The notion of this lapse of awareness disturbed him. *What am I doing?* He looked down at the heavy pistols in his hands. He was unprepared, inexperienced, and underskilled—he confessed of himself. *Heaven's sword?* he deliberated. *Was it was all in my head? What if God hadn't chosen me after all?*

The Sword had built up such lofty expectations over the last year. Maybe he was just fooling himself. He was one man against so many; a favorable outcome was bleak, he now knew. Reality was catching up to him. He was no killer. The hands beneath his pistols were not those of a hardworking man. He further reflected had a privileged life. This was all wrong. His hands shook with overwhelming apprehension. And to think he was so confident just minutes ago.

Lowering his heavy arms, he again closed his burning eyes. With butterflies in his gut, the Sword somehow allowed himself a moment to come to grips with his fluttering emotions. Galvanizing his fleeting confidence, he began. The earth around him was so dark, there was no way to cast a silhouette. And he did, in fact, look around the wagons before he pulled into the open. There was no way to peer through the wooden top. And though he hadn't factored in potential occupants in said wagon, at least he had the presence of mind to roll down the hill; that had to count for something. Maybe God was guiding his subconscious mind. *No,* he told himself, *this is my destiny. If not me, who? If not now, when?* he reasoned.

Opening his eyes, he cautioned himself, *Pull it together.* Still crouching low, he rocked his body to a duckwalk over toward the four-horse-drawn stagecoach. The multicolored elegantly crafted wooden carriage was gracefully designed. It seemed someone in the group of heathens was of a wealthy purse. This was an expensive ride, not commonly seen in this area of the state. The extended cab carriage was rocking up and down with a soft shimmer. The subtle creek in the well-constructed wooden bass was being easily drowned out by the high-pitched squeals of a woman willfully taking the brunt of what force the man between her thighs could offer her.

The Sword pulled to within a yard of the carriage. His black pistols were locked and loaded. All his energetic tenacity had returned—the fire back in his self-assured swagger. He could easily swing around the side window and empty into the preoccupied couple—death before climax, blood to taint their yet unfulfilled sweaty juncture. *But no, not the gun,* he wordlessly assessed. The gun was too loud, and those within the wagon needed to be silently reaped for not to alert the band ahead.

Holstering his pistols, the black-masked worn patron slid his hunting knife from its leather casing. Long deep breaths served to keep his fleeting nerves at a manageable calm. Timing was essential. As soon as he made his presence known, the demons would continue to fall until he or the field was no more.

His stomach was in a knot, but the discomfort was tolerable. His hands were slick with perspiration; still he managed a tight grip on his sharp metal blade. Edging toward the opening of the stagecoach, his heart thumped and his throat dried, but he pushed on.

Crouching low, the Sword hesitantly marched one baby step at a time. Steadily he advanced, careful not to make a sound. *This is for my father,* he declared as he neared the opening. *This is for my color, my race.* He stepped further still.

The loud pleasure-invoked cries of a man letting into his woman exited the wagon's interior, stalling the Sword's advance. He was literally inches from the entrance of the wagon, hidden on its side. A woman's giggles teased the air, exciting a hushed conversation between the couple. Violently the wagon began to rock as one or both its occupants began to rustle around the cab. Peeking around the side, everything seemed to be happening at a hesitant speed.

Suddenly the gate of the wagon opened wide, and a pair of bare feet sprung from the opening. The Sword instinctively pushed back on his hamstrings, readying his posture. A thickly hung, full-bearded white man hopped down from the carriage crevice; his eyes twisted in opposition to where they might be facing if he were to have any chance at some sort of life-saving resistance.

A brief hesitation on the Sword's end allowed the yawning half-naked Caucasian an abbreviated glimpse of his attacker, a hair second before he was tackled to the cushioned lawn. With overpowering strength, the Sword jumped atop the man, holding one hand across his furry mouth and the other tightly around the hilt of the knife he had plunged into the man's chest. A sharp twist of the wrist quelled the man's struggles before they really even began.

The Sword could feel the dying man's spirit fading away beneath him. Surprisingly, a pleased and invisible smile spread across the masked Negro's mental zing. His first cleansing, he processed, was so special. If only his victim could have fathomed how important his end had been. His tiny, insignificant death had ushered in a new era in justice. Suddenly the Sword wished he had known the man's name. On cue, he heard the woman in the stagecoach call out, "Marty?" Now a physical smile curled the Sword's lips.

"Marty?" the woman called again. "Stop messing. Who's out there?"

Keeping low, the Sword dragged Marty's dead body around the side of the wagon, a fresh trail of blood hidden in the night's blackened grass.

"Marty! Answer me! This isn't funny. Do not send anyone else in here! You promised. I'll not let anyone else lay with me tonight. I swear it."

A small barrage of gunfire from the other side of the field interrupted the woman's statement. The gun-crackling explosions dragged on for what seemed like minutes, and when it finally subsided, drunken cheers of encouragement immediately followed.

The Sword snatched his ridged dagger from Marty's chest with a savage yank. Warm runny blood and caked-on flesh occupied the teeth of the weapon. Apparently sick of being ignored, the loudmouthed, overzealous female's feet pushed out of the wagon. In one fluent acceleration, the Sword whipped around and grabbed the woman by her throat. Tightening his fist, he pulled her to her feet. His giant hands were clamped so harshly around the still-nude woman's windpipe, in addition to deterring her attempted scream, he unintentionally sent her an involuntary seductive jiggle.

The woman had taken him. He was not himself. He could feel it. His first kill had occurred only seconds ago, yet he already had a thirst for more. However, the naked white woman in front of him was influencing a different craving.

The Sword's iron grip was unrelenting. He could feel the woman's canty pulse bubbling beneath his closed palm. He squeezed harder, his fingers cramping from the applied pressure in which they were being subjected. He liked the pain; it served to insinuate the mortal connection the woman and he had.

Pulling her close with a bend of the elbow, the Sword examined her goods. Her fully nude body convulsed beneath his will. She was engrossed in the fight of her life, while he was calm—mesmerized by her moving parts. With a need for precision, adjusting to the dark, his eyes swam from her smooth skin. She was a darling specimen, he assessed. The shapely female's perky breast danced unrestrained as she struggled to free herself. Tiny hands pulled, scratched, and squeezed at his large wrist. Her face was heaven-sent. Even in her immediate state of panic, her flawless features warmed his loins.

Fear had begun to abandon her blue eyes, as the realization of inevitability began to wash over her. Her pretty little mouth sat gaped open as she inertly struggled to breathe. The woman's blemish-less pearl-colored skin gleamed in the dim moonlight. *The things he could do with her had he had the time.*

Thin but shapely, her hundred pounds cradled her five-foot-three frame perfectly. The Sword practically had her airborne—her small bare feet scraping grass and dirt while struggling to remain planted up under her. Spying down the untrimmed hairs on the inside of her thighs, the Sword thought it looked so soft—blonde, matching the shoulder-length wig hung down around his fingers. White women, beautiful white women—through all he had been through, still he could not overcome the power they had over him.

With his hand securely cemented around her throat, the Sword felt the young woman's struggles start to falter. With alarm, he loosened his grip just enough to allow her to pull in a nice breath; then not to spoil her, he squeezed it tight once more. Again but with less vigor, this time the woman's perky boobs bounced up and down as her body convulsed. Boy, did he want to take her. And he could have; he had time, and there was nothing she could do to stop him. A devilish smile parted the Sword's veiled mouth. *Enough fun for one night.* He straightened up. He was a righteous man, not a pale devil. Rape was a barbaric act; besides, there was work to be done. Reluctantly, he lifted his knife hand over his head. *Something,* he thought, *something is delaying my hand.* For several seconds, he stood, hand thrust above his head, with the female's naked body forcefully positioned before him. Then his killing arm fell altogether. He couldn't do it. She was too lovely to die in such a manner. No, she was not to feel his blade—not yet at least. He would save her for last. She did not participate in the party's transgressions. Just being in this valley proved she wasn't exactly innocent, but she hadn't physically engaged in the assault.

The woman was a pleasure-giver as far as he was concerned. Yes, he would give her a second chance, a choice. Death or dessert, he rationed. She would live to show him her gifts or die if she'd insist he show her his.

The naked woman began to nod off in his hand. But before she went, the Sword raised his blade and came down on the back of her neck with the handle. Her body plopped to the ground with a thud and lay still.

"Dessert," he reiterated as he looked down at his night's reward. Then putting away his blade, he pulled his two sidearms. He was ready for the main course.

CHAPTER 19

Blake felt low, spineless, and unworthy of the Townsman name—the name his gracious late Caucasian father felt so inclined to bestow upon him. Here he was, curled up half-naked and lying atop a comfortable plush-cushioned mattress being pampered while, because of him, his Caucasian brother was in town—possibly somewhere lying facedown.

All this is my fault, Blake mentally berated himself. All this was because he foolishly made the mistake of sticking his Negro penis in the wrong white woman. *My life has gone to* shit, Blake internally griped as salty tears continually raced down both sides of his face. He could have done anything and become anything—the state's first Negro lawyer, doctor, deputy, or maybe even sheriff. Before this slipup, his image was golden. In his town, he felt as notable a figure as any white man. But now, now he wasn't even sure if he could ever publicly show his face again—not without worrying about getting it blown off.

It was sickening how far he'd fallen—from Georgia's leading Negro gentleman to maybe one of the more despised persons in the entire state. It was so cliché—his fall from grace. The one thing a free black man was deprived was, of course, what he craved most: a good white woman.

His father was dead; he mournfully churn. His darling father was dead, and there was no way to bring him back. Blake hadn't cried this much his whole life. Dejected, he spent the last day and a half crying himself to sleep, only to wake up to begin again. Nearly all the liquid nourishment in his body had escaped from his eyes. Totally distraught, he couldn't eat or drink; all he wanted to do was lie there and die.

Blake's supple will to live had faltered. His mental resolve had waned, and it seemed even his body had begun to wave the white flag. His muscles convulsed, his limbs ached, and his head throbbed from a combination of dehydration, the lack of exertion, and the severe beating he'd undertaken the previous night.

Darla—he damned the thought of her. This was all her doing—her and her forthcoming demon child. The two amounted to a biblical plague on his world. *I should have killed her,* Blake revived. *I should have done it the night she told me she was pregnant.* No one would have been the wiser. This entire scenario would have died with her in that barn. None of this would have materialized. His soul might have been destined for a black hell, but that would have been exactly what he deserved. At least his precious brother, Michael, wouldn't have to share his fate. And most of all, his darling father would still be alive.

An agonizing moan upchucked his grungy body. His father was gone. He cried warm tears, damping his pillow. Blake's inside felt completely drained. With every wet tear that bled down his cheek, his feeble ribs would ache from the loss of substance.

A diversified lunch tray that Lory (Blake's new favorite female slave) had fixed for him laid undisturbed on his bedside. The smell of the cooling food was irritating to his sensitive stomach, but this was the third meal Lory prepared, with him turning the first two away. Doubled over by a pain he'd never been subjected, Blake knew unequivocally that he needed to get something into his stomach.

"Lory," Blake spoke with not much more effort than a whisper, "I'm ready to eat."

With sympathetic eyes, Lory pushed off the edge of the bed where she had been occupying his left flank. Wearing a tiny skintight skirt that barely covered her ample behind, she walked over to the nightstand and lifted the tray. Laboring to a seated position, Blake sat back to allow her to place the food across his lap.

"Please, Masta Blake," Lory began with tenderness in her voice, "eat as much as you could. I's be right back. I's gonna make you some tea."

A stern look from Lory implored Lila to also lift off the bed. Lila, Blake's second favorite, had been rubbing his back as she occupied his right flank, as he skittishly did her through the night. Lila, who was at least a decade older than Lory, was topless, wearing only a short thin-fabric red skirt that Meissa had gifted her a month earlier. Blake loved the shape and texture of Lila's perky breasts and insisted that she wear them out whenever she was in the house.

"I's be back too," Lila promised before she and Lory exited the room. Every bite hurt. Blake felt like his swollen throat was on fire, ripping a little with each strained swallow. Forcing himself to endure, he ingested small portions, chewing slowly and using water to help it down. It took him all twenty minutes to finish. In the process, he actually pushed the tray aside twice; but willing himself, he finally cleared the entire platter.

Lory and Lila returned a minute later. By their icy demeanor, Blake could tell that for whatever reason, the two women were at odds. Sliding onto the bed, Lila returned to her subsequent position, her swollen upper cushioning pressed up against Blake's bare back. Moving with a slow deliberate drag while throwing a darting if-looks-could-kill scowl in Lila's direction, Lory trudged over and placed the tea on the bedside table before returning to her previous spot on the other side of the bed.

Blake moaned gently. From the way Lila was pressed against him, he knew precisely what the wanton woman was trying to initiate; but the way he was feeling, an erratic escapade was definitely not in the cards. Turning toward Lila, Blake positioned the top-heavy woman flat on her back. After giving both boobies a good fondling, he stretched out, relaxing his lazy body as he lay against her soft pillows. Tired from being tired, he closed his eyes.

Close to an hour later, Blake woke up to a small puddle of drool on Lila's stomach. Smiling politely, the dark-complexioned middle-aged field woman didn't appear to mind the warm murky slobber. Lila's dark oval breasts were magnetic. Giving her chocolate nipples a playful bite, Blake's manhood swelled with anticipation. He wanted to. He contemplated while looking down at Lory, still asleep at the foot. Nonetheless, sitting up, he ruefully elected against it.

Pushing to his feet for the first time in thirty-some-odd hours, Blake's body felt a bit stronger than it had just moments ago. After dressing, he made his way down to the outhouse.

The sky outside was just beginning to gray. There was a cool breeze blowing in from the north. Taking in the stimuli, the fresh air served as a natural healing agent. Blake's face, though swollen and bloody a mere day ago, held only a small gash across his right cheek. Other than that, he looked good as new.

Stretching his still-sore muscles and bones, Blake thought about riding into town. Pessimistic about his unknown, he needed to find his brother. He needed to know if he was safe; he needed to see his face. But first, he had to check on his mother. His last image of her was morose.

Regretfully ordering Lila to get fully dressed, Blake had her saddle his horse. At this time, the male slaves were still out in the field, and Lila was somewhat of a full-service servant.

Mounting the tall stallion, Blake learned just how sore he really was. The bounce from the horse trotting the short distance to the main house convinced Blake that a ride to town would no doubt had to be postponed. Every inch, from his calves to his forehead, was in pain by the time he climbed off the horse.

From the fence at the back house, Blake could see inside the property's huge storage stable. Immediately he noticed that their parents' newest stagecoach had gone missing. *What would Michael need a four-horse carriage for?* Blake quietly pondered. Entering his parents' home from the rear, a weird feeling of displacement washed over him. The house seemed spooky, quieter, and even a bit more spacious now that his father wasn't around to fill the material void.

Pushing through the entire bottom floor before making his way up to the second, Blake aimlessly searched for his mother. Only the pounding of his raking feet could be heard, as his apprehensive voice seemed to be lodged behind paralyzing despair, which, at least to this point, stood yet unfound. Door after door, he found rooms deserted. Torturing himself, he latched open doors to rooms he knew his mother wouldn't be in. Nearing the end of the hall, he held his breath with self-inflicted incendiary anticipation. Pushing open the door without bothering to knock, he found his father's study also empty. Entering slowly, he noticed a single sheet of paper laying across his father's desk. Reaching apprehensively while allowing the moist tension to build, Blake took hold of the letter. Inhaling a deep breath, he read the letter:

> To Michael and Blake:
> I have decided to take your father's body with me to Connecticut to give him a proper burial. Also, there are some people up North whom I must meet with in honor of your father's passing. Your father was a very important man. His business endeavors were complex and must be handled delicately. I will be back as soon as I can—maybe a month, maybe more. I have all the confidence that you two will meet any problems head-on and without prejudice. Take care of each other at all cost. You are the last two people I truly love. Protect your brother with everything you have. And that unborn child is a Townsman. You keep that woman safe.
> Mommy loves you both. See you soon.
> X. Mom

By the end of the letter, Blake yet again had a face full of tears. His mother's words were a sobering indication that Darla and her child were a life sentence he would have to forever endure. They were his family now—his blood—and there was no changing that.

Moping, Blake made his way down to Mary's room at the back of the house. Politely he instructed her to prepare a big showstopping dinner. Michael would be back soon (he hoped), and his hero brother deserved a good meal.

Climbing the stairs, emotionally and physically drained, Blake made his way up to his parents' bedroom. Feeling exhausted, he climbed into their huge bed and lay down. Holding the note against his chest, he closed his eyes for what seemed like a second; and when he opened them, Michael was standing over the bed with their mother's letter in hand.

"Dinner's ready," Michael announced, his face ungiving and relentless. Turning and walking to the door, he crumpled the sheet of paper in his fist. "And," he said without turning around as he stopped in the doorway, "you're going to want to change."

For the first time, Blake noticed that Michael was wearing one of his favorite suits.

"Wear something spiffy. Your child's mother is waiting for us at the table. She and Meissa are both wearing their best," Michael informed, and with that, he made his exit.

Blake lay in the bed another minute stewing silently, letting the stark reality of his life consume him. "Darla," he whispered her name as if repercussion might follow the word. But no reciprocation was likely to upstage the devastation the woman had already caused. Consequences be damned. Darla was here, and she was here to stay.

CHAPTER 20

It had been a long emotional few weeks. Losing her husband was like losing her hands. Even worse, it was like losing her arms at the shoulder. To Mrs. Townsman, her husband was her all. To her, he embodied everything good about the American spirit. He was a loyal husband, a hardworking provider, and the most generous and kind father to his sons and loved ones alike.

Before the merciful day when Mr. Townsman rescued her from the life of being a destitute, poverty-stricken farm hen, Mrs. Townsman was no more than a close-minded skinny fifteen-year-old tomboy whose only view of the world was from and around the confines of her family's farm. A semisuccessful gunsmith at the time, Mr. Townsman eventually took a shine to the young gamine woman, as she was never too far removed from the showroom foyer of his shop.

At a very young age, Mrs. Townsman developed an intense and unexpected fixation for firearms. Her father, a third-generation struggling livestock farmer, would sometimes allow her the privilege of putting the fatal bullet between the eyes of a pig or cow once the animal's time had come. When her then future husband opened his gun shop only five walking minutes away from her farm, Mrs. Townsman made it a priority to work in a visit to the overly ingrained gunpowder-incensed storefront every chance she got.

The initial union between the two served to benefit all parties involved. Mrs. Townsman grew up an only child, but with her father's family-inherited farm being so disadvantageous, even tending to the needs of one child got to be burdensome. Mr. Townsman's proposal to take the young woman off her father's hands was an offer accepted with bouncing approval.

Mrs. Townsman could not have dreamed of choosing a more ideal mate—a husband with an exciting profitable profession that she had a genuine interest in whose only demand of her were to cook, clean, and bare him children. Mrs. Townsman felt like the luckiest woman alive. She had been cooking and cleaning since the moment she was able, so taking care of home was like one nature to her, and procreation was assumed to be the most unambiguous part of the deal. Bearing her husband a son was supposed to be an artless act. Notwithstanding, as fate would have it, this apparent straightforward task didn't turn out to be so simple. Eventually having to move across the country after an unexpected turn of events left some of their family members (his family members) feeling resentment toward her, and no matter the explanation, some of them still blamed her for the relocation. And now here she was, on her way back to her home state to face her lawfully related critics with her purported all-purpose bodyguard's quickly decomposing body in tow.

Nothing about the trip from Georgia to Connecticut was simple. Every step of the journey had its hurdles. Just the process of getting his body across the state while trying to keep concealed the news of his passing was a venture in and of itself.

Cautious not to draw any unwanted attention to her task, Mrs. Townsman loaded her husband's corpse into her gigantic four-horse-drawn stagecoach and set off under the cover of nightfall, traveling from Atlanta to Sylvania. There she proceeded to acquire the guide services of a longtime friend and business partner of her husband. Ridley Booker, a self-proclaimed world-renowned multifashioned merchant, was contracted under the cloak of confidentiality to escort her and her husband's remains to the city of New Haven,

Connecticut. Mrs. Townsman, even if it meant traveling thousands of miles on short notice, was determined to lay her husband's body to rest where the news of his untimely demise would not immediately be discovered by the nosy, gossipy, happy townsfolk there in Georgia. Ridley, as he always appeared to her, was a constant professional. The six-foot, heavily bearded, overweight, and well-dressed tradesman first went out and acquired an airtight casket. Then he booked a last-minute ferry ride that was scheduled to depart from Georgia to New York in two days' time. From New York, they would cart Mr. Townsman's body to New Haven, Connecticut, where she could finally give him a proper funeral.

Providing the love of her life a proper burial was one of her main reasons for taking him back to Connecticut. With what had taken place that night, Mrs. Townsman loathed the task of detailing the specifics of her husband's death to the clumsy so-called legal authority down in Georgia. Whoever had come to her home that night were likely to have loved ones questioning after them, and her husband's death may arouse suspicion into why they hadn't made it home—especially if whoever did it was to let their intentions slip to someone.

Brownie (her loyal stableman) and Tywin (one of her more well-spoken field slaves) accompanied Mrs. Townsman on this trip. Mrs. Townsman would have actually preferred it had been only her and her black help, but a white woman traveling with two male slaves was considered dangerous in some people's eyes. Of course, she wasn't worried about her slaves misbehaving. Still, so not to arouse a would-be issue, Ridley's presence served to alleviate any unwanted attention.

Ridley Booker was what some would consider a modern-day renaissance man. He was well-traveled, he spoke three languages fluently (English, Spanish, and French), and he had contacts with different statesmen spread across the county. He didn't really need her money. Mrs. Townsman knew the only reason he agreed to accompany her was in hopes of a future favor being paid in return. Mrs. Townsman didn't mind being in Ridley's debt. Though he was far from being her favorite person, she had known him since before her sons were born. He and her husband had been investing in horse ranches for longer than she could remember; thusly, this business relationship was what she was banking on to keep the man tight-lipped. Still, Mrs. Townsman told him no more than she was required, and Ridley didn't ask too many questions. Mrs. Townsman never fully trusted Ridley. The fact that he disagreed with them raising Blake as a son placed him in a category of merely a business associate and not a friend.

Mrs. Townsman and her two slaves remained with the body in the wagon, while Ridley rode the horseback. The four traveled from the horse ranch to the shore, where a midday ferry had docked in the shipping bay. Mrs. Townsman's mouth fell open in disgust. The overall appearance of the undersized ship was just about enough to make her change her mind. The dirty sailboat looked to be threadbare. The ragged and white cloths were beige, dingy, and even ripped in certain areas. On top of that, the deck and bow both seemed to be holding more equipment than it could safely carry across the water. The thought of being recognized boating in such shabby conditions turned her stomach. Mrs. Townsman was accustomed to a more luxurious travel. When she and her husband sailed, it was on the finest ships the sea had to offer. Catered meals and private rooms supplemented an average journey for her. With all things being fair, she couldn't complain too much. This was apparently the only route to be had on such short notice.

Mrs. Townsman loitered the hull of her huge stagecoach as the overstocked multipurpose freight ferry dragged sluggishly across the open water. Already upset about the savage accommodations, she was then forced to suffer through the ship's vocational course as it made four tiresome stops. Picking up and dropping off passengers and merchantable goods, the boat proceeded about its weekly routine before ultimately landing them in New York City days later.

On any and every occasion, Mrs. Townsman loved visiting New York; suffice to say, this was no ordinary visit. Be that as it may, the excitement of the city was undeniable. There were buildings stacked five- to seven-stories high on both sides of the roads. Outside restaurants were worked by colorfully dressed persons in fancy little numbers. People, young and old, were everywhere hustling and bustling about, fighting for their perceived slice of the proverbial pie.

The New York City walkways were a beautiful frenetic song of wonderful poetic insanity. There were single-ridden horses of various colors (brown, black, white, red, and blue). Mrs. Townsman was confused at why some thought it clever to dye their animals' coat, but the imagery was entertaining nonetheless. Always, as in competition, there was every style of a stagecoach (old and new) being paraded up and down the intersection carrying impatient passengers to and fro.

Brownie's and Tywin's eyes were wide as their pupils darted in circles, trying to keep up with the madness. Amused, Mrs. Townsman imagined that the place must have looked as foreign to them as flying swine. Exaggerated gasps and hesitant smiles were shared between the two whenever an unsupervised crop of black faces was spotted in the crowd.

Ridley's experience frequenting the great Northeastern city proved essential. In no time at all, he had them fed, supplied, boarded, and on their way up the road heading across the bridge. A second wagon was rented from a vintage carriage repair shop that Ridley was familiar with to carry Mr. Townsman's body, which, in the smoggy tow of the ship, had begun to smell through the alleged airtight coffin.

In the absence of the capacious metal box, Mrs. Townsman was able to stretch her cramped legs. Finally, after days of scarcely taken vertical naps, the soon-to-be-grandmother was able to lean back comfortably and close her heavy eyelids. Tywin rode up front with Brownie, while Ridley populated the opposite side of the wagon hall.

The vibration of the rocky drift was relaxing. Breathing a warm sigh of relief, Mrs. Townsman finally let her guard down. She was nearly home free. Temporarily assuaged, she allowed her thoughts to stream. The unchecked vision of her faraway sons dominated her daydreams. She knew they were just fine.

The peaceful East Coast air cooled as the evening progressed. As the wagon crawled along, a nice fresh-water draft poured in from an open slit in the window. The breeze felt good on her face. She didn't even realize she had dozed off until Ridley was shaking her awake many hours later announcing their arrival. It was the dead of the night by the time the four pulled to a stop in front of a petite constructed motel. Mr. Townsman's body was immediately transferred back over to their original wagon, as the driver of the rented carriage seemed eager to be rid of the offensive scent of rotting flesh.

Ready to be done with the day, Mrs. Townsman pounded on the empty counter, screaming for whoever could hear, as it took more than twenty minutes to get hold of the building's desk clerk. When they finally found him, Mrs. Townsman and Ridley both purchased rooms in the front of the two-by-four motel, while Brownie and Tywin shared one of the rooms in the back, which were reserved for people of color.

The comfort of a cushioned mattress on their backs was a welcomed delicacy, yet early the next morning, Mrs. Townsman was up at first light, focusing on making her rounds of obligation. Ridley and Tywin stayed at the motel, while she and Brownie set off.

Downtown New Haven was a busy aristocratic area. Even this early, the city had begun to come alive. Farmers and merchandisers were up early, trying to get a jump on the competition. Vending tables of all sorts were being set up, and discount store doors were beginning to open. Even the bar owners were up and at them. And as sure as day follows night, the local boozehounds were pushing through the entrances.

Mrs. Townsman's wagon dragged patiently across the dirt as she took in the activities. This was her childhood home after all. Looking from her window, she enjoyed watching the ins and outs of the neighborhood. There were young blacks spit shining shoes and washing horses. Whores with thickly caked-on makeup and low-cut tops sat the porches of their apparent pleasure house. The business establishments that she passed all had big signs hung above their doors, advertising the services provided within. This section of New Haven was ever vibrant; the overall vibe was pleasant.

Pulling into a significantly less urgent part of the city, Mrs. Townsman's first stop was to the home of her late husband's parents. The news of their son's untimely departure was unearthed with a hysteric ear. A loud scream from his mother garnered the attention of everyone on the property. There were seven homes on this land. Brothers, sisters, aunts, and uncles all came out to share in the distress.

Scorn, sadness, and anger spilled into the air as family members, young and old, cursed the gods for taking their champion breadwinner. Strained words of comfort were offered to the grieving widow, but the dark looks she was receiving from her estranged kinfolk told her their true thinking of her. The visual of Mr. Townsman's decaying corpse lying in the metal box only served to heighten the family's heartache. Leaving the casket with his parents, Mrs. Townsman excused herself, vowing to return the following day for the funeral.

Initially planning to visit her husband's bank that evening, Mrs. Townsman was emotionally drained by the time she pulled out of her in-laws' lot. Her day essentially at its end, she stopped by the motel and grabbed Tywin, and she and her blacks headed over to her mother's house. Mrs. Townsman's mother, Clare, was only fourteen years her elder. Wrinkle-free with a head full of pretty blonde hair, the passing years had been good to the old woman. At times, in passing, people would suggest the two looked more like sisters rather than mother and daughter.

Mrs. Townsman's surprise visit was originally met with enthusiastic cheer, but the mood quickly turned when the motivation surrounding her Connecticut visit was revealed. Her mother, Clare, loved her daughter's husband; ten years back, he purchased her the beautiful fifteen acres that neighbored her old farm. He also hired builders to construct the two-story, four-bed, two-washroom home that she loved so much. There were vegetable gardens, two barns, a chicken coop, pigsty, and horse stable. In the back of the property was the old two-room shack that Mrs. Townsman had grown up in. This was where Mrs. Clare housed her hired black help. Brownie and Tywin both were allowed to take refuge here. Two elderly black women who had worked for Mrs. Townsman's family since she was a young girl also stayed there.

CHAPTER 21

The funeral took place at noon the next day. Mr. Townsman's family put out the word faster than Mrs. Townsman thought possible. Nearly sixty people showed up to say their goodbyes. Though he lived thousands of miles away, Mr. Townsman's affluence rang loud throughout the small city. He had a lot of property in and around the state of Connecticut. His horse ranches and gun shops were still very profitable in this state, and his firearms factory provided plenty of much-needed good-wage jobs in the region.

Mr. Townsman came from a very big family. He had four brothers, three sisters, and a league of cousins, aunts, and uncles; most of whom were in attendance that evening. For the most part, everyone at the funeral was adequately cordial to her, but there was that select percentage who still blamed her for dragging him down South in the first place. In respect to the deceased, Mrs. Townsman took the rolled eyes and sideways comments with a grain of salt.

All and all, the funeral went off without a hitch. Mrs. Townsman's only regret was that her sons weren't there to see their father off. Their absence was no doubt the topic of a lot of the undertalk. Still, some were genuinely disappointed they weren't there. Several who hadn't met Blake but had heard about him expressed an interest in doing so.

This brought Mrs. Townsman's spirits up. The mention of her sons' hotel was even brought up. This was a surprise to her. Her boys had amassed a buzz all the way up North. She was impressed. *Maybe she shouldn't be so judgmental about their little venture.*

Though Mrs. Clare was adequately enthusiastic, Mrs. Townsman thought it best that she not allow her mother to come to the funeral. With tensions so strained, Mrs. Townsman was skeptical about her husband's family being able to control their offensive tongues, and she didn't want to bring her mother into any type of controversy.

Mrs. Clare was a widow herself. Several years back, her husband (Mrs. Townsman's father) passed, leaving her to tend to the farming alone. Fortunately for her, her son-in-law made it so that farming for a profit was no longer a requisite. Mrs. Townsman despised coming back to Connecticut for many reasons, but visiting her darling mother was not one of them. She loved her mother; to her, the woman was the equivalence of a glass of refreshing lemonade. She was studious, kind, and soothing in every way. At a time so filled with loss, Mrs. Clare's presence was the one bright spot in her daughter's day.

CHAPTER 22

When her husband died, Mrs. Clare, who was still very physically alluring, chose not to remarry. Mrs. Townsman thought her mother and her were a lot alike in that regard. She was sure there was no another man who could ever replace the love that she lost.

Returning to her parents' home after the funeral that evening, her mother met her at the front door. "Sweetheart," she began with sorrow in her eyes, "are you all right?"

"Yes, Mother," Mrs. Townsman began. "I'm fine, and the funeral was nice. A lot more people than I had expected to show came out. I'm sorry you couldn't be there. I hope you understand."

"Oh no, Mary, I can totally sympathize." With a shy smile, her mothered continued, "I'm just glad you're back. Sherry has just taken the bird out of the oven. I had her fix a big dinner for you and your guests tonight."

Mrs. Clare knew that Brownie and Tywin were her daughter's slaves, but she refused to address them as such. Mrs. Townsman was fine with the oversight. Here in Connecticut, slavery was considered inhumane. Besides, for the most part, she didn't consider her black slaves in the same sense as most slave masters did. She felt her blacks, and she had an understanding. They provided her a service; and in return, she fed, clothed, and gave them a place to stay. The matter of ownership was immaterial, merely in title.

"Thank you, Mother," Mrs. Townsman said, pushing into the foyer. "Everything smells delicious."

"Sherry has gotten very creative in the kitchen. You are in for a real treat. And her apple pie...now mm-hmm," her mother embellished.

"I can't wait." Mrs. Townsman smiled.

"Well, it's nearly dinnertime. Why don't you go get cleaned up, and I'll have Sherry set the table."

Mrs. Townsman gave her mother a nod before turning and heading for her room.

CHAPTER 23

When she came back downstairs, the dining table was alive with so much food that Mrs. Townsman thought her mother must have been expecting a dinner party. But the feast was only for the two of them. Brownie and Tywin's meals had already been sent to the guesthouse.

"Mother, this is a little...over the top."

Her mother smiled. "I know. I told her to make a good amount of food. I thought maybe you might bring home a guest from the... and Sherry got carried away. But don't worry. It won't go to waste. Whatever we don't eat, we'll send back to the blacks. Negroes have an appetite akin to hogs." She laughed. "And I guess we can save some of this chicken to go with some eggs in the morning."

"That will be nice," Mrs. Townsman agreed.

The two women ate in relative silence, only breaking calm to comment on this dish and that. Her mother smiled politely throughout, but Mrs. Townsman knew she had a question behind those cheeks. They hadn't discussed her husband's death since the subject first broke upon arrival, and Mrs. Townsman knew that her mother was far too polite to openly address such a sensitive topic. With that in mind, she could tell that the subject was eating at the woman, so she gave the assist.

"My husband would've loved these sweet potatoes. I only wish they were on the table last time we were in town."

"Oh, honey, that would've been lovely," Mrs. Clare jumped right in. "I'm so sorry about Michael, dear. I know how much you loved him. He was a good man. He's surely watching over you right now."

"Thank you, Mother," Mrs. Townsman said with a quaint smile.

"How are my grandsons taking the loss?"

Mrs. Townsman's face registered a measured look of surprise. Her mother never before put the *s* on the word *grandson*. Her mother smiled at her only daughter. Her acceptance of Blake into the family was clearly appreciated by her daughter. With eyes glossed over, Mrs. Townsman answered, "They're managing. They were so close to Michael. It's been rough on all of us, but we'll get through."

A silence lingered over the table for a moment. Mrs. Clare wanted to say something in regard to Blake, but the words came up absent.

"So," Mrs. Clare began as she stood to pour herself a healthy serving of thick-creamed gravy, "are you...financially set? I mean, did he leave you a means to get by? I..." Mrs. Clare paused, her eyes darting back and forth between her cram-full plate and her daughter's stoic face. Though visually uncomfortable conversing about such a sensitive matter, Mrs. Clare felt the issue was one that needed to be addressed. Enduring, she lifted her head confidently and eyed her only child. "I'm just asking because I'm...he died so suddenly. It's difficult to imagine he had time to...prepare or... I don't know. I'm sorry," Mrs. Clare rambled.

Mrs. Townsman loved her mother's milky-sweet manner—how timid she was. Her mother's skittish demeanor was a big part of her feminine charm. Covertly amused, Mrs. Townsman was tempted to let her mother stumble about for another minute or so, but rescuing her drowning mom, she admitted, finally breaking her guileful silence, "We're fine, Mother. Yes, Michael left us plenty of money. I'm actually meeting with his lawyers this coming week."

"Oh, that's wonderful." Clare exhaled, relieved. "I was so worried. When you first told me, I didn't know how to ask. But thank goodness," she said, dipping her fork into her mashed potatoes. "I should have known. Michael was such a reliable young man."

"Thank you, Mother," Mrs. Townsman replied, a gentle smile parting her red-wine painted lips.

Satisfied that her daughter's alimony was soundly intact, Mrs. Clare began to loosen up. With the underlined tension eased, before long the two giggly women were laughing, teasing, and chitchatting about this, that, and nothing at all.

The entire meal was exquisite—every dish as good as advertised. This was the first dinner the mother-and-daughter duo had shared alone in nearly forever. Gorging for whatever reason, the two proceed to shave away as much of the large dinner as they could safely consume.

After dinner, some hour and change later, Mrs. Townsman, stuffed to the point of cramping, excused herself from the table. The home's sole toilet was to the rear of the house. There were two entrances leading to this private room. There was a door that could be reached for the downstairs den, and another that could be accessed from the outside. Craving a bit of fresh air, Mrs. Townsman chose to take a stroll around the exterior of the home.

Right outside the door, immediately to the left of the privy, was a small but very swank rose garden. Even in the dead of night, the uniquely shaped flowers provided a beautiful image. Still, even more glaring was the natural fragrance furnished thereof. Oddly, in spite of the fact that she enjoyed the popular red-petalled plant's scent, that same romance-setting aroma served to bring Mrs. Townsman's favorable mood down a notch. Unfortunately, the fragrance reminded Mrs. Townsman of the beautiful bouquet of roses she received from her husband only a little over a month past.

Her private-room activity concluded, Mrs. Townsman again chose the external route around. The fresh air seemed to help blot some of the apprehension that had crept into her subconscious. Finding her way to the back porch, she took a lazy seat on the wooden bench in front of a rear bay window.

At this point, her emotions had begun pulling her in ten different directions. There were no words that could express how much she missed her husband. Traveling to Connecticut to bury him was a bold move, one she hoped he would approve of. Mrs. Townsman knew in her heart that he was watching. Everything she was doing was to protect their boys; she prayed he understood this. Still, being all the way up North while her sons were all the way South, the disquiet of the unknown was mentally draining. Ultimately, all she could do was try to stay positive, but second-guessing her decision to leave so abruptly was unavoidable.

Rerunning the scenario in her head, Mrs. Townsman oh so wished she could go back in time and wait just a couple of days to be sure no repercussions followed the dead men who had foolishly come storming onto her property. However, senseless wishing was a moot point. If she'd been awarded the gift of just one wish, her husband would have survived that fatal wound. Or rather, those cowards would have never dawned her land. Or even better still, her reckless, bounteous son would have never impregnated that whore in the first place. But everything had played out the way it had, and here she was in Connecticut while her sons were miles away in Georgia.

She reassured herself her sons were survivors. They didn't need their mother there to hold their hands. She had to do her part. Burying her husband was priority number one. Now she needed to meet with his business partner and lawyers to take care of the financial end of her trip. Although Mr. Townsman had business dealings in numerous states, the vast majority of his banking was conducted in Connecticut. His gun factory along with the law firm that handled his stock investments were both located in New Haven.

It seemed hours had passed with Mrs. Townsman sitting on that bench—alone with only her hopes and regrets to comfort her. Peeling herself off that hardwood seat with tomorrow's demands urging her to call it a night, the still pack-full newly widowed mother of two pushed into the back door and sluggishly climbed the troublesome stairs up to the second floor. Bypassing the washroom, Mrs. Townsman entered her room, stripped down to her underclothes, and fell into bed. Drowsy from dinner, her body lay dead-man still. However, for some reason, her active mind continually loitered.

Insomnia had never been an issue for her in the past, so now lying in bed helplessly vigilant, Mrs. Townsman had no cure, ideal, or remedy hence to rely upon to quell her active consciousness. The pestering sound of crickets coming through her slightly cracked window accompanied her through the lingering restless binge. The howling of a canine of some sort creased the air in the distance. *Sounds of the jaded Connecticut country backdrop,* Mrs. Townsman reckoned as she lay uncomfortably, finally contempt with having to suffer through the rigors of a slumberless night.

Eyes open, Mrs. Townsman traced the outlines of the moonlight rectangle on the wall. She busied herself trying to denominate identities to what darken shadows in the room resembled when the sound of dragging footsteps rustling across the dirt outside caught her attention. Too lazy to get up and go over to the window, Mrs. Townsman merely opened her sound receptors a bit wider, concentrating on the pitter-patter washing in through the inch-high lift in her window.

Mrs. Townsman's room was located on the second floor in the back of the house. When she heard the back door creak open and her mother's hushed voice followed in transaction by another, Mrs. Townsman's cognizant mind roused that much more. *Who would be paying my dear old mom a look-in at this time of night?*

Curiosity coaxed a desire to go downstairs to see what all the fuss was about, but thinking better of it, Mrs. Townsman elected to stay put. There was only one out of the two species of human who'd show up to a known widow's home this time of night. And though the prospect of her mother having such a friend to keep her pleasantly occupied, Mrs. Townsman was nowhere near ready to meet such a person. Her mother's business was her own. As far as she was concerned, her father was the only man she wanted to associate her mother to.

A short moment after the whispered conversation fell silent, Mrs. Townsman heard hurried feet ascending the steps on the way up to the closed door of her room. In a panic, Mrs. Townsman squeezed shut her lids and pretended to sleep.

A light tap on the door was ignored. Then the door latch was twisted free, and the door pushed open. "Mary... Mary, are you awake?" Mrs. Clare looked in.

Relaxing her lids, Mrs. Townsman's eyes were narrow slits as she peeked to see if her mother was alone.

"Mary," Mrs. Clare called again, but her attempt was again ignored. Without putting forth too much of an effort, Mrs. Clare backed out of the room and closed the door behind her.

How dare she try to introduce me to someone at this hour? Mrs. Townsman thought with a smile. *Maybe my mother isn't so timid a Northern belle after all.* The ideal of it tickled her. Overthinking the possibilities, she finally dozed off, a narrow smirk curling her mouth.

The following morning, met by the crowing of the property's one-eyed rooster, Mrs. Townsman was up at first light, again crossing the yard on her way to the outer door of the privy. Never again would she indulge in such gluttony.

After relieving herself, Mrs. Townsman washed, got dressed, and entered the kitchen pantry. To her surprise, all the leftover food from the previous night's dinner extravaganza was gone. She wasn't exactly hungry, but with such a full schedule ahead, she planned to pack a basket. Nothing was left. *My mother's friend must have really been hungry.* Walking out into the awaiting morning, she prepared herself. *This day's undertakings are of the utmost importance.*

It was very early, arbitrary to her normal lax schedule; still, the factory was more than ten miles out, and Mrs. Townsman wanted to get there relatively early. Not bothering to send for Brownie, she readied her mother's single-horse carriage and set off.

At the funeral, Ridley informed her that he decided to check out of the small shabby hotel where he was staying in and checked in to a more upscale establishment. With her husband safely in the ground, Mrs. Townsman really had no further use for Ridley, at least not until it was time for her to head home. Nevertheless, since the hotel was on the way, she gathered it would be a nice gesture to pay him a visit.

Bob Sullivan was a very successful sixty-three-year-old former cattle farmer from the West who had relocated to New Haven some twenty-five years back. Now a long-standing cash cow in the community, Old Man Sullivan (as he was often referred) garnered much political influence and unflappable respect from the local townspeople. Mrs. Townsman hated the sight of the old geezer. The man sat out front of his hotel for hours on in with a large double-barrel shotgun, eyeing the passing crowds of colored people as if hoping for a reason to empty his weapon.

Bob Sullivan was a hard man—a man with long-standing confederate values and a starch hatred for the spoiled, freed Northern blacks. No man of color was allowed within twenty yards of his hotel, which stood the most celebrated in the city. With that said, of course, this was where Ridley chose to hold up.

Walking into Sullivan's hotel lobby, Mrs. Townsman was met by a slew of thirsty stares. Sullivan's played host to a diverse gathering of up-and-coming to veteran swindlers. New Haven was a relatively small city; outsiders (which she was essentially) were easily recognized (wealthy-dressed strangers even more so). Felicitous salesmen stirred anxiously as she walked up to the counter.

"Good morning, miss," a wiry-built, clean-shaven middle-aged man in a dirty-looking dark-gray suit opened before she could reach the hotel patron behind the bar.

Pretending not to have heard him, Mrs. Townsman hustled past his outreached hand on the way to the service counter.

"Excuse me. I'm looking for Ridley Booker. He was supposed to check in to this hotel a day or two ago," Mrs. Townsman explained to the desk clerk.

With a nod, the overweight man sitting in a cushioned bucket chair behind the desk gestured over to a table in the corner of the bar, where a group of hard-faced gentlemen were engaged in a heated-looking card game. Ridley was among the fray. His eyes met hers as she looked over.

"Excuse me, woman!" the suited man she had brushed off asserted, stepping in front of her. "Did you hear me talking to you over there when you walked in?"

"Whatever it is you're selling, I'm not interested."

The stranger just smiled at her. "But you haven't heard my sales pitch."

Mrs. Townsman wasn't moved. "I am very sorry if I came off as dismissive, but I am really not in the mood to be…socially engaged," she warned with not a hint of warmth in her tone.

Not to be outdone, the domineering man countered just as sternly. "At least allow me to show you my collection," he insisted, grabbing her by the arm in an attempt to lead her over to the table where he had his suitcase opened in display.

"Mary," Ridley growled, stepping in between the two.

"Ridley…you know this fine lady?" the man asked, disappointment in his voice.

Ridley was nearly a half-foot his superior and a good sixty pounds heavier.

"Yes, and I'm pretty sure I heard her tell you that she wasn't interested," Ridley barked.

"No problem," the suit began, backing away with both hands raised, palms out. "I'm just trying to make an honest buck."

"Thank you," Mrs. Townsman said once the pest was out of earshot. "I would have hated to have put him down this early in the day," she said, flashing Ridley a look at the single-shot derringer she had slipped out of the small pocket she had sewn into her dress. Ridley shook his head. "A friend of yours?" she continued.

"Hardly," he replied, motioning for her to put the pistol back in its hiding place. "He's harmless really," Ridley began, "unless you're a runaway."

"A runaway?"

"Yeah. He's a slave chaser. His name's Tommy White. His brother, Buck, is over there getting the shirt torn off his back in a game of seven card. I met the two awhile back in Mississippi. They're down here following a lead on a ring of runners who are pushing back and forth across the country, smuggling slaves from down South up here."

"Slave chasers—some job," Mrs. Townsman said, glancing over at Tommy who was at the bar drinking from a large mug. "He would be the type of person to hold such employment," she snorted.

"Yeah, but someone's gotta do it."

"I guess. Well, I just came to check on you."

"I'm touched," Ridley jeered.

Mrs. Townsman rolled her eyes.

"Kidding," Ridley declared. "Do you need me to help you with something today?"

"No, I'm fine. We should be ready to head back in four to five days."

"I'm ready when you are," Ridley admitted.

"I'll be back to check in on you in a day or two."

Ridley nodded. "Don't shoot anyone," he half-joked.

And with a curtsy, Mrs. Townsman turned to go, leaving Ridley to finish his card game.

CHAPTER 24

Sylvester's Pistols was a large shipping and manufacturing company as well as a brand. The building stood two-stories high and measured at least half an acre in diameter. Pumping out the latest standard in weaponry, the place was a full-service concrete fortress of modernized warfare.

When Mrs. Townsman walked in through the double doors of the lobby, the day-shift supervisor, Peter Blanch, was just coming off the ground floor. Doing a double-take, Mrs. Townsman and he spotted each other seconds before she reached the desk clerk sitting behind the counter.

"Oh my!" Peter began as he laid his cupped beverage on the counter. "Hello, Mrs. Townsman. Back so soon?"

"How are you, Peter?" Mrs. Townsman greeted the well-mannered young man.

"Good. And yourself?" Peter asked, turning his head ever so slightly in an attempt to mask the slight smell of alcohol on his breath. His eyes roamed as he stuck out his hand.

"I'm well," Mrs. Townsman answered before firmly shaking Peter's hand.

Smiling politely, Peter casually gave the double doors behind her a couple of subtle glances. Then he looked Mrs. Townsman over strangely. "Are we waiting for Mr. Townsman?"

"No, I'm here alone," Mrs. Townsman said emotionlessly. "I was wondering if Sylvester was in this morning."

"Oh, certainly. You know that man practically lives in the building," Peter said with humorous indication in his words.

Mrs. Townsman didn't laugh.

"Well, right this way." Peter gestured with a wave.

Dozens of people scurried about, tightly engaged in their dutiful activities. Kind smiles and an occasional hand movement greeted Mrs. Townsman as she passed. Escorting her through the craft-work area of the facility, up some stairs, and then down a hall, Peter talked nonstop about the recent developments the company was making.

Sylvester Blackwell's office was on the upper floor at the back of the building. Taking the lead, Peter knocked on the wide wooden door before sticking his head in and announcing Mrs. Townsman's presence. Standing only a couple yards behind Peter, Mrs. Townsman heard Sylvester's husky voice clear as if she were in the room. Pushing the door open wide for her, Peter smiled. "He said to come on in."

Sylvester was up and walking toward her when she entered the room. "Mary, what a lovely surprise," Sylvester greeted his longtime business partner's wife. "To what do I owe the pleasure?" He grabbed and repeatedly kissed the back of her two hands. Her husband always did the same thing to Sylvester's wife; it was something both men got a kick out of. "What a lovely surprise. Please have a seat," he said, ushering her over to a cushioned chair. Sylvester's spacious redwood-heavy office was expensively furnished, with exotic-looking African-inspired paintings lining the walls.

While Mr. Townsman did most of the traveling for the company, Sylvester remained at the factory overseeing day-to-day operations. Peter Blanch was one of the more prestigious young men brought in to front as company manager. He and Barry Wells were two Sylvester-friendly individuals whose Caucasian faces served to pacify the natives. These young men were alleged to stand in as Mr. Townsman's physical presence when he was away. They supposedly spoke with his tongue, but in all actuality, they took their orders from Sylvester.

Peter and Barry were merely a face for the workers to identify, so not to feel as if they were being led by a black man. A colored man running such a lucrative association was like a stiff elbow to the racist, elitist white-male-dominated society. Mr. Blackwell was content with sitting in his office, rifling through papers while reaping the financial rewards.

"Sylvester, it is so nice to see you again," Mrs. Townsman began. "It looks plenty busy downstairs. Seems business is booming."

"Well," Mr. Blackwell stirred modestly, "we're making do. The new nickel-plated .45s are in high demand. The things are selling out faster than we can ship them. And the new Townswell your husband designed should be ready for mass production by year's end. Yeah, I say we are doing quite well. This is going to be a big year for us. So where is Mr. Michael? Or did he send you down here just to put a smile on my face?"

"My husband has passed," Mrs. Townsman informed impassively.

It took a second or two for Mr. Blackwell to register what she had said. Then jarred, he looked at her strangely, like he thought she might be joking, but Mrs. Townsman's face held no sign of befooling. Mr. Blackwell's mouth fell wide, and a deflating breath left his body. Befuddled, he searched for words, but his brain was momentarily locked. Involuntarily, his eyes fell to the floor. Startled, he didn't even have the presence of mind to offer his condolences. Mr. Townsman was his best friend in the world—the best white man he had ever known.

"Sylvester," Mrs. Townsman called.

Holding up an instructive finger, the large black man stood up with his face diverted and spent, his back to her. It was the last domino. This show of emotion was the push over the edge for her. She hadn't cried since the night it happened. To see Sylvester come apart like this made her break down as well. Before Mrs. Townsman could stop herself, she had pushed up from her chair and walked over and grabbed Sylvester in a strong hug. Slowly the big man threw his oversize arms around her and held her close. The two stayed like this, silently sharing praises for her late husband. The man meant so much to each of them; they both pitied how bad the loss was affecting each other. After a long time, the two pulled apart. No words were spoken, but they were each aware that they had just been brought closer by this tragedy.

Sylvester cleared his throat then handed Mrs. Townsman a handkerchief from his inner breast pocket. He then walked over to a small hanging wall cabinet and retrieved a second cloth napkin for himself. "Please sit," he offered her a seat while valiantly attempting to straighten himself as expeditiously as possible. "Would you like a drink?" Not waiting for an answer, he poured two glasses—one for each of them.

Besides her husband, Mrs. Townsman could not remember ever crying in front of a man. Growing up with nothing to now holding a prestigious position among men, she prided herself on being a strong female.

Sipping the hard liquor periodically, the two most unlikely of friends remained quiet for a time. Though their relationship had indeed grown in the waning minutes, the awkwardness of the moment harvested words unspoken.

Mr. Blackwell was first to empty his glass. Letting out a long breath, he composed himself. "How?" he asked.

"He was murdered," Mrs. Townsman answered plainly.

"By whom?"

"They're all dead now. My son took care of them," she declared proudly.

"Michael? Really?" Mr. Blackwell smirked.

Sylvester's distinct assumption surprised her. It was strange to her that he automatically went with Michael over Blake. But brushing it aside, she admitted, "Yes. Michael chased them down and killed all five of them. Could have been six." She embellished.

Sylvester knew she was putting a little on it. "Are your boys okay?" he asked.

"Of course, they're fine. He and Blake will always take care of each other."

Mr. Blackwell gave a weak attempt at a smile. "Still," he continued, "who would do something like this? Your husband was…" Mr. Blackwell paused again, overcame with emotion.

Mrs. Townsman cut in. "It doesn't matter now. It's over. All that matters now is my sons' future in this company. The business, Sylvester," she voiced with emphasis.

"Yes, um, well, did you speak with his lawyers?"

"No. I wanted to come talk with you first."

"Oh, well, here on this end, you and your boys are definitely secure. All of you are the beneficiaries of 50 percent of Sylvester's Pistols. Your interest here is solid. Your husband and I had written parameters contracted to ensure our families be forever taken care of should anything tragic befall either of us. I just never would have thought… I'm just at a loss."

Shaking her head with a sense of relief glittered beneath her eyes, Mrs. Townsend said, "I don't want anything to change. I will be heading back to Georgia within the next month—after I meet with the lawyer."

"Of course, of course," Mr. Blackwell began, also harboring something beneath glaring eyes. "If there's anything I can do—"

"Well, I was wondering if you could find me a safe place up here. Somewhere out of the way."

"You're planning to move up North?" Sylvester asked, surprised.

"No. I just need a nice secluded place. Something for my son."

"Why? Is Blake in some kind of trouble?"

Again with the accusations. She just told him Michael had gunned down a half-dozen people, and he asked if Blake was in trouble.

"Some men came to the house to lynch him the day Michael died," she confessed. "They bound his hands and dragged him away after murdering my husband. My son tracked them down before they could escape the property."

Sylvester's eyes wandered, and he looked to be deep in thought.

Mrs. Townsman continued, "Blake, in a foolish attempt to keep stride with his brother, has somehow managed to get some white whore pregnant."

Mr. Blackwell's head snapped around in dismay.

"Yes," Mrs. Townsman stated further. "And I'm afraid once this child arrives, the drama will begin again."

"I see," Mr. Blackwell agreed, pushing back into his chair. "Yes, I believe I have just the spot for Mr. Blake. How old is he now?"

"They're nineteen."

Blackwell smiled, amused, reminded of how close her sons were in age. "Very good," he continued. "And as soon as you can," he said, standing to walk around the desk, "bring me the names of the men who were involved and any who may want to do Blake harm."

"No, Sylvester. I don't want any more trouble."

"No trouble. But your family is my family. And as I'm sure you know, looking after you and yours is nothing less than your husband would have done for mine."

"Sylvester…"

"Mary, it's settled. I'm going to at least have someone check into this."

"Sylvester," Mrs. Townsman pleaded as she rose, but Mr. Blackwell waved her coming concerns.

"Mary." He walked over to her and grabbed her two hands in his, kissing each one. "I am going to send someone back with you. You give him all the information you have on these men, no matter how minute. He is a professional problem solver, and he will be very discreet."

Mrs. Townsman wanted to say something in protest, but all she could muster was a timid nod. "Thank you, Sylvester," she said, stepping into his willing embrace.

Mr. Townsman shared with her the rumors surrounding Sylvester's art of handling problems. He said a black man doesn't get to Sylvester's level of success by conversational persuasion alone. Sylvester was sending her back with a problem solver. And though part of her was apprehensive about it, she mostly felt a refreshing sense of relief. Her two sons were all she had now. If a hired gun was what was needed to keep them safe, then so be it.

Leaving the factory cradling a new compact, low-caliber five-shot nickel-plated hand pistol, Mrs. Townsman had an extra bounce in her step. Exhaling some, she felt a large weight had been lifted off her shoulders. Mr. Blackwell's words had a way of making her feel at ease. There was something about his calm that was contagious.

Restraining an impulsive snicker, Mrs. Townsman remembered back to when her husband first told her that he was thinking about sinking all their hard-earned money into a venture with the man. Mrs. Townsman was starchily against it. More than against it, she was horrified at the notion. Angry words exchanged during heated discussions accompanied the couple to bed several straight nights as she did her best to talk him out of it. Her husband, who normally crumbled under her nagging petitioning, kept insisting that she wait until Sylvester explains to her the brilliance of it. He assured her that Sylvester would show her how misplaced her reservations were. Sure enough, after hearing the details and all proof safeguards from the large black man's wide lips, Mrs. Townsman, though still skeptical, had begun to warm to the idea of becoming rich and famous in the firearms manufacturing and retail market.

From the factory, Mrs. Townsman stopped by the bank and, for the following evening, booked an appointment with her husband's lawyer. As she anticipated, the bank had already been apprised of her tragic loss and was expecting her arrival. Sorrow-filled greetings and exaggerated words of condolences accelerated her decampment from the bank. Hopping back into her awaiting carriage, Mrs. Townsman crisscrossed through town while openly fiddling with her beautiful chrome-encrusted handgun. She wished she had had the gun this morning when the handsy slave runner was harassing her at the hotel. The pistol was so gorgeous, she would have practically been obligated to end his Negro-chasing days in a beautiful nickel-plated style. Twisting the pistol in her fist, she smiled into her reflection. She was definitely going to pull this on someone—even if only to show it off.

Plump gray clouds moving in sequence had begun to congregate above as she pulled onto her parents' farm. Spurring her horse to a hastened trot, she coerced up the property's carefully kept, gravel-laid entrails. Taking in the beauty of the agriculturally furnished compass, Mrs. Townsman was reminded of just how hard her parents had to work to keep the place up and running when she was a child.

Now the property had more than doubled, and her father was not around to help keep the place up.

From her vantage point, the land appeared relatively flawless. The blossoming gardens were obviously being pruned regularly, and all the animals looked well-fed and properly groomed. And as far as she could see, even the farm's infrastructure (barns, gates, and grounds) showed no sign of neglect. *My mother must be working the two black women eighteen hours a day, trying to keep up with the demand! Maybe I should let Tywin stick around to provide assistance,* she reasoned.

Leading the wagon past the house, Mrs. Townsman rode over to the old shack-like home, where Brownie and Tywin were staying with her mother's round-the-clock service women. In Connecticut, they were service workers or servants, not slaves; though most were still treated as such.

Essentially free men who could walk away at any time, the blacks—as long as they were properly fed, housed, and fairly treated—would work long and hard without complaint. Room and board accompanied by a few pennies a month easily earned most of the Northeast Negroes' loyalty. Wage negotiations were a one-sided affair. The blacks were paid what they were offered, which, in nearly all cases, was practically nothing. Still, turning down a place to reside was a moot possibility. Most were left with little choice. At this time in this country, there weren't many opportunities provided for those of color. This made a man like Sylvester all the more admirable for accomplishing what he had under such daunting circumstances.

The tiny two-bedroom cabin that she once called home was now used to house her mother's female help. The place was nearly one hundred yards in front of her. The sky had begun to darken due to the pending storm, but the chimney atop the small house… She could smell that someone was cooking. Mrs. Townsman delight-fully speculated that maybe Sherry was throwing together one of her megameals. Smiling big, she connived she was going to have to crash their little dinner party and steal herself a plate.

Setting her horse in front of the old house, she thought, *Funny. There was no gate out front when I lived here.* She mused further that in fact, she was positive that this gate was not up when she was here not a year prior. Mrs. Townsman confirmed her mother was really going all out for her blacks as she hopped down from the wagon. Cutting through the warm murky air, a trickle of rain drifted down and kissed her exposed skin, instantly cooling her wary body. The chilling sprinkles sprawling down from the sky were a welcomed treat. This past week's spring climate had a midsummer feel as of late. And just thinking about it, she was certain that this was the first bit of rain she had witnessed her entire trip. That was odd for the Northeast this time of year.

Taking a deep breath, Mrs. Townsman lifted her face to the clouds and began a pacified march toward the intoxicating sweet aroma of roasted nourishment, which was seducing her toward the tiny cabin. With hoggish determination in her stride, Mrs. Townsman slowly stumbled across the yard. Only a dozen steps from the door, her gawky advance was rudely thwarted by a couple of unwieldy little birds that boorishly swooped past her—one of them only missing her face by inches. The two playful feathered pests swirled the dampening air in a carefree dance before one of them landed on top of the roof of the protruding brick water well inside the front yard of the little house to her right.

An irreproachable smile creased her cherry lips as she thought back to her adolescent years where she would use a slingshot her father had given her to shoot down birds, squirrels, and other small animals that happened to mistakenly land on that notable well. For as long as she could recall, that old stone-encased water well had been bone-dry—never a splish or a splash, just the breaking sound of pulp and tissue hitting earth. That and the muffled chirp every time her speeding rocks hurled its unsuspecting targets to the bottom. Mrs. Townsman could only imagine just how many decaying vermin skeletons lay crumbled below.

Turning back toward the scent of what smelled to her like some kind of fruit-filled pie being baked, Mrs. Townsman's feet dragged her ahead. Subsequently, she only managed a couple small steps before a curious sound stalled her progress. Startled, she swung around in search of the strange noise. It was coming from somewhere—a dragging moan or some type of humming. *What is it?* she wondered as her eyes darted back and forth. The harder she listened, the more pronounced the clamor became. It was a song or melody of some sort. She wasn't crazy. She was hearing something, and it wasn't coming from the direction of the house.

Spinning in a semicircle, Mrs. Townsman's eyes fell once again on the old water well. *Is something or someone down there? It can't be,* she reasoned. *No, there better not be,* she rephrased, grabbing her new chrome companion. She took a couple steps toward the well, and the aberrant noise had come down a notch. A couple more steps, and the sound was completely gone.

Leaning over the rim of the old well and looking down into the darkness, Mrs. Townsman listened for any sign of life. "Anyone down there?" she yelled into the dark hole and immediately felt silly for doing so.

Suddenly a booming crash broke, prompting a violent bounce out of her. The large thunder blast hit so massively, it shook the ground beneath her. The hellish barking overhead that lasted several prolonged seconds was followed by an inflamed bolt of lightning. In an instant, the world around her was being bombarded by thick droplets of chilled rainwater that smashed against the earth like the hooves of a million galloping ponies.

Belting out a narrow scream, Mrs. Townsman grabbed down at her flowing beige-and-white dress and ran as fast as she could toward her old home. Snatching open the door, she threw herself inside and slammed it closed behind her. Completely drenched, her sandy-blonde hair clung to her face, as her multilayered dress hung heavily against her base.

Outside, the dark clouds had eclipsed the afternoon sky so profound that the two windows in the room she was in only managed to provide a spartan illumination. The rapid midday dim in itself was spooky, but something on the horizon seemed even more peculiar. She was only seconds into the room when for whatever reason, the deafening quiet caused the instinctive hairs on the back of her neck to rise. Turning to face the room shrouded by a baneful black shadow, she knew even before her vision adjusted to the hue that something was amiss.

As her pupils dilated to adapt, she noticed to her left that there were a number of persons sitting at or around a table. The room was so dark she couldn't equate faces to torsos, but she did a brief calculation. There were five blacks, and by her recollection, there should be only four. Without it even registering, her pistol was in hand. There were five persons, and only one of them appeared to be female. There was something off about this setting.

All remained quiet. It was as if she were engaged in a standoff. She waited for them to blink...and they, her. Beginning to agitate, Mrs. Townsman postured in defense. The adjustment did not go unnoticed. It seemed even in the most obscure lighting, the unmistakable sound of a hammer being thumbed back seldom failed to inspire. Nervous whispers and the sound of people squirming in their chairs began to circulate.

"Hel-lo," Mrs. Townsman articulated, a calm malice present in her tone. She was stock-still with her pistol down by her leg but not hidden from the five. She wouldn't hesitate, but she sincerely hoped she wouldn't be forced to lift it.

"Hello," she said again. And again, her universal greeting went unanswered. Every once and again, the clouds outside would shift in a way where they allowed a bit of light into the room. Squinting, she scanned the five and again gathered that only one of them appeared female.

"Brownie?" Mrs. Townsman inquired, but there was still only silence from the group of Negroes now stirring nervously.

Out of the blue, the door to the kitchen was pushed open, and in walked another. Oblivious to the one-sided standoff, this individual marched in snickering softly to himself. Like a cornered rabbi, the man was halted when he noticed Mrs. Townsman standing in the room.

"That's six," she declared, lifting her weapon to a more progressive angle. "What's going on here?" Mrs. Townsman demanded while pointing the short stalk of her weapon directly at the unfamiliar man's face. "Who are you, and what are you doing on my mother's land?"

"I… I… I work here. We work here," he stuttered in a heavy Southern field slave accent.

"Get over there," she directed, using her pistol to divert him over toward the others.

In assumed total control of the entire situation, Mrs. Townsman stood with her back to the front door, switching her weight from one foot to the other desperately to get her head around what she was seeing. Then again, the kitchen door was pushed open. This time from the opening, in walked Brownie. His hands instantly went up when he saw the gun in his master's hand.

"No, no, Madam Mrs. Mary, please."

"Brownie, who are these people?" Mrs. Townsman growled.

"They work for your mother. They work the farm."

Shaking her head from side to side, dismissing his claims, she said, "My mother told me nothing about these men living here." She put emphasis on *men*.

"Madam, I swear it. Just ask Mrs. Clare."

"You… All of you stand up," Mrs. Townsman ordered the half-dozen people to her left.

Jumping to, the Negro flock did as they were bid.

"Back up against the wall. Hurry up. I'll shoot you where you stand," she threatened a slow-moving man taking his time inching sternward.

"Please, Madam Mrs. Mary," Brownie cried.

"Brownie, what is going on here?"

"Your mother has been helping them."

"Who else is in here?"

"Come in here," Brownie called to the other room, and one by one, Negro persons came pouring into the room—a man, another man, and a woman holding a candle.

Mrs. Townsman's body shook as a shocking image entered into view. Blinking wide eyes, she couldn't believe it. Her breath quickened, and her knees weakened. But her grip on the pistol instantly tightened.

The new arrivals crowded in behind Brownie. There were now eleven people in the room—six on the wall and five in front of her—but Mrs. Townsman's pistol was only raised on one of them.

"Where is Tywin?" she barked through gritted teeth.

"He's down in the well," Brownie answered.

"How many in the well?"

Brownie thought for a moment. "Ten…eleven," he corrected.

Mrs. Townsman's body burned at the thought. She knew Brownie would never lie to her, but this made little sense. Her mother was no brave woman. It was difficult to fathom her somehow involved in hiding slaves. These runaways were the ones taking care of the grounds, she assessed. They were the ones who ate the leftovers the day before. Why would her mother be hiding this from her? How long had this been going on, and why the hell was this person holding the candle standing in front of her? It had been a long painstaking, rough voyage (so she was told) to the state of Virginia some two decades ago. This said hard-ridden journey was supposed to forever rid her of the walking infestation standing before her.

Struggling to grasp the gravity of the moment, Mrs. Townsman's jittered mind shimmered a flash of Bob Sullivan's old pale spotted puss. The sly, opportunist old fart, who was mistakenly entrusted the task of cleaning her of this cancerous scoundrel, had obviously deceived her.

Now standing before her, holding a bright single-wicked candle a foot below her tan-brown unmistakable identifier, Lizzy—her darling youngest son's biological mother—had returned. Looking straight ahead, Lizzy's soft brown eyes—her son's eyes—showed not a hint of fear as she squinted. Her blinking peepers were enchanted in the room's bantam lighting.

Mrs. Townsman mentally jolted and peered wide-eyed right through the three men standing a touch ahead of the hated Negro woman from her past. In fact, in that moment, everyone else in the room seemed to dematerialize. Mrs. Townsman felt like she had aged ten years as Lizzy's hauntingly seductive gaze bit into her, taunting her more and more with each passing second.

Holding the gun now with two hands, Mrs. Townsman's body trembled as she fought the temptation to squeeze all five rounds into Lizzy's wildly inviting young frame. It was like a bad dream, a nightmare—her decaying past coming back to gash her after all these years. Mrs. Townsman spurned that Lizzy had aged well. Not a wrinkle adorned her timeless mask. She appeared healthy, vibrant, and full of life. This was not the portrait of a woman condemned to the demanding cotton fields of a Southern plantation. In Mrs. Townsman's assessment, Lizzy looked as if she hadn't been made to do a hard day's work her entire life. This was her paid decree. Mrs. Townsman steamed. Lizzy was to be worked till it hurt—savagely each day for the rest of her life. This was what she had paid for. Lizzy was to be sold to a heavy-handed Southern slave owner who would make sure she broke under the burning sun. Bob Sullivan promised as much. He assured her he had the exact plantation in mind to punish her thusly. However, looking at her glowing exterior, Mrs. Townsman knew that he lied. He fooled her out of her money and disregarded her desires.

It was as if the world began to move in slow motion, and after a time, the gun in her hands seemed to gain ten additional pounds. Her arms doddered and her palms moisturized so much that Mrs. Townsman was forced to cradle her elbows against her body in order to keep the barrel pointed directly at Lizzy's face. In her mind, it was only the two of them in the room.

Mrs. Townsman hadn't thought of this woman in a decade. Lizzy's manipulative black ass had been a distant memory—an embarrassing hurdle previously thought forever removed. Now with this resurfacing, Mrs. Townsman's blood boiled again with the renewed hatred once thought lost.

Vaguely, Mrs. Townsman could hear the humming of Brownie's frantic words, pleading for her to lower the gun; but in her enraged state, his verbiage was akin to gibberish.

The roaring storm's thunder belches along with the heavily pounding droplets of rainwater were like dramatic theme music to the scene of Lizzy's head jerking back as Mrs. Townsman's imagination saw her pulling the trigger over and over again. But holding form a morticious long minute, Mrs. Townsman just stood there in silence still stunned, not totally believing what her eyes were conveying.

Then just as a blazing blast of thunder erupted, the back door to her back was flung open. Everything happened like a scene out of a scary story. The lightning outside struck with a furious multiblast, peppering the room with a strobing light show. Again the sky cried out with a pounding crash, shaking the house all the way to the floor. Mrs. Townsman, still with her pistol locked onto its immediate target, turned her head to see her mother rushing in behind her.

"Mary," Mrs. Clare called.

Startled at the sight of her mother barging in or panicked by the size of the earth-shattering thunder explosion or maybe just because the collection of mitigating circumstances seemed to give her the reason, Mrs. Townsman pulled the trigger.

An exaggerated bright flash filled the room as the lively weapon roared with ferocious authority. The contained yet blunt blast convulsed, evoking a multitude of shocked responses from everyone in the room.

"Mary, no!" Mrs. Clare screamed before running past her daughter toward the fallen woman.

Mrs. Townsman—shaken, embarrassed, and suddenly apprehensive—allowed the pistol to drag down to her side. A small chorus of horrid gasps and irate murmurs populated the small home as faceless eyes stared at her from the dark corners of the somber room.

Down on her knees now, Mrs. Clare continued to scream. Her retching physically scratched her daughter's mentality.

Harboring the guilt, pressure, and acquiescent gratification of her actions, Mrs. Townsman silently sank out through the open door and slowly dragged into the pouring rain.

It took her much longer than it should have to make it from the small black shack to the stairs of her mother's home. In that time, Mrs. Townsman had gone through all the appropriate and inappropriate states of grief. She laughed, cried, and daydreamed a thousand different thoughts as the thick beads of water drummed down on her uncovered head.

Mrs. Townsman was soaking wet by the time she made it to the house. Letting her soggy clothes fall to her bedroom floor, she dried herself off as best she could before climbing into the bed born-day clean. Pulling her cream-and-brown comforter shoulder-high, she lay back with only her pretty chrome coconspirator to occupy the reverse side of the pillow.

The smell of a properly seasoned, freshly cooked meal awoke Mrs. Townsman from a well-earned slumber. Waking up drowsy, her brain had gone through so much thinking that her errant nerves actually hurt. And allied tickling the corner of her left eye was an early sign of a coming headache.

Her room was pitch-black. With a mediocre moonlight providing little in the way of visible illumination, Mrs. Townsman could hardly see her own hand in front of her face.

Lifting herself to a seated position, she felt the unfamiliar swing in her restrained cleavage and realized that she was still butterball naked. Startled, she threw an arm over her exposed chest as if the walls were watching. Her pulse had quickened; for whatever reason, she had heightened sense of uneasiness. Grabbing a secure hold of her pistol, she rolled out of bed and clothed herself as fast as she could. The wayward hairs on her arms were raised in concern. *This is my mother's house,* she insecurely reasoned. Composing herself, she shook her arms and rubbed her face in an attempt to hush her fickle nerves.

Stepping lightly, the halls were brightened, each with a single candle cradled onto custom-crafted holsters carved into the walls. Through the hall and down the stairs, she made her way to the brightly lamp-lit kitchen, where her mother, Brownie, and Sherry had all congregated. With her pistol safely tucked into the front of her pants, beneath her thin-fabric day jacket, Mrs. Townsman took a deep breath and moseyed through the open doorway.

"Hello, Mother," she announced herself, moving at an animated speed. "Brownie." She nodded. "Good evening, Sherry. The food smells wonderful as usual," Mrs. Townsman spat, speaking at a breakneck speed yet trying to sound as casual as she dared.

Portraying a cloak of confidence, Mrs. Townsman smiled and motioned appropriately as if what happened never happened. She had had many hours to come to terms with what took place. Mulling it over, she decided that what was done was unimpeachable at the very least, if not altogether warranted. At the very, very least, she was convinced that conservative mistakes had transpired on both sides and there was no cause for anyone to grudge over it now. A runaway died—happened all the time.

"Where's Tywin?" she spoke to Brownie, authentic concern in her expression.

Brownie opened his mouth to speak, but his reply audio was lost at the moment. The three surrounding individuals just stared blankly at her as if the words she spoke held no tenor.

"I see you sat down to eat without me," Mrs. Townsman teased, looking across at the near-empty plate of food in front of her mother. Still, Mrs. Clare provided no return dialogue.

Letting out a frustrated breath, she asked Sherry, "Can you please set me a dish?" She had spent less than a minute in the room, but already she was beginning to anger.

As if hearing the magic words, Mrs. Clare, snapping out of her nauseated haze, blinked alive. "Yes, Sherry, please. And set me another as well. And pour us both a glass of wine and a shot of brandy. In fact," she said, nodding at her daughter, "bring the whole bottle."

Mrs. Townsman smiled at her mother, who returned the expression in kind.

"Maybe two bottles," Mrs. Clare comically corrected.

While they ate, the conversation regarding that night's events started with Mrs. Clare apologizing to her daughter for her having to find out in the manner she had. The explanation on how she got started helping the runaways held the earmarks of a speech duly rehearsed. Mrs. Townsman listened intently, aware that her mother's words were obviously designed to pull at her emotional heartstrings. In short, Mrs. Clare relayed that the relationship her daughter had with her adopted son, Blake, played a large part in why she initially decided to help. Eventually after more and more began to show, she started to develop a real sense of gallantry—like her life finally held some significance. She was helping people, truly helping people—human beings who would probably die without her. After a time, Mrs. Clare informed the conjunction became equally beneficial. She provided a place to hide, and in return, they worked her farm.

Brownie, who was ashamed of his part in the deception, apologized for not telling her earlier about what he knew of the situation. Keeping a secret from his beloved madam killed him. It took for him, he explained, to try and avoid her altogether in order for him to keep quiet about this ruse. But Mrs. Clare swore him to secrecy. She insisted that she be the one to tell her. In her defense, she made the attempt the night of the big feast. Mrs. Townsman smiled when she thought back on that night.

My mother—the freedom fighter. She was astonished. And though she worried about the potential dangers, she was actually proud of her mom, and she expressed that sentiment before apologizing for her own impulsive actions.

"You burst in…the lightning, thunder… I was just… I'm just so sorry about the woman. It…it was an accident," Mrs. Townsman gave a synthetic admission of regret.

"Oh, darling, it's fine. Everything is fine. No one's faulting you for reacting the way you did. It was a lot to take in," Mrs. Clare consoled.

"Yeah, but that poor woman," Mrs. Townsman overcolored, shaking her head for effect.

"It's fine, Mary. She'll be fine."

This caught Mrs. Townsman off guard. "The woman?" she asked.

"Yes, Lizzy's all right. She just got a small bump on the head from the fall. You did put a scare into her."

"Bump on the head? The woman I shot?"

"Oh, dear, you didn't shoot her." Mrs. Clare laughed. "She just fell. Fainted. Poor thing. That woman's a fragile one." Mrs. Clare laughed again.

"Bu… But… But… I…"

"Mary, she's fine."

The news hit Mrs. Townsman like a mule kick to the gut. Lizzy was still alive—not even shot, nothing. Though she hadn't intentionally, exactly, positively tried to shoot her, Mrs. Townsman had come to terms with the fact that it happened. She had forgiven herself—rationalized that it was painted to play out the way it had. Now!

At this time, Mrs. Townsman was already on her second glass of wine. Up until this point, she hadn't even touched the brandy; but reaching over the table, she grabbed and tilted the bottle over her wineglass, holding it steady for a healthy pour. Mrs. Clare nodded her acknowledgment as she continued to ramble, totally unaware of the negative change in her daughter's disposition.

Mrs. Townsman was caught in a stupor—her appetite instantly lost. Sitting slouched over, nursing her brandy-wine mixture, the headache previously held in check seemed to double at that point—the thumping pain punishing her for her premature celebration.

Smiling, drinking, nodding, and thinking, Mrs. Townsman managed to keep up an exemplary charade while combating her mother's vocal engagements in shot. Doing the moral calculations in her head, she weighed her options as the strong liquor in her cup continued to dissipate with growing frequency. After long, she could hardly keep her head straight.

Now only half-hearing her mother's regurgitating rant, Mrs. Townsman's clouded thoughts began to trail off, running down potential solutions to this delicate dilemma. Fully drunk now, she contemplated marching right back out to that shack and sure a bullet right into Lizzy's peanut head. She considered dragging Lizzy over to Bob Sullivan and demanding he make good on the deal they struck so many years ago. She pondered the option of simply going over and demanding her off her mother's property. But the truth was, she thought it most appropriate to finally set her bias aside and allow Blake the chance to meet his birth mother.

It was a hard decision with all her options, with pros and cons on all sides. Still, though the Bob Sullivan angle sounded righteous enough, Mrs. Townsman knew what had to be done. How could any woman, regardless of race, possibly choose to deny another the opportunity to reunite with their child? This thinking followed her all the way to bed and rocked her to sleep, and in the morning, she was convinced that bringing Lizzy back with her to Georgia was the Christian thing to do.

When it came right down to it, Mrs. Townsman reasoned that it wasn't Lizzy's decision to procreate with her husband. Committing adultery was a sin surely forced on her. It was her darling husband who broke his vow. In all actuality, Lizzy was just a warm body conveniently prancing around. Mrs. Townsman apprised that however it happened, it happened, and a beautiful baby boy was the product. Blake was a blessing in and of itself. And she knew that if her husband were still alive, bringing Lizzy to Georgia to meet her son would be what he'd want.

Shelving the whole Lizzy issue, at least for that morning, Mrs. Townsman had Brownie ready the carriage. Escorted by her loyal black help, she set off into town. This was the morning of her very important meeting at her husband's bank.

Harvey Baker, her late husband's lawyer and financial adviser, met her in the back office of the bank with a stern handshake and a mouth full of pearly-white teeth. A tall fairly handsome older gentleman, Harvey began their meeting with a brief yet powerful synopsis on her and her husband's lucrative conjoined relationship. Simply put, he explained the various investments and business ventures in which her inherited money was involved.

Nodding repeatedly while utilizing a plethora of one-word answers, Mrs. Townsman, though trying to appear receptive, was overwhelmed by the vastness of the fiscal world. From real estate hubs to overseas imports, Mrs. Townsman realized that her husband had his hands in everything.

She tried to remember her husband's horse ranches through all the different cities and all the funny names of companies she couldn't quite pronounce; the only thing Mrs. Townsman truly understood was the bottom line. Harvey Baker, after totaling out her net worth, informed Mrs. Townsman that she was worth over $1,740,000.

Mrs. Townsman's mouth dropped. $1,740,000—she had no idea her husband was so wealthy. And to top it off, Harvey explained that in another few years, if she kept all her investments in one place, she could be looking at well over a million plus.

Mrs. Townsman was walking on air by the time she left the bank that morning. Sylvester, also a client of Harvey, told him to send her over to meet with him at the conclusion of their meeting.

Riding passenger beside Brownie, Mrs. Townsman interlocked her hands in prayer, silently thanking her husband for being the grand provider he was. Speaking to his ghostly spirit, she promised to use the money to bolster their family's legacy to the heavens, where he could directly bathe in their success.

Still a few hours before noon, Mrs. Townsman sashayed into Sylvester's gun factory like Queen Elizabeth walking into her palace. This time, Peter (the day-shift manager), anxiously expecting her, was waiting in the lobby sober as a priest. Having heard the awful news by now, he offered his sincerest condolences and said how sorry he was for not doing so before.

A naturally easygoing young man, Peter chatted her up as they walked over to Sylvester's office. After announcing her presence, Peter excused himself, allowing Mrs. Townsman to walk past him into the office alone.

"Mary," Sylvester began. He and a younger Caucasian gentleman stood to receive her. "I wasn't expecting you for another hour," he said, taking and kissing her hand.

"Hello," Mrs. Townsman replied, looking over Sylvester's shoulder at the well-dressed strapping young stranger in the room.

"Oh." Sylvester smiled. "Let me introduce you to Mr. Barry McCoy."

"A pleasure," Mrs. Townsman admitted, grabbing and shaking his hand.

"Barry here will be heading back with you on your trip back to Georgia."

Mrs. Townsman smiled but said nothing.

"Barry's the best—"

"Sylvester, um…can I speak to you in private?" Mrs. Townsman politely asked, not wanting to be rude.

"Sure, sure," Sylvester replied. "Barry, can you give us a second?"

Barry nodded and, without a word, walked past Mrs. Townsman toward the door.

As soon as Barry was out of earshot, Mrs. Townsman proceeded to address her concerns. Traveling across the country chaperoned by some strange gunman was not her idea of a safe trip. Moreover, for her to entertain the notion of having such an individual around her plantation, her sons! To say it was skeptical would be putting it mildly.

Nevertheless, being the smooth-talking, savvy salesman he was, in less than ten minutes, Sylvester was not only able to convince Mrs. Townsman that bringing Barry back with her to Georgia was what her husband would have wanted but he also set the blueprint to his living situation.

So not to make her uncomfortable, Barry was to be housed at her son's hotel where he would be hired to help provide security. In addition, with her husband gone, Barry could be used to help Blake work the gun shop. Barry's contract was paid through for ninety days. For those three months, he was to be at Mrs. Townsman's beck and call. If nothing transpired out of the information he'd gather about the dead men who rode out to her plantation, no harm, no foul. Barry was to return to Connecticut once his three months had run its course.

Riding back across town quietly laughing to herself, Mrs. Townsman was in awe at how she always managed to let Sylvester outtalk her. *The man could sell a fur coat to a grizzly bear,* Mrs. Townsman quietly joked. She was to pick Barry up at the hotel the day after tomorrow. She left the house with her husband in a box only to return with a gunfighter, a million dollars plus, and a new lease on life.

It was still quite early that afternoon, 4:00 maybe 5:00 p.m., yet with so much activity revolving in her head, Mrs. Townsman was physically and mentally exhausted. What an aggressive chain of events the last month delivered—husband gone, grandchild pending, Lizzy back for the abyss, and now money beyond her wildest dreams. $1,740,000—the number seemed unreal.

Throwing her head back, she used her fingers to comb her thick blonde lock of hair. Overwhelmed, the newly rich widow roughly took in and exhaled a hard breath of fatigue.

Sitting on the back porch looking off into the large farm garden, Mrs. Townsman marveled openly at the army of free blacks ahead of her. Now that the cat was out of the bag, her mother had her Negro workers out in full force. There was a pleasant vibe from where she stood. The scene surrounding her parents' property reminded her of home. Slaves or servants, to her the line was blurred. Mrs. Townsman felt the slaves on her plantation were just as fortunate as the upbeat blacks she was spying presently.

Watching over the grounds, there were Negroes everywhere. No wonder the farm was so flawless, Mrs. Townsman admitted. Raking, pruning, painting, and cleaning, the workers here were a lively bunch. Not one appeared lazy or unwilling to pull their weight. It was a beautiful thing that her mother had created. Not slaves but free workers—Mrs. Townsman applauded the premise.

Then out of the corner of her eye… It was typically what she imagined she'd have to expect from such a pretentious woman. Coming down the roadway, sitting beside Brownie who was steering her mother's single-horse-pulled wagon, was who else but prissy Lizzy. *Who does this woman think she is, being ushered around the farm by carriage while the others worked?* Mrs. Townsman steamed, irate. A warm hate-fueled fever brushed against the underskin of her body as she watched Lizzy from afar. Though she had resolved to go ahead and take Lizzy back with her to Georgia, that didn't automatically mean she had to like her.

Growing mad enough to spit, Mrs. Townsman shook her head in anguish, forethinking on the long week or so she would have to share in close quarters with this abhorrent woman. But worst of all was how she knew Blake would instantly fall for her. Blake being the perfect gentleman she had raised, Mrs. Townsman was positive her baby boy would make it his life's goal not to have his birth mother ever have to lift a finger. From the moment he'd meet her, Mrs. Townsman was sure Lizzy would become royalty in his eyes. Mrs. Townsman could see her brown baby now gushing over this woman he never met. She struggled to think how short her mommy time would be cut with Lizzy in the picture. This line of thinking helped elicit a knotting tightness in her lower back. *Damn indecisive conscious.*

Raising her hand, Mrs. Townsman got Brownie's attention as he pulled toward the horse stable smiling like a rat on a cheese farm. Mrs. Townsman stirred, annoyed; she never saw Brownie so embarrassingly giddy over a woman before. Lizzy had the man entangled within her black widow web.

Redirecting the carriage toward the house, Mrs. Townsman watched as Lizzy gestured for him to stop and let her out. Garnering her attention, Mrs. Townsman instructed him to bring her along. Mrs. Townsman could see the two openly conversing. Obviously, Lizzy did not want to comply. Eventually, Brownie convinced her to do as bid.

There was only negative condemnation being processed as the carriage briskly trotted across the yard. Cursing under her breath, Mrs. Townsman damned her blasted kind heart. If she'd had any sense at all, she'd pull out her pistol and put a bullet right between Lizzy's eyes.

Pompous runaway slave whore, Mrs. Townsman mentally griped while watching Brownie climb down to help Lizzy out of the cart. Using the back of her hand in a dismissive manner, Mrs. Townsman waved Brownie away to speak to Lizzy in private.

"Have a seat," Mrs. Townsman instructed. Though peeved, she mustered up a measured yet inviting smile.

"Thank you, ma'am." Lizzy smiled in return, her facial expression just as deceivingly manufactured as her host.

"How long have you been here?" Mrs. Townsman quizzed.

Lizzy shrugged. "I don't know. Maybe a year. Your mother is very nice to us. We try to work hard as we can."

Maybe the others work as hard as they can, Mrs. Townsman mentally retorted.

Lizzy continued, "I love it here. Anything Mrs. Clare ask me to do, I's—"

Cutting her short, Mrs. Townsman said, dropping her phony smile, "You know who I am, yes?" Stabbing sharp as needles, her piercing brown eyes tore into Lizzy. They were both young women at the time, but there was no way to forget such an ordeal.

Also choosing to forfeit her fraudulent tenor, Lizzy let her pink pouty lips uncurl. Staring right back at Mrs. Townsman, defiantly she replied, "Yes. I remember."

The two strong-willed women just stared at each other for a short intense moment, neither of them wanting to be the first to flinch. Then allowing a tiny smirk, Mrs. Townsman nodded. Covertly, she somewhat admired Lizzy's toughness—the woman had heart. Dropping her cement gaze before refocusing, Mrs. Townsman opened, "I'd like to apologize to you." Lizzy didn't respond. Continuing, she said, "I was wrong and impulsive and... No, there's no excuse. I was wrong."

The beautiful, proud black woman's facial expression remained fixed, but after a while, her eyes fell to the floor. "Thank you," she said in a near whisper.

With the stone wall lifted, sitting a foot and a half apart, (slowly at first) the two women talked for hours. Mrs. Townsman informed her that her husband had recently passed, and Lizzy explained that Old Man Bob kept her on his property all these years. Under his repulsive concuss, she admitted to birthing the man two sons—one of which he killed in a fit of rage and the other she'd brought along with her.

According to Lizzy, the majority of the free-service workers here on the farm were those who had run away from the illegal plantation owners here in the North. She asserted that Bob Sullivan had a half-dozen slaves working his giant plantation. Keeping his slaves well-isolated from society, none of them were aware that Connecticut awarded blacks their unarrested freedom.

Mrs. Townsman recognized that Lizzy spoke well for a former slave. She told her sad stories with sensitivity and conviction. After a while, Mrs. Townsman, taken aback, began to talk less and listen more. In truth, Mrs. Townsman was procrastinating, nervously contemplating how she was going to approach the topic of Blake being raised as her own. And apparently, Lizzy was intent on not inquiring about him altogether.

Nonetheless, folding her hands across her lap, Mrs. Townsman just let out with it. "We've named your son Blake, and we've raised him an equal to his brother, my son Michael."

Lizzy's mouth parted a fraction, and her eyes seemed to lose focus. Then raising a hand to her face, she began to cry. Leaning back on the bench ashamed, Mrs. Townsman let the woman have a moment. She could not imagine someone taking one of her boys from her, which was terribly ironic being she was now consoling the victimized mother of the boy she'd taken.

If not a miracle, Lizzy knew not what to call it. For almost two decades, she wondered pessimistically about the well-being of her firstborn. Sitting and talking to Mrs. Townsman, she tried her damnedest to put it out of her thoughts. Being how violently Mrs. Townsman had reacted a night ago, Lizzy, rather than to hear a heart-breaker, chose to hear nothing at all. But now! To know her son had been raised a free man in a prestigious white family brightened her heart. Mr. Michael Townsman, her first and only love, had kept his promise.

When Mrs. Townsman offered to bring her and her eight-year-old son, Deacon, to meet his brother, Blake, it was like a dream come true. Lizzy had to restrain herself from hugging the woman she hated more than almost anything in life for twenty years. Lizzy was excited beyond words. In her happiest dreams, she'd prayed this day would come. She'd meet her beautiful baby boy—her Master Michael's free born son. "Blake," she let the name linger on her tongue.

*****

The Sword

He was ready for the main course.

First, the Sword untied each of the twelve horses one by one, smacking them hard on the rear to send them scurrying up the hill and into the woods. Then climbing onto one of the two four-horse stagecoaches, the Sword sat behind the reins and stared off at the hateful party congregated nearly two hundred yards ahead. *This won't be easy.*

A pulverizing start was absolutely essential to his chances of success. In order to inflict as much damage as he could, he needed to get as close as possible without being seen. This being said, with so many eyes among the enemy flock, sneaking up behind them posed a difficult task. Peering over at the other stagecoach, the Sword resolved he might had just the vehicle to carry out such a beginning.

The impromptu outdoor festival was in full swing. The happy group of twenty were totally preoccupied—eating, drinking, and letting off their rifles. Busy partying, they were left unaware of the large wagon trotting over until it was right on them.

"What in the hell," Rolen, the leader of the outfit, cursed.

Pulling off his simple white mask, Ned—a thin short hard-faced fellow—stared off at the now-circling wagon. Then squinting his eyes, he looked back to the empty lot of horses at the entrance of the valley. "Where the hell are the…the horses?" he spoke out loud to himself. "Marty!" Ned called.

"Rolen! What the fuck is going on with your cousin?" one of the women who was in charge of the children called. This was a rather gaudy oversize female. "Marty, stop your nonsense!" she called to the still-moving wagon. "Rolen!" she screamed, now addressing their host. "I told you he shouldn't have been allowed to bring that whore." Standing to her feet, she charged, pointing an accusatory finger at him. "This is your doing."

"Marty!" Rolen called to the wagon as it passed only thirty feet from where he stood. "This isn't funny."

"Marty!" one of the other men called.

The ignorant crowd stirred in animation. In a chorus of complaints, everyone began speaking at once or calling the dead man's name. A young boy who had mistakenly dropped his plate of food when another child bumped him began to wail audibly.

"Maybe something startled them, and somehow they got loose," Rolen began. "Ed, why don't you—" Rolen was cut off when out of the darkness, the other stagecoach appeared. Crawling considerably slower than the previous, the large carriage pulled across the field.

"Marty, you asshole," Rolen declared with a tickle in his statement.

The large hard-topped wagon pulled to a stop ten yards away from the picnic area. But when his eyes focused, Rolen saw that there was no one at the reins.

Ed, a clean-shaven medium-built middle-aged country bumpkin, shaking his head in frustration, started off. An overweight short fellow named Charley followed behind him. Rolen, sensing something amiss, cautiously hung back. Watching attentively, he loaded his double-barrel shotgun.

Irritated, Ed grabbed hold of the rail and climbed on the cart. *Boom! Boom! Boom!* Gunfire exploded from within the cab. Two shots through Ed from the foothold, and another tore into the man behind him, dropping him to a knee. The sizable hole in his chest poured as Charley scurried backward, but his retreat was spoiled when another gunshot broke through his sternum.

Hasty, the wagon spit forward, rushing toward the heart of the crowd before taking a sharp right turn, passing by the blazing fire. *Boom, boom, boom!* The Sword's revolvers unleashed a furious assault, his powerful bullets meeting flesh and bone with every shot fired. Even in the dark of night, the Sword's expert shooting cut with precision. The crowd's screams shook the air as man, woman, and child caught flying metal flush.

Rolen rolled out of the way of the speeding wagon as it bore down on his position. Tumbling to the earth, his fall landed him on top of a thin child who had taken a bullet to the stomach. Rolen's eyes instantly swelled with liquid sorrow as his eldest child shook with pain. The red essence spilled from Jessy's body at an unsustainable rate. Within seconds, Jessy had gone limp in his father's arms. His hands shook as a rage he never felt solicited the shotgun from the earth. Standing to his feet with no fear of consequence, Rolen put both barrels into the side panel of the passing carriage. Rolen gave a horrific howl that shook several of the other men to raise their arms in defense.

The lone Negro climbed back to the front of the wagon. Only grabbing the reins when compelled, he led the huge stagecoach around the rim of the valley while reloading his pistols. His adrenaline was bubbling over. The Sword kept to the outskirts of the field now that measured gunfire followed him about.

Holding on to their rifles for dear life, the cowardly gunmen were more than frantic now that the aggression was forthcoming. Aiming in no particular direction, they emptied their weapons into the darkness.

One of the women, delirious with fear, took two of the younger children by the arm and made a beeline toward the entrance of the blood-drenched park. This was a terrible idea. Her ill-advised decision made a perfect target. With a toothy smile threatening to shine right through the mask, the Sword aimed the horses down on them. The four muscle-bound animals pulling the large wooden cart pushed full speed, trampling over the poor would-be-deserters like a rockslide.

Fatigued with the mobile assault approach, the Sword jumped from the moving wagon. Only the woman who was leading the retreat was noticeably vitally conscious. An accurately placed shell remedied that problem.

In a matter of minutes, the party of twenty was quickly reduced to under ten. Two women, three children, and four men stood huddled together around the bright fire, desperately trying to figure a way out of the nightmarish juncture they were involved.

On his stomach, crawling through the beautiful velvety grass, the Sword watched as Rolen, an ex-army sergeant, tried to calm the masses. "All right, everybody. Everybody just shut up," he pleaded. But the frightened children wouldn't shush.

Howling her head off, a pained ten-year-old who had taken a bullet in the arm filled the arena with her song. Equally as vocal was the girl's mother, who was holding the screaming girl against her chest. Shaking with anger, she cried bloody murder, "She's only ten, you bastards. Why are you doing this!"

Rolen, still beside himself with the grief of his lost son, stilled himself enough to create a plan of escape. He grabbed Braddick, a twenty-seven-year-old drunk, by the arm.

"That's them," Brad, as he was called for short, spoke first. The man was scared witless. "That's them Indian savages who kill—"

"Brad," Rolen cut him off, "pull it together." But just the mention of the savage Indian horde excited Rolen's feet.

"We're all going to die. They're going to scalp us," Brad said, grabbing a handful of his shaggy-cut hair.

Snatching him by the shoulder, Rolen animated, "Brad!"

"They're going—"

"Stop it. You're scaring the children," Rolen cautioned him while gesturing with a nod over to the women and children who had somewhat quieted to hear them.

The other wagon that had first drew their attention had parked itself by a crease in the valley wall.

"Go get the carriage," Rolen instructed Brad.

Brad was beside himself with fear and looked at Rolen like he was speaking a foreign language.

"Go!" Rolen said, flicking back the hammer on his shotgun. The expression on his face read "or else." "Get the carriage," he challenged again. "We have to get these women out of here."

"Okay," Brad agreed reluctantly.

The scene dragged in slow motion. Brad, who had retrieved the runaway wagon, pulled up beside the eight besieged. Expeditiously and with pep, the feeble group hustled into the horse-drawn vehicle. The four powerful animals stirred nervously as if cognizant of the imminent danger plaguing them. Brad and another man road up front, while Rolen and an older gentleman sat in the back with the more vulnerable.

The Sword was only yards away, lying between the coming wagon and the valley exit. *These devils are not going to evade this punishment,* he vowed. The stagecoach was barreling down on him. The four potent working beasts sluggishly muscled the full load. Gingerly, so as not to give away his position, the Sword rolled over onto his back and flipped his body so that his feet were pointed toward the coming wagon.

"There," the man sitting up front with Brad called seconds before the Sword's dual revolvers exploded, ripping the two lead men to pieces. Still firing, the Sword stopped the two front horses, riddling them from midbreast to head with deadly bullet fire. The two downed horses stalled the party's departure. Shrieking violently, the two remaining horses bucked and bounced, hopelessly trying to pull around their dead colleagues.

Frantic and without ample cause, the older man who was riding in the back with Rolen and the others climbed to the front of the cab and stuck his head through the opening. A patiently fired slug caught him square between the eyes, shoving him back into the frenzied crowd minus a lot of his face.

The Sword was standing upright now, raining small metal balls of death into the side of the fully stocked wagon. To the applauding quills of the people inside, he squeezed his large revolvers empty. Hearing the hollow sound of metal clanging against metal, he holstered his overworked firearms, swapping them for their identical twins at his back.

Sidestepping, the Sword worked his way around the near-silent carriage, his weapons pointed and ready. Circling, he spotted a woman coming out of the open door.

"Please," she cried as she saw him. A stray bullet, which had grazed her in the side, had her doubled over in pain. However, calling on all her strength, she held a small child cradled in her arms. The Sword hesitated. *I am not a monster,* he rationalized. The boy she was holding was the youngest of the lot—just a toddler really. *He couldn't have done so much, if anything, to warrant such an end,* the Sword quickly processed. *Truthfully, he may not even remember this night when he matures.* The Sword lowered his guns.

"Thank you. Please. Thank you," the woman pleaded.

No, the Sword reasoned. The child might be innocent, but the woman—*boom! boom!* He caught her in the upper thigh, causing her to drop the little boy. *Boom! Boom!* Two more shots ripped her high in the chest as she was stumbling backward.

Outside of the screaming baby and the agitated horses, the valley lay still. Easing around the wagon, the Sword aimed his guns at the silent cab; there was no sign of life. Self-composing, he let his guns fall to his side. Then from behind the wagon, the sound of a shotgun blast rocked him back. The blow struck him in the shoulder. It wasn't a clean hit, but it was enough to send him stumbling to the turf. Rolen, who had rolled out of the wagon the first instant the first shots were fired, was now charging forward, his double-barrel shotgun arched against his shoulder.

The entire left side of the Sword's body seemed frozen-stiff. Frantically he rolled. *Boom!* The shot from Rolen's rifle rained down, missing the Sword by half a foot. Baring his teeth, Rolen lifted his rifle by the stalk and charged the grounded man. Coming down with a violent swing, he struck him square across the chest with the bunt of his shotgun. The blow invoked a resounding gruff from the downed assailant. A second attempted strike hit dirt, as the Sword rolled onto his side a horse's second before impact. Off balance, Rolen was caught with a sweeping kick that took his legs out from under him. Not stopping to gather himself, Rolen lunged right up and onto his opponent. With power-filled strikes, Rolen began pounding and hammering down with aggressive fists.

"Son of a bitch, those were children," he cursed, forcing one fist after the other into the masked man's face. "My son!" He was red with rage as he attempted to beat the man to death with his bare hands.

With only one good arm, the Sword's efforts to slow the enraged Caucasian were futile; and after long, he stopped trying altogether. Exhausted physically and mentally, the Sword went limp. Succumbing to the emotion of the moment, Rolen then threw his massive hands around the masked man's neck. There was a long instant of satisfaction as Rolen felt his victim's neck pulsating beneath his tight grip.

No longer subject to the rigors of pain and agony, the Sword lay eyes open, looking into the face of the man on top of him—his vision blinking in and out. He was still conscious but barely. *This can't be my end. I can't die like this.* All the oxygen had left his lungs, and he was close to the point of brain failure when Rolen released his hold. Spotting one of the Sword's fallen pistols lying in the grass only a few feet away, Rolen postured up. The weapon, which had matted the fluffy grass around it, looked like supper to a starving man. The temptation of killing the slayer of his eldest son with his own pistol intrigued the man. Lethargic, the newly grieving father crawled off his near-unconscious victim in pursuit of the weapon that lay just beyond his reach.

The cries from the young child shook the Sword from his virtual dream state. *I am not done yet. My Lord still has work for me.* It took all he had to lift up enough to reach his knife. Pulling his back off the ground, the Sword swallowed a big gulp of air before turning to find Rolen in the dark. Rolen had the pistol in his hand, but he couldn't find the hammer in which to thumb it back. The gun was unlike any he had encountered. It was nearly twice as heavy, and when he went to squeeze, Rolen yanked at the trigger. *Boom!* The weapon went off. Turning back to his fallen foe, Rolen was surprised to see that the man was not as he left him but up on his feet lunging toward him.

With a burst, the Sword tackled Rolen to the ground. His knife, crusted with dried blood, caught Rolen in the neck. There was absolutely no resistance as the blade plunged up through the neck and into the brain. Rolling off Rolen onto his back, the Sword exhaled. His chest heaved in and out as the sound of his breathing challenged the sobs of the still-crying child.

Taking a minute to assuage, he lifted himself off the ground. The Sword was shot and in need of medical attention, but he was alive. He was shot, exhausted, and bleeding profusely; yet his main concern was to get as far away from the blood-soaked valley as soon as possible. He needed to be miles away by the time reinforcements came.

With little help from his left arm, the Sword managed to collect his pistol from Rolen's dead hands; and though timing was of the essence, he kneeled there beside the dead man and reloaded all four of his guns. His mentor had installed in him a stern practice: "Always ride with weapons fully loaded."

While squatting there, pushing the last few bullets into the cylinder, the Sword noticed a shadow creeping up from his left. Turning his posture to meet the threat, he cradled his injured arm across his chest and aimed his other.

"Hello!" the coming person called with a female belch. The naked woman was walking through the blinding darkness toward the burning flame, her eyes focused on the stalled wagon. The Sword dropped his outreached arm as he remembered who she was. Slowly he lay back against Rolen's stiff corpse, not moving as he allowed the woman to approach.

The Sword was lying on his stomach across Rolen's legs with his pistol hand hidden under his chest. The naked white woman saw the two bodies and gave a sharp yelp. Moving on, she spotted the dead persons by the wagon and let her voice sound unrestricted.

The Sword's shoulder was beginning to burn, but he lay quiet. He could see the woman was beautiful through the darkness. It had been ages since he felt the insides of a white woman. Her hesitant strides carried her gracefully through the carnage he left behind.

"Where are you?" she called to the child, whose cries had become a fixture in the moment. Still inching around, she made it to the door of the wagon. "Ah!" she screamed when she looked inside. Taking hastened steps back, she unintentionally tripped over the child who had come up behind her.

The Sword labored up to a seated position. His left arm was now all but useless; still his right held the weight of a long black revolver. The naked woman was on her feet now, holding the child in her arms in a way to shield him from the devastation left hence. The Sword was also standing now, his feet silently carrying him toward the only two whites left alive.

She meant nothing to him. In his present condition, he couldn't enjoy her the way he wanted even if she begged for it. As he crept inch by inch, the woman seemed to be unaware of his presence until he was right behind her. The gun felt heavy in his hand as he held it out pointed less than a yard away from the back of her head. The nude woman stood stiff, holding the whiny kid close against her breast. She knew he was there, and he knew she knew. Without turning around, "Please" was all she said as she took a step forward then another and another until she had begun to dim in the surrounding night.

The Sword let his pistol fall as the woman walked off with her life and the life of the baby boy she held. The Sword turned and, with a heavy heart, walked out of the murderous valley for the last time.

CHAPTER 25

"Come here" was all that was said. Two words, which out of his mouth, on that plantation held all the sway of a formal mandate.

Blake, who was not required to be in town that morning, was up at dusk all the same. Nonchalant, out for a routine stroll of the property absentmindedly, he veered to the left, coursing through the middle of the huge vegetable garden, where a single female worker was out pruning and deweeding. Bessy, the awkwardly tall wide-built middle-aged slave responsible for that portion of the garden, was squatted down in a three-point stance tending to a premature tomato bush. "Come here" was all it took to put a wide chapped-lipped smile on her irregularly small face.

For a woman, Bessy was on the wrong side of six feet, but the size of her head suggested it'd be better fit for a small child's body. Bessy's head was so disproportioned in contrast to her height that Blake figured her birth had to be a product of incest.

Laying down her hedge clippers, Bessy stood to her full height; and with high arching steps, she began climbing over small tomato bushes on her way to where Blake was standing. Blake cringed as the homely designed voluminous woman approached. Bessy was anything but attractive. Her overall appearance made the superficial young black slave master want to turn away.

Bessy's thin sweat-stained sleeveless shirt clung to her upper body like loose skin on an old cow—the imprint insinuating the long flat sagging breasts beneath the fabric, old perennial breasts forged from years of spitting out potential hardworking slave children for her former owner.

Bessy had long leather-whip-inspired scars dragged all across her arms and down the uncovers of her upper back. From what Blake could casually inspect, every aspect of this woman's physical presence was repellent. He had a few experimental stumbles with some of the plantation's less enchanting, but as for a slave woman, Bessy was among the underbelly of the lot. There was no way he could, in good conscience, voluntarily ever think to stick his golden woman tamer in the womb of such an unsightly female. *Who would do such a thing?* He looked at her in astonishment. *It took a desperate man to enter that snake trap.* But her mouth on the other hand—her mouth was a different story.

"Here, drink this," he said, offering her the last of his fresh squeezed lemonade. "And lick your lips." He hated a dry, cotton-mouthed woman. Bessy's thick pouted lips were white from dehydration, and Blake needed those babies fluffed and lubricated. He was stretching the front of his breeches just anticipating the pleasures to come.

The basket she used to collect the tomatoes was also the stool she normally used to sit on when offering him fellatio. Flipping the basket over, she placed it down in front of Blake as he undid his trousers. The basket set upside down was just at the right height to put her face waist-level. The hot ground was killer on her knees, and crouching with them bent got to be uncomfortable after long, and Blake usually took a while.

Now out of all the slaves on their plantation, Bessy did not exactly possess the most capable mouth; and in no way, shape, or form was she anywhere as skilled as his soon-to-be child's mother. But what made him seek her out time after time was the woman was passionate about her oral duties. Bessy took pride in being called to the forefront, and she went at it head-on, with a starch relentlessness that impressed him.

Slow shallow mouthfuls as she rotated her head and neck in small semicircles was how she knew he liked her to begin. "Don't be so eager to get it out," Blake would tell her. "You have to work it up. Just be attentive. I'll tell you when to speed up," he'd instruct.

Blake had his hands on his waist, with his pelvis thrust forward. His eyes searched the fluffy cloud-heavy skies as he relaxingly enjoyed the warmth of Bessy's inner cheeks. Bessy had strong jaws, which allowed her to pull him in and out for an unusually long amount of time, but Blake wasn't in the mood to stand there all day. Growing restless, he gave her a tap on the head, which usually indicated to her that he wanted her to speed up the process.

Four nappy thick corn braids were pulled down the back of her head. Bessy was going at a nice spill, but Blake grabbed a grip of her loosely woven braids and began aggressively forcing her on to him. The woman was a trooper, her wet mouth able and willing. Still, there was a limit to the amount of force her small throat could absorb. Though her tolerance was reasonably high, Bessy's capabilities had their restrictions, and Blake was dangerously poking at its threshhold.

After long, Bessy began slobbering heavily and gagging after every few pushes. Beginning to tire of her cringing, Blake pulled free of her soft full lips, allowing her some time to regain her bearings. Bessy took a few deep breaths while rotating her neck and shoulders in a manner that suggested she needed to loosen her posture. Blake could tell by her expression that she was disappointed in herself. "You're doing good," he spoke reassuringly. He loved that about her. Bessy was a stickler when it came to performing a task. Like her vegetable garden, she'd stay at it all day until she got the job done.

Peering down at her small face, Blake laid his large penis across her head. Bessy smiled beneath him. Her tiny pea-head looked even smaller under his massive manhood. Scrolling down the length of her face, he began sliding his penis from side to side. Bessy had her small mouth gaped wide, trying to catch him as he teasingly smacked her from cheek to cheek. Bessy laughed giddily with all the joy of a small child playing with a favorite toy.

Blake smiled lightheartedly at her amusement. He knew how much she liked it when he played with her like this. He wouldn't let her use her hands. The game was, she had to try and capture the prize using only her mouth.

When Bessy finally got a hold of him, for a while, he allowed her to go at her own pace. She loved the thrill of being so intimate with Blake. She'd sit on that tomato basket for hours if he'd let her, and on occasion, she sat for quite some time. Blake found it difficult to orgasm with her. She was very active, and her pull was decent, but somehow, she seemed to lack the punch necessary to extract his seed. Most times, he found himself using his hand to help her, but today he wanted her to get it out under her own power.

"Come on," he urged. "Get it… Harder… Faster… Deeper… Make it drag across the top of your mouth. You don't always have to get It all the way back. Just every three strokes," he coached. Still, after a while, he again found himself with his hand on her head thrusting her into a gagging cough.

Her body jerked and convulsed as she started to choke and gag after nearly every other push. Still, Bessy did not pull away. Blake had both hands on her head pumping urgently with a reserved but steady rhythm. Bessy's head snapped back forcefully as he quickened his pace. Gripping her small head, he ignored her exaggerated gasp as he bucked back and forth, feeling the urge grip him. His brink was just about at its breaking when Bessy pulled free of his cuffed hands and leaned to the side, heaving up an orange milky liquid on the side of a nearby tomato bush. Blake stepped back as Bessy followed up with a nasty slime-inspired spit. Blake was disappointed. He was almost there.

Looking down at the tomato bush, Bessy whispered embarrassedly, "I's clean it." Her face was sad and contrite. Opening and closing her mouth, she tried to relax her jaw. Blake was tempted to reenter the polluted solace, but disheartened, he elected against it.

"I's sorry," Bessy began. "I's sorry, Masta Blake. I's ready. I won't spit up again."

"Just…finish the tomatoes and clean that up," Blake said, tucking away.

"I's sorry."

"No, you did good," he assured, giving her a polite smile. Fastening his belt, he turned to make his exit.

"Bye," Bessy called after him.

Blake held up a lusterless hand and kept stepping. "Shit!" he cursed as he headed back up the winding trail. There were more people out now. Blake greeted the hardworking flock of blacks with a stoic smile and lazy hand gestures. He was in no mood to be overly social.

Blake wanted to finish that orgasm. Bad! His penis was still three-quarters-of-the-way hard. He couldn't end the morning like this, but Lory—his favorite—was on her monthly bleed. And Blake hated the way it smelled when they bled; plus it was sticky, red, and just more trouble than it was worth. Already irritated, he didn't have the energy to run down any of the others.

"Shit," Blake cursed again as he headed up to the main house. He knew what he had to do, and though part of him wanted to, he loathed the task all the same.

Darla had gained thirty pounds during the last nine months, and a good portion of the weight landed directly in her rear. Darla had been staying in Blake's old room at the main house while his mother was away. Maybe one time in the last month did he slip up and let her talk him into laying with her, but ever since then, he had been starving her of the pleasure.

This is going to be regrettable, he mentally grumbled.

After washing off Bessy's saliva, Blake walked into his room and found Darla lying on her side in the middle of the bed. She had on a thin long slip that unfortunately made her giant protruding belly look even bigger.

Damn. He detested having to do this. Blake stood over the bed for a long time looking down as she looked right back up at him. Both were quiet for nearly a whole minute, as neither one of their faces showed the slightest hint of reverence for the other.

"What?" Darla finally spat, breaking the silent standoff.

The two had been on bad terms for too long, with Blake not willing to work with her to fix their relationship. Darla had just about given up on her dream of building a loving family with him. She wanted to tell him to get out, but just the sight of him drove her hormones in a pulsating uproar.

"Take your clothes off," Blake ordered as he began unbuckling his belt.

"No," Darla barked defiantly.

Shrugging his shoulders as if to say "Your loss," Blake pretended to buckle his belt.

"All right." She smiled. "You know I was just playing. I couldn't refuse if I wanted to." She wasn't telling him anything he didn't already know. "I need you so bad," she admitted while rocking to a seated position.

Darla was fully nude in a flash, puffing her chest out; she finally had a decent amount of cushioning atop her circular midsection. Pulling out of his shorts, Blake put his head down, hiding a devilish grin. His little flat-chested Caucasian had come a long way.

Darla was up on her knees in the middle of the bed. As Blake approached, she crawled over to meet him at the edge. When she grabbed him in her hand, he promptly hardened at her touch. Dipping her head, she angled for a collision, but Blake stopped her. Darla was startled. She knew how much he loved to be pleasured in that way; what type of game was he playing? She stared at him puzzled.

"Lean over," he instructed, brushing her head to the side. *I had had enough mouth for one morning.* Darla didn't mind him shoving her in that way; she sometimes preferred it rough. Besides, she was so horny, he could have spit in her face right now and she'd still be game. Spinning on all fours, she stuck her big pale behind off the edge of the bed. Darla had a nice ass, he had to admit. Her perfectly shaped rear was one of the things he could definitely tolerate about her. For a white woman, her ass was well above average.

Blake pulled in behind her and slid his long stick across her moist slit. Darla gyrated as he teased her hungry vagina. Playing on her eagerness, he put two fingers inside her hairy sex box and felt her insides tense from the lightly applied pressure. *It had been too long,* he reasoned.

Darla was so wet and inviting. *Pregnant pussy,* he rationed. Rubbing her juices around the curve of her spongy rear, he pulled into position. Angling his head, he gripped her cheeks, held her still, and with a sharp push, he plunged inside. Blake felt Darla shudder as the first thrust navigated all the way to her rear wall.

"Hmm, baby," she moaned willingly as his long strokes dragged back and forth at a leisurely forum. He was letting into her with hesitant powerful thrusts to watch her soft ample rump vibrate against his pelvis. No, he definitely didn't hate her from this angle. Fast then slow, grinding against the right wall then the left, round and round—yeah, he was having more fun than he could have foretold.

"Hmm…hmm, baby. Blake, I… I love you. I love you so much… I'm sorry," she declared in between moans. It was weird. At this moment, he actually felt sorry for her. She truly loved him. He allowed himself to process as he dug even deeper still. He knew how much she cared for him, but he also knew that he would never feel the same way about her. No. He could not give her love. She'd just have to settle for some top-notch dick.

The art of lovemaking was a skill he had mastered. He had the tools to pound a woman into a pile of steaming mush. He was giving it to her good when he realized that she was crying. "You okay?" he asked.

"Mm-hmm," she responded wordlessly.

That was confirmation enough for him. Grabbing two handfuls of her thick round rear, he bent the cushioning forward and proceeded to plow her into the next world.

"Hmm, ah, oh, hmm," Darla reverberated, moaning like she lost her tongue. After a minute or two of this, she grabbed the sheets in two tight fists. Blake felt her body go tense, as she was about to orgasm.

"Yes, hmm… Baby, don't stop," she demanded. As she grabbed back at his wrist, Blake stopped. One would have thought the world had ended. "What…you…what happened? Are you okay? What's going on?" she inquired excitedly.

Blake didn't answer her. He just held his position until he was sure her sensitivity had eased. Then he started back up again. *Bam, bam, bam, bam, bam*—he drilled down into her. When he felt her tense up again, he stopped again.

"Blake. What? Why? Why are you stopping?" she begged, reaching back at his behind and trying to force him into her. She attempted to push back on him, but he had her by the ass, holding her stiff.

Blake refused to let her control this encounter. *Dick runs this relationship, not cunt.* He laughed. Then giving her a hard slap on the rear, he rushed deep inside her. There would be no more delays. He held her at the waist, forcing her to take every bit of him as he pounded her until she screamed out in ecstasy. He came right behind her. *Damn, it had been too long.* He exhaled. And the fact was, he actually missed her.

Blake was done, but his soon-to-be baby's mother was campaigning for more. Darla twirled her lustrous hips, surging back on him as she tried to milk every last ounce of substance out his rapidly softening pleasure stick. Biting her bottom lip, she swallowed him into her, as she didn't know how long it would be before the next time she'd get to enjoy him in this way.

Blake's legs gave after a time, and he collapsed over her and rolled onto the bed.

Turning to face him, Darla admitted, "I missed you so much, Blake." She was still shaking as she lay on her side staring into his eyes. "I missed you so much. I'm sorry. Whatever I did. I'm sorry, Blake."

Blake smiled a big triumphant smile. He spent a long few seconds staring at the woman he was, at least for the immediate future, allied to. "Tell me you love me," he demanded.

"I love you, Blake. I love you, baby," Darla admitted eagerly. "I love you with all my heart."

Blake smiled again. "I love you too, Darla," he said before leaning forward, kissing her softly on the lips.

Darla's eyes glossed over instantly, and she ducked her head into his chest. "Thank you…thank you, baby," she cried.

Blake took her in his arms and held her tightly. He kissed her on the top of the head, allowing her her moment.

*****

Boston Harbor, Friday, twelve noon was when the ship routed to carry them back to Georgia was scheduled to dock. Locked and loaded, the interracial assembly of six set out the evening before in order to make the appointed time slot. Leading the jaunt from Connecticut to Massachusetts was Ridley who rode horseback, while Mrs. Townsman, Barry, McCoy, Lizzy, and her son Deacon occupied the cab of the stagecoach. Brownie was behind the reins.

Unwilling to sacrifice another solitary moment apart from her sons, Mrs. Townsman stubbornly insisted on catching the very first available boat back home. After rigorously petitioning, she got Sylvester to pull some strings, eventually booking her and her small party aboard a huge freight ferry he had recently contracted to carry a shipment of firearms South.

The six rode from dawn on Thursday to early morning Friday. The long late hour ride in the back of the wagon was exhausting and very uncomfortable. Though constructed to carry six, the cab of Mrs. Townsman's stagecoach felt cramped with only four. Luckily for them, Tywin, who'd taken a shine to one of the women at the farm, had conveniently elected to stay behind.

Mrs. Townsman was happy for the newly freed slave. Drawing up freedom papers for the man was an unnecessary provision up North. However, airing on the side of prudence, she planned to contract a copy just so he could have it. The last past weeks on her mother's farm opened her eyes. Meeting the runaways there made her want to emancipate all her blacks. It'd be a favor for a favor— paid servants, free Negroes living on her land, working to earn their keep. It seemed only right.

This wasn't the first time the notion of liberating her plantation had been broached. She and her husband had canvassed the pros and cons of this option many times, yet for some reason or another, the actual procedural process always seemed to suggest such a move would present more trouble than it was worth.

But today was a new day. It was the 1800s, and the world was changing. People, even the most avid critics, were beginning to admit that blacks, if given the opportunity, were just as likely as whites of doing the right thing. To free her loyal black servants felt like the honorable thing to do. *Complications be damned. My mother pulled it off, and so should I.*

After riding hard all night on into the morning hours, her carriage pulled into the Boston Harbor well ahead of schedule. Drifting across the busy docks, Lizzy's and Deacon's eyes were glued to the window as they watched in awe all the debonair black faces roaming about.

Following a scarcely slept night, in which the four were forced to remain seated upright, Mrs. Townsman and her guests were uncomfortably fatigued. Thankfully when the carriage stopped, Barry, who had been positioned on the bench next to Mrs. Townsman, got out to acquire about their travel arrangements. Mrs. Townsman wasted no time filling his spot with outstretched legs.

Pulling the drapes on the window, Mrs. Townsman shut her eyes and leaned all the way back; and before she knew it, she was in a deep sleep. Being so tired, the dream fairy came to visit with immediacy. A little over an hour later, sucking in an impetus breath, she shot straight up out of her slumber. Sitting upright, gasping as if starved for oxygen, Mrs. Townsman wiped with a slow deliberate motion her wrinkled brow that was dotted with nervous perspiration. Though only out a short stint, in that lapse, a sobering dream quickly made her realize the terrible mistake she was making.

Still breathing irregularly, Mrs. Townsman's body trembled with the horrid knowledge of the colossal error she'd almost committed. No, Lizzy would not be accompanying her back to Georgia. She and Blake would never be allowed to cross paths. This was a premonition, an intimate look into the future.

She had had a hellish dream, a nightmare of epic proportions. In her vision, Blake had taken to Lizzy like a hawk takes to flight— all hugs and kisses for his Negro birth mother back from the dead.

Mrs. Townsman's heart raced as she remembered this Negro woman's immediate and indefensible betrayal.

Oriel-eyed, Mrs. Townsman stared over at the sneaky yet extremely virulent black woman who had just tried to ruin her life. Lizzy, sitting across the aisle, was slouched back with her head against the wall. Her son, who was relatively small for his age, was lying on the bench, his head cradled in his mother's lap.

Seeing red, Mrs. Townsman's forehead curled with the arch only a defending parent could properly maneuver. Her hand instinctively went for her pistol as she astonished at how Lizzy tried to sabotage her already-fragile world. This after she mercifully rescued her from having to live down in a dusty well. In her dream, the nigger woman wasn't five minutes into the house and the first thing she did was tell Blake that it was her who sold her off so many years ago. *Ungrateful, deceitful, unwed, adulteress whore,* Mrs. Townsman grumbled. There was no justification. Her baby Blake wouldn't even allow her to explain. Surprisingly, even Michael got behind Lizzy and her treacherous ploy. Aghast, Mrs. Townsman was being ramrodded; neither one of her boys stopped barking at her long enough to listen to reason—especially her gentle Blake. Mrs. Townsman's heart ached as she again heard her brown baby boy promise to take his whore and unborn child away to live with Lizzy, never to see her again.

"My grandbaby!" Mrs. Townsman muttered as she turned and pulled the curtain on the window.

The bright unimpeded sunlight shot into the wagon, shocking Lizzy awake. Groggy, she opened her eyes to the sight of an all-too-familiar chrome revolver being held a foot from her face. Lizzy took a quick breath and grabbed down at her son. Yawning awake, the small beige child turned in his mother's lap.

"Please, no, please!" Lizzy quietly begged.

"Shut your filthy mouth!" Mrs. Townsman warned.

"Mom!" Deacon cried, turning and shoving his face into his mother's bosom.

"I raised him, not you," Mrs. Townsman gave. "He hasn't been your son for nineteen years." The scowl on her face was menacing.

Lizzy stirred in confusion.

Holding silent, Mrs. Townsman let her thoughts swirl as she actively relived the nightmare.

"Mom," Deacon squealed.

"Shh," Lizzy hissed, quieting her son. There was murder a foot from her, and she didn't want to excite an aggressive reaction in any way.

Extended seconds turned to forever minutes as Mrs. Townsman's unblinking gaze lay across from the helpless mother and son. For a long moment, all was still. After peeking in the window, Brownie snatched the door wide.

"Madam, no!" he implored.

"Please help us," Lizzy yelped hysterically. "Brownie, please."

The stifled black man was in shock. "Madam, please," he cried.

Mrs. Townsman was still, her revolver pointed directly at Lizzy's tiny nose.

"Where's Barry?" she asked after a long few seconds.

"I…think…should I go get him?" Brownie stuttered.

"Go get him," Mrs. Townsman instructed, never taking her eyes off her target.

"Yes…ma'am," Brownie agreed. "Please don't shoot her," he beseeched with pleading eyes before pushing shut the door as he took off, running to find Barry.

In minutes, Brownie returned with Barry, who was holding a tray full of food.

"Get in," Mrs. Townsman charged.

Without flinching, Barry climbed into the cab.

"Please help us," Lizzy again tried her hand.

But Barry paid her no attention. With a calm demeanor, he began, "Two dead Negroes on this dock can garner us some very unpleasant attention."

"I'm not going to kill them," Mrs. Townsman admitted. Then slowly as if fighting with herself, she let her pistol fall to her lap. "I see there are quite a few Negroes working this dock," Mrs. Townsman began, talking to Barry while never taking her eyes off Lizzy.

"Yes," answered Barry.

"Are all of them free men?"

"I suppose. Though I don't have intricate knowledge of their liberal status."

"Are you familiar with this part of town?"

"Some."

"Are there Negro landowners anywhere near?"

"Yes, there's an entire town full of blacks…just… I'll say…" He thought. "Ten, maybe fifteen, miles west of here."

"Can you find someone to take her to this town?"

"Absolutely."

"Please," Mrs. Townsman said finally, turning to face him, "tend to that right now."

Placing the box of breakfast on the seat, Barry said before turning and exiting the wagon, "Will do."

Brownie, who had been eavesdropping, was standing by the door. His face etched in subsiding anguish.

"Get in," Mrs. Townsman directed.

"Madam, I—" Barry began, only to be shushed when Mrs. Townsman put up a hand stopping his utterance.

Looking over at Lizzy then at the box of breakfast, Mrs. Townsman ordered, "Eat."

Lizzy didn't move.

"Everything is fine, woman. You and your boy should eat something."

Lizzy remained still.

Adjusting the pistol in her lap, Mrs. Townsman insinuated, "I won't ask again." She wouldn't have shot the woman for refusing a meal, but the authority the weapon gave her made it hard not to abuse. Lizzy grabbed an apple out of the box and bit it. Her son, following suit, grabbed a bread roll.

"I see you've developed a relationship with this woman."

"Oh no, madam, I's… Madam Mary, I—"

"It's okay, Brownie. She's a beautiful girl."

Lowering his gaze to the cab floor, Brownie didn't respond.

"Do you want them?" Mrs. Townsman asked nonchalantly.

Brownie was muddled. His face came up with a questioning expression.

Mrs. Townsman enlightened him. "Her and the boy. Do you want them? To take care of them?" she elaborated.

Brownie didn't know how to answer.

Mrs. Townsman went on, "These two are not coming with us." She paused for a moment. "You three are not coming with me."

Digging into her bag, she pulled out the $9,000 she'd taken out of the bank, splitting the billfold in half. "This is enough money to buy a nice piece of land. You are a free man now. This woman and child will be your responsibility. I am leaving them in your care."

Brownie was taken aback. *A free man.* On one hand, what she was suggesting was foreign and almost frightening. On the other hand, how could he protest?

Mrs. Townsman pointed her revolver at Lizzy's son. "If you ever go back to my mother's farm, "I'll kill him then you," she threatened Lizzy, who had cradled her boy to her breast.

Lizzy was surprisingly calm now that she was reasonably sure she wasn't going to die.

"I'm giving him a lot of money. You be a good wife to him. Brownie's a fine man. You should count yourself fortunate." Turning to Brownie, she said, "When you get settled, I will send someone to keep an eye on you. You're a good man. You're smart, and you can count. Don't let anyone take advantage of you and never show anyone all this money." She handed him a wad of cash. "Put it in your pocket," she instructed.

"I'm sorry," Mrs. Townsman said to Lizzy, and her eyes suggested that she was sincere. Nonetheless, pointing her pistol, she said, "Get out. Stand outside until your escort comes to collect you. I need to talk to my friend alone."

Mrs. Townsman's words for Brownie were heartfelt and emotion-driven. As a slave, Brownie was as loyal a worker as they came. As a friend, he was unmatched. Leaving him was a difficult decision, but it was a decision that had to be made.

When Barry came back, he was with a short Negro man in a gray suit. Barry explained that the man was a longtime employee on these docks and that he and Sylvester used him for many jobs. Barry assured that the man could be trusted.

After a long interrogation, where the man explained that he knew a bank that serviced blacks and a few vacant lots available in the Negro town of Bridgewater, Mrs. Townsman gave the man a healthy tip and promised he'd be found if anything unspeakable happened to her friends.

The ship they were waiting for was just pulling in when she and Brownie said their final goodbyes. She'd miss him, but she was heading home, and he was about to find a new one.

"You take care of these two," she told Brownie. "They are Blake's family—his mother and brother." *A mother and brother he'd never get to meet,* she rationed.

CHAPTER 26

It was June 13, 1852. The naturally ingrained temperament surrounding the normally peaceful plantation was as it always was. Yet on this midcalendar hump day, somehow it wasn't. Late morning until early evening, Michael, Blake, and Meissa were all in town tending to their respective workweek responsibilities. Only Darla, kept social via a multitude of bondage-born help, remained behind.

Outside the Townsmans' master home, plantation life went on as usual. Like any other day, the farm animals were fed, field slaves worked, and the younger adolescent children played. On the surface, the courtly environment looked to be the picture of tranquility. However, inside the home, Mary and Lory were virtually being run ragged.

With no pause and no solace in sight, Mary and Lory were readily assaulted with all manners of verbal and mental attacks, at times even having to endure some physical amercement. All this was at the frail hand of a less-than-stable-minded white woman who, as the morning progressed, was becoming more and more unhinged.

When Blake and Michael were away, Darla was the field master; and today, more than any other, she had become a horrid, world-beating dictator. Unfortunate for having to evade flying projectile objects being flung with surprising velocity, Lory received the lion's share of Darla's merciless fury. Darla knew Blake was frequently laying with the wide-hipped, long-legged, and nappy-headed Negro woman, and she detested the thought. There was little she hated more than a dark-brown slave who thought she was cute, and a dark-brown slave who was fucking her man was one of them. However, at the moment, Darla's aggression toward Lory was not solely retribution-related. This day, no one in her path would have been safe from her fire. Not even Mary, whom Darla relatively fancied, was provided any commiseration.

The notion of who they were held no relevance at this point. It wasn't about ethnicity, class, or even color. The fact was, in Darla's opinion, today everyone was categorically inadequate. The whole world and everyone in it were on her shit list.

Darla was out of her mind with hysteria. Every nasty word she had ever spat came flowing readily from her quivering lips. She pounded her fist, hollered from her gut, and flung at the two women whatever she could get her hands on. Fidgeting violently, Darla cursed the heavens as she proceeded to throw a fit for the ages. She was a scorned, unruly, noncooperative, and overbearing woman; but most of all, she was a woman in labor.

"Ah…you stupid black…ah! It's trying to come out. Do something!" Darla ordered. "Oh! Why are you standing there? Why is she just standing there?" she asked Mary of Lory's lack of productive activity.

"Calm down, ma'am. Please. Everything is going to be all right," Mary tried reassuring her. But Darla was having none of it.

"Shut up and do something. It's trying to kill me. Ah…it's going to rip something inside me."

"Just breathe."

"I'm breathing, bitch! Get it out!"

"Oh, ma'am, yous have to relax. Yous can't keep movin' around."

Darla was practically climbing out of the bed. "Ah!" she screamed. "Oh shit, it's… Oh!" Her bottom lifted off the mattress as a severe contraction coursed through her body. "Help me, please."

Both her feet were in the air, her legs spread-eagle. Darla was crying uncontrollably, as she could feel another contraction building in her mid to lower region. "Ah!" It hit, causing her to involuntarily release her bowels all over the bed. "Oh God, you don't know what you're doing. You're just a slave. Ah! No, no, no. Black…you better… oh! Oh! Huh!" Darla moaned as she gave it her all.

"Aw…see…there we go," Mary said, lifting the newborn free.

Exhausted and queer, Darla rolled onto her side and stuck her hand in between her thighs in an attempt to allow her tortured body a chance to compose.

Now Mary had seen it all. The baby in her hands, she smiled a triumphant smile. This was truly a joyous occasion. As far as she knew, this was the first of its kind. She had just extracted a Negro baby from the vagina of a white woman. This was definitely something to be celebrated. This was the inconceivable coming to fruition.

Lory was right behind her smiling just as bright. Blake had done it, and they were both witnesses. He had conquered white America.

CHAPTER 27

Ever the alert recipient of angry slants and suspicious gazes, the well-spoken, sharp-attired black man, wildly rumored to have engaged in inappropriate relations with the hotel's white head hostess, was back about town, frequenting freely. A restless heart, it was only so long he could stay hidden within the confines of the plantation. Blake needed the excitement of the everyday in-town theater. He was lost without it—a shell of himself. Michael noticed the despair in his brother and could stand it no more. One building block at a time, he commenced setting in place pillars in which to acclimate Blake back into the urban fray.

At this point, Loner's had taken on a sublime identity akin to civil royalty. The place was a wonderland to the growing city. It was a focal median for new businesses that were sprouting from the ground up. It was as if round-the-clock construction was molding new buildings two and three structures at a time. A refashioning had taken hold. The atmosphere around Atlanta was slowly beginning to mutate as more and more out-of-town folk flocked to the transforming district. And with the arrival of these outsiders came the inflation of currency and progressive cultural-defying ideas.

With this vast population increase, now he and Blake were meeting free Negroes—Negroes carrying papers proving their liberty. Some of these blacks were men and women who were recently freed from neighboring plantations around the state, and others had just taken to the city in search of less discriminatory opportunity. Michael knew this surge in enfranchisement was, in large part, because of his brother's relationship to the city, and the thought filled him with pride.

As the days passed, Loner's continued to thrive, garnering the brothers a healthy prestige along with some political power among the public. As a result, Blake was now able to work in a few delimited appearances at the hotel. Apprehensive at first, he would poke his head in here and there until he was eventually able to convince Michael it was okay to sketch him in a couple of hours of grill work. Blake missed cooking in his barbecue pit, and for the most part, his presence was greeted with acceptance.

Humbly, Blake took every opportunity to increase his public standing around town-now decades less showy than he was just months past. Blake tiptoed through town cautiously and on his best behavior.

Back working his father's gun store, he was kept even by a couple ambitious men brought in to suave any and all potential confrontation. Raised from humble beginnings, these two ruffians were ideal candidates to pair beside the controversial plaqued black man.

Billy and Lowel Dunkin, sons of Danelle Dunkin (one of the hotel's older working women), were a sixteen- and eighteen-year-old headstrong duo who were receptive to taking orders from their sandy-brown-skinned manager. Billy, the oldest, was heavyset and six foot one with a full beard. Lowel, a shade shorter but equally as stocky, could only manage a fuzzy tickle above his upper lip. Though essentially kids, Billy and Lowel were spitball aggressive when it came to customers talking down to Blake. To set off their adolescent-age disadvantage, each of the boys was fitted with giant pearl-handled black .45s that bulged off their wide hips with the presence of a double-edged Viking sword.

On weekends, in an attempt to bond with his young security team, Blake would take the boys out shooting, teaching them tricks to sharpen their aim. Billy and Lowel were astonished at the way Blake could fire accurately with both hands. Gripping huge twin handguns that he had designed to fire without having to be recocked, Blake danced around the makeshift firing range bursting bottles, centering bullseyes and ripping down low-hung branches from designated trees.

Always by his side, Billy and Lowel were starch protagonist when it came to Blake campaigning for a stable position at the hotel. Working the gun store was candyland for the two, and Blake always keeping a couple slave whores at their disposal was certainly not a dealbreaker.

At 7:00 p.m. that evening, Blake had already closed up the shop. Truth be told, he contemplated running out several hours earlier; he was so charged. This night, he was to sit in as acting manager of the hotel. Michael and Meissa were heading back to the plantation for the night, and Michael had given him the go-ahead to spend the night at the hotel.

Blake's nerves were on the fritz. This was his first time managing the spot since before his father's passing. Looking around at the colorfully dressed whores being unattended, his manhood swelled with anticipation—just thinking about the multifeminine juncture he would be privy to this night. Also amply stocked were his teenage bodyguards who were invited to accompany him on his post.

Being midweek, Loner's was as composed as could be expected for such a raunchy establishment. Crossing his fingers, Michael felt it was a good time as any to allow Blake a test run. Of course, taking no chances, the Fighter and his entire team were instructed to remain vigilant. Nothing was to happen to his brother.

Michael and Meissa were looking forward to the night ahead. Being built to embody a luxurious stay, Loner's still got to be a bit overwhelming to one tasked with enduring the rigors of its most questionable values for a long unrestricted stretch. It was a night away from the boozing and laughter, the sex and gambling, and the music and whoring. Being back to the simple life of the plantation was a welcomed benefaction.

Michael took his brand-new three-horse wagon, which was fitted with a full-length fluffy goose-feathered, cushioned black leather front seat. An absolute attention grabber, the wagon was plush. It had a red cloth top; red, white, and black-painted metal spoked wheels; a unique oakwood-crafted base with the name Loner's painted across the side; and again a thick-cushioned leather seat that made one feel as if he were seated on a cloud. The day he purchased the wagon, all he could think about was one day lying back on that leather bench as he navigated the open road and his exposed penis firmly wedged in the throat of a woman positioned comfortably beside him.

Forever her master's fantasy, Meissa made sure his premonition was brought into existence as she inhaled his full length in a dragging slow deep throat that had Michael yanking the reins in an involuntary lean. With expert technique, Meissa sucked him hard and long, taking her time as they had plenty, for the ride home was rich with capacious privacy.

It had to have been close to two hours of off-and-on activity before she began to swallow fluently without missing a beat. Using plenty of tongue and cheek, she sucked him all the way down to a flaccid wobble, cleaning him off as they pulled into the property entrance.

The sky was clear as a glass of water this night—pearly black, with the stars looking like sparkling diamonds. The country's enlarged moon was full and appeared to be a lot closer to the earth than usual.

Helping his lady down from the carriage, Michael's bright eyes held Meissa's oval-shaped peepers for a long moment. He loved this woman. Black, white, brown, or blue—he knew the feelings he held for her were as true as the Word of God. She was his forever, his to have and to hold for better or worse.

Climbing the stairs of the big house, her head tucked securely under his arm, the door swam open before they stepped a foot on the porch. Meissa knew right away. Her mother had the biggest smile across her round face. Lila, whom Michael couldn't remember the last time he saw her inside wearing a top, was behind Mary, also shining a mouthful. It was written all over their exteriors. The two women were excited in a way they hadn't been in years.

"She had a boy!" Mary announced joyously.

"Oh my!" Meissa screeched before shoving her two hands across her mouth in an attempt to suppress her bellowing scream that whistled from beneath her palms. "Where is he? Is he awake? Is he okay? Upstairs?" Meissa rambled as her antsy feet kicked about in a ragged dance.

"Yes, upstairs," Mary confirmed.

"He's beautiful," Lila added, also shuffling around to a soundless tune—Meissa's excitement obviously infectious.

Hissing and whaling like young girls in play, the two took off speed-walking through the house, leaving Mary and Michael standing in the doorway.

The electricity around the plantation was abuzz; Michael now realized he'd felt it the moment he turned onto the roadway. Still, his jaw fixed in a locked position, Michael was a lot less enthusiastic. Realizing this, Mary instantly curbed her emotions accordingly.

"I need a drink... Scotch," Michael instructed the portly Negro woman. "On my day off," he griped quietly. Feeling a tightening in his muscles, his recently pleasant posture had quickly taken a downward spiral. Obviously he was aware that this day was fast approaching, but now that it was here, it felt like a planned ambush. *Damn, what a night to come home.*

Michael took the young glass of scotch down in two heavy pulls before sending Mary back to fetch him a taller fill. Michael needed to calm his bouncing nerves before he confronted this child.

"Please no," he whispered. Life would be so much less controlled if this baby were of Caucasian descent.

Slowly walking with weighted feet, Michael strolled through the house, this time taking measured sips of his voluminous glass. Every step toward the truth felt like a hammer being plunged into the nail that was to seal his brother's coffin. "Please don't let this be Blake's child" was his revolving chant as he went.

For every couple yards he gained, the more the inclination was for him to turn back. He didn't want to face the child, but he had to see for himself if this was indeed his brother's son. Brimming with mixed emotions, Michael ascended the staircase. There was so much being processed in his brain that he physically felt faint. If this child was anything less than beige, Darla and her troublesome kid would be on their way out the door tonight. Michael imagined giving her a swift kick in the ass as she left.

"Please let this not be Blake's," Michael began anew as he neared Darla's designated living quarters.

The door to her room was half-cocked, and from the spit, Michael could see Meissa standing over Darla's bed, fluctuating from foot to foot in a soft yet dicey sequence. Sitting her back against the bedpost, Darla had the child wrapped in her arms with a light-blue-and-white blanket pulled up to its chin.

Every step Michael took seemed to decrease in diameter until he was pushing open the door; he was literally inching toward the bed.

As soon as Darla noticed him, she smiled with all the bluster of a woman being anointed. Michael didn't even have to see the kid; her expression said it all. She had her prize. Still rebelliously holding out hope, Michael continued to push forward. "Please," he begged as he leaned over.

Triumphantly positioning her golden egg to reveal him to her skeptics, Darla held her son up for the world to see. Pulling the blanket back a bit, she proudly exposed her trophy. Michael shortened an inch at the moment. It was like Darla wasn't even involved. The child was his father's spitting image—baby Blake all over again. His mother was going to cry a river when she returned.

"Here," Darla spoke a whispered song. "Meet your nephew," she said, lifting the child, offering him to Michael.

Meissa took the scotch from his hand and sat it on the dresser.

His fears realized, Michael's morale was down a notch, and his energy seemed deflated, but hesitantly he reached shivered hands out to receive his nephew. "Beautiful," Michael spoke almost without a word.

"Hold his head up… Put your hand under his bottom… Yeah, like… Yeah," Meissa instructed, helpfully reaching out to adjust Michael's posture to properly hold the newborn.

The moment was surreal. The first touch had done it. This was his brother's child, he reasoned. This was his mother's long-awaited first grandbaby. He swallowed a lump in his throat. This was his soon-to-be spoiled nephew. The kid was angelic, by far the most beautiful thing he had ever encountered. Michael's emotions had taken him. With a scratch in his voice, he asked, "What's his name?"

Darla shot him a look that suggested his question was absurd. "Michael, of course," she answered matter-of-factly. "Blake insisted that if we were to be blessed with a son, we would name him after you and your father."

That did it. He felt the thick tear roll down his face at the conclusion of her statement. *Yeah,* Michael thought as he and the surprisingly aware newborn locked eyes; he was going to spoil this baby rotten.

He was perfect. Little Michael was so calm and comfortable in his uncle's hands; it was like destiny. He was a rather large day-old, Michael reasoned. A kiss on the forehead brought a squeak and a resounding wiggle out of the baby boy. Michael took that as an acknowledgment of the bond that had just been forged. An inner smile spread across Uncle Michael's heart, reaching all the way to his mouth.

"Thank you," Michael whispered. This was just what he needed—a living bundle of innocence to keep him grounded. Baby Michael.

A night away—twelve, maybe fourteen, hours. They left Wednesday evening to be back at noon on Thursday. This was the initial concept—the contractual span in which Michael was willing to leave his hotel under the care of another. Insert Baby Michael, and that immediately thwarted the premise.

It was love at first contact. Courting his nephew trumped all other previously set engagements. The rising sun hadn't even properly glittered the sky before Michael, Meissa, and Mary were all up knocking at Darla's bedroom door.

It was bedlam. This child had the entire plantation in a complete frenzy. Everyone, from the oldest field slaves to the smallest child, was rallying to get a glimpse of the newest Townsman addition.

After a while, in order to satisfy the soaring demand and adequately settle the populace, Meissa was able to talk Michael into bringing the baby down to the tenement in the back of the house, where they then allowed five people in at a time to visit.

There were goo-goos and gah-gahs all around. It was as if Baby Michael was built for this position. Only days old, he held his eyes open, worked his tiny hands, and smiled for the locals. He was a fabulous little host, well far from a whiny child. Confident and a regular superstar, the boy knew he was loved. There was no frivolous crying or shallow fussing when being handled by different people. Baby Michael seemed content in the arms of whoever was holding him.

A simple night away quickly morphed into a three-day vacation. It would have been longer, but beginning to guilt-trip, Michael reasoned it was far time Blake found out he was officially a dad.

CHAPTER 28

Navigating the beaten path to town, Michael said, "Debra Teamaker." Michael snickered. *Who else would clear a villa like this?* he thought as he and Meissa pulled across the near-empty roadway heading toward Loner's Hotel. Man, was he happy he opted to come back when he did.

Completely caught up in the alluring rapture that was his nephew, Michael had forgotten about this evening's eminent first-rate party at the hotel. To miss today's event after all the work he and Meissa put into planning this show would have been a goof that haunted him for the next year.

It was only a hair past twelve noon, and already out, almost two hundred yards, they could clearly hear the rumblings of the ruckus crowd noise fighting against the bellows of various instruments coming from the courtyard of the hotel.

Debra Teamaker, the beautiful Negro songstress, was the most sought-after female vocalist in the state of Georgia. The lead performer in an all-female biracial band of five, Debra was easily the biggest single draw Michael had ever booked to play at his young hotel.

The ideal venue for a citywide festival, Loner's had a three-hundred-square-foot stage built into the courtyard. On select days, events ranging from amateur singing contests to professional-style comedic plays were featured in that adored field. No matter what the performance, almost every event helped pull in a successful single-evening take. But there was nothing in the hotel's recent history that compared to the big spending crowds Debra and her band could turn out.

For the last month, the return of Debra Teamaker was the talk of the town. Large colorful posters and signs promoting her arrival could be found hung up all around the county. For weeks now, Meissa had the girls working the hotel chatting up customers and boasting this event; and so easily occupied, Michael and she had nearly missed it.

Pushing his briskly trotting carriage down the scarcely populated roadway, Michael could practically see dollar signs dancing above his head. The normally lively intersection was a shadow on itself. It was as if the entire town collectively chose to put their everyday responsibilities aside in order to attend the hotel's festivities.

"Debra!" Michael smiled. The woman was phenomenal.

Debra grew up on the Teamaker plantation a privileged slave much like Meissa had. David Teamaker, her widely publicized significant other, was the youngest son of the state's leading peach and apple wine distributor. With the Teamaker name being used as a door opener, David easily began booking his lady small gigs all over the state.

An incredible talent, Debra's reputation quickly began to spread from town to town. Hooking up with a pair of multiple instruments-playing white women at a talent show, David then went off and purchased two of the prettiest slaves he could find to pair with the three. After teaching these two Negro women to sing backup and strum a banjo, the band was complete.

Singing, dancing, and pushing the audience to participate in an interactive choir of sorts, Debra and her band instantly became fan favorites. Their performances were legendary.

Debra's inventive style of engagement was forcing audiences to see and judge her for her talent and not just the color of her skin. The woman was sweeping across color barriers like Michael had never seen before. Every bar and hoedown she played at left leagues of white men lusting after her and green-eyed white women envying her. Debra Teamaker was a trailblazer of the highest order—a Negro woman not to be fooled with.

Michael and Meissa were met at the door by one of the newest members of the Fighter's security team. A man with one name—Donald—was a three-hundred-pound-plus, six-foot-seven, bald-headed mountain of a man. Pushing through shoulder-to-shoulder traffic, Donald ushered the hotel's power couple to the front of the stage.

At the back of the courtyard, sitting legs crossed on the edge of the performance platform, Debra had her arm draped across some lucky fellow as she led the drunken crowd in a sing-along that, with so many slurring their words, sounded more like a mumbled carol rather than an actual song.

In full control of the assembly, it only took one raised hand for Debra to silence the masses when she wanted to be heard. A virtual puppeteer, the woman had the entire courtyard on a string, pulling and twisting the field as she saw fit.

My, how Michael wished he had her on his roster. But the woman was definitely not for sale. In fact, she had been issued her freedom papers years ago; and to Blake's detriment, she was emphatically spoken for. David Teamaker, Debra's lover and starch supporter, was a Caucasian man as color-blind as a bloodhound when it came to his Nubian princess. If the way Michael paraded Meissa around turned heads, David and Debra would be giving folks whiplash. The two were a couple by no small means. Head over heels and chin-deep in love, David was actively campaigning for legislation to provide legal standings for him and his lady to be formally married. And Michael couldn't blame him. Not only did she have the voice of an angel but the woman was also drop-dead gorgeous.

Debra had a reddish-brown complexion with long straight hair that stopped right above the ample hump on her back. Debra's impossibly green eyes, when caught in the right amount of sunlight, changed from green to hazel like a magic trick. And all this was accessorized by a perky rack that was almost intriguing enough to curb a stampeding herd of buffalo. The woman had the full package.

Debra Teamaker was the perfect woman to lead the change in aiding the world closer to racial acceptance. In fact, there was only one quality Michael admired more about her than her ability to transform people, and that was her ability to generate income for his hotel.

Looking to his left, Michael saw that his outside bar was jam-packed with rowdy loose-pocket customers looking for an opportunity to force their money into the hands of his low-top-wearing barmaids. Looking to his right, the barbecue pit was being circled like someone found gold in the potato salad. Squinting to see over the mob of hungry customers, Michael saw that his brother was not behind the grill. This was no huge surprise.

Shaking his head, Michael leaned onto the elevated stage and pushed himself up. Peering past the overdone decorations, he spotted Blake right where he speculated he'd be—sitting at a half-hidden table in the back of the stage, spying Debra from behind. Michael knew Blake wanted a chance at Debra bad. The first time she played at Loner's, he and David nearly had an issue over Blake's zealous propositioning.

Debra had played at Loner's only once before. This was when the place had just opened. In that weekend, blocked by David's persistent shadowing, Blake found himself lodged between the cocoa-brown thighs of the band's Negro banjo players. But, of course, Debra was still the initial objective.

Standing onstage, Michael turned and raised his hands in acknowledgment for such a great turnout and got a very receptive cheer. Debra, recognizing his presence, walked over and threw her arms around his neck, provoking a hearty roar out of the audience. David, who was also present onstage, threw up two playful fists warning Michael away from his woman. Backing away, palms out, Michael gestured he wanted no quarrel. The scene was highly comical to the attentive crowd, who whistled, screamed absurdities, and clapped in amusement.

Meissa was next to climb the stage. David spotted his chance and took a few quick steps toward her, and now it was Michael's turn to play determent. The crowd erupted in hearty laughter.

After the excitement had died down, Michael walked over to where Blake was standing. Proudly and with rhapsody, he put a rough arm across his sibling's shoulders. Leaning in to where no one but Blake was able to hear him, he said, "It's a boy."

Smirking but confused, Blake turned to face his brother. It seemed Michael's words didn't immediately register with him. But smiling hard, Michael began nodding his head in acknowledgment, confirming what Blake thought he heard.

Next, like clockwork, it was Meissa who came over for a hug. "Congratulations," she whispered in his ear. "Your son is so beautiful—a perfect little gentleman."

Blake was flabbergasted. His face held the look of a man standing in front of a loaded rifle. His mouth parted slightly as his lips quivered with words unsaid. He had a million questions, but all of them basically centered around the child's paternity. But from Michael's and Meissa's faces, he already knew the answer.

"Go on," Michael urged. "Get out of here." He smiled. And with a head nod, not wanting to speak out loud in fear of his words being picked up, he gestured for his brother to go be with his newborn son.

Beginning to back away before he even realized he was doing so, Blake, with uneasy eyes, made his exit.

Michael, still smiling, grabbed Meissa from the back in a tight hug as he watched his brother hit the stage stairs.

"He'll be all right." Michael laughed before kissing Meissa on the neck.

Meissa didn't respond; she couldn't. She was caught in her own world. Putting her arms around her petite stomach, she let out a heavy breath. She wanted one.

CHAPTER 29

A knotted gut uncomfortably accompanied Blake on the rigorous horse ride home. Michael and Meissa seemed so enthused about the situation, yet Blake was pessimistically reserved.

Now that the paternity was no longer mere speculation, the ramifications of his future-to-be were really hitting home. He was a father now. He had a woman to take care of—a white woman, a frighteningly unpredictable white woman. Still, what was even more terrifying was the realization that he had to grow up.

It was a Sunday afternoon when he came trotting onto the property. The slaves out working the grounds provided him a hero's welcome. Subconsciously, Blake knew what they were actually cheering. He could see it in their emotion-filled eyes. He felt it in the way they smiled and extended their arms to the sky. Inadvertently, without realizing he had, in some small way and categorically, he had struck a blow, avenging their long-standing oppression.

Nearly all the slaves on the Townsman Plantation had been purchased from another, and more than half of the women had been made to bear young biracial slave children for their previous white owners. The men had wives and daughters who were often subjected to unfavorable reproductive perforation. Blake knew how much his child meant to them without anyone having to say it. His child represented a symbolic win—score one for the Negroes.

Blake had transcended. Lifting a hand, he waved on his way past his gratified votary. Entering the house, brisk legs carried him through the deserted first floor. Up the stairs, he made a beeline toward Darla's room. Slowing as he neared, his breathing became ragged as his cowardly spine threatened to embarrassingly betray him. Peering in through the open door, he found Darla lying on her stomach looking across the room at Mary, Lory, and Lila playing with his child on another bed that had been added to the room.

All the women froze as Blake walked in. For an instant, there was a brief moment of eerie, uncomfortable silence. The whole setting was just inappropriately off. Coincidentally (or not), he was actively sexing three of the four women in the room. And for a brief second, it seemed the shocked expressions on their faces were in subscription to the product of these proceedings.

Breaking the stale tension, Blake went over and gave Darla's thick upright booty a hard slap before sitting beside her on the bed. Pulling her in, he gave her a hug and kiss. This brought a big gawking smile to Darla's face.

"Mary, bring me my baby." A confident smile was shining his parted mouth. "Thank you," he said, taking his mini-me from Mary's willing arms. "Can you leave us alone for a while?" he asked, politely dismissing the crowd. With little haste, the three women picked up and exited the room, all working pleasant grins.

This is it. Holding Baby Michael felt as natural to him as breathing. At the present juncture, Blake was at peace. Overcame, he kissed down at his son's face. Sitting back against the headboard, his son in one arm and Darla in the other, he felt like everything was as it was supposed to be. This was the beginning of his new life. This was his unconventional little family taking form. Sure, they had come together under erratic circumstances, and there were some definite hurdles to overcome. But they were together, and at that moment, that was all that mattered.

CHAPTER 30

Darla couldn't contain the facial muscles driving her cheesy smile. Every top-cushioned happy day was a blessing. She had breasts—perky, soft, and squeezable breasts. Her milk-available chest was like candy to his eyes. She had them both out when feeding. With the straps of her gown hung about her shoulders, she looked into the full-length mirror she had set up across from her bed. Twisting moderately, she stood and marveled at her brand-new set of desirables as her baby boy fed.

Her feminine frontal lumps were not overly sized by any means, but compared to her previous mass, they were a definite upgrade. Seemingly more academic rather than functional, from one to the other, she had to alter her greedy newborn as he emptied both her feed bags on nearly each and every feeding.

A concerned dad worried about the nutrition intake of his child, Blake insisted that Darla remain well-hydrated, drinking plenty of milk, fruit juices, and water. Blake made it his business to personally prepare her healthy protein-heavy meals every chance he got. Rubbing her feet and massaging her shoulders and back had also become part of his daily routine and spousal ritual. He was spending more time with her in the last week than he had their entire relationship. Blake's newfound acquiescence, though at times appeared forced, gave Darla an optimistic, rose-colored glance into their future together.

The former most-unlikely-to-succeed parent duo's relationship had undergone dramatic reconstruction. Passionate touching, grins instead of frowns, hugs, laughs, and loving kisses were frequently shared between the two. Their priceless infant baby boy washed over their past disagreements and controversies to provide them with a fresh start—a newfound foundation on which to anchor. Darla was the most auspicious mother in the world, and Blake was a careful, attentive father. Burping, changing, and bathing his son were now his life's joy. He was also becoming a receptive, loving helpmate. Darla wasn't entirely healed in regard to her son's parturition, but she was confident by the time she was capable of being handled in that fashion, her man was going to make the wait well worth it.

On that same subject, she was definitely going to insist that he pull out from now on. This pregnancy had taken her through hell. Never again, she vowed. One child was enough for her. Little Michael would have no siblings—at least not any pushing out of her womb.

Darla kissed the top of her newborn son's head. He had done his duty. He had taken her from the depths of the whorehouse to the bedroom of a mansion. He had brought her and her once-improbable soul mate closer together and ensured she'd never have to skirmish for another dime as long as she lived. Her beautiful son, without scarring her quickly dissolving stomach, had single-handedly enhanced her bust from near-nothing to a respectable volume. Her miracle child, her knight-in-cushioned under pants, had brought stability to her otherwise debilitated being. She was now a mother, a life bringer, and a female determinant in one of the most prestigious families in the state.

Everything was perfect. The plan was to allow little Michael a few months to mature enough to comfortably sustain an extended travel. This was at the insistence of his overly protective uncle Michael, who was taking no chances with the health of his nephew. Michael wouldn't even consent to allowing her to carry his nephew out on the porch in fear of him being attacked by, as he put it, any number of filthy sickness-carrying insects.

Michael, Meissa, Mary, and even Lory were all head over heels over little Michael. There would be no lack of babysitting on this plantation and even less chances of avoiding her son being spoiled rotten. Someone always had him in their arms; even when he slept, he was often cradled against someone's loving embrace.

In a baffling turn of events, Darla herself had become a celebrity. The entire plantation, from the most minute field slave up, was now bewitched with her. Affectionate smiles and enthusiastic verbiage followed her around the property. Even Michael began treating her like a respectable human being—no more dirty-whore taunts or evil glaring stares. Michael spoke to her now with an ounce of warmth in his tone. He was, in essence, her brother-in-law now. Although she and Blake could never be married, she was a Townsman now. "Darla Townsman," she practiced. The name had a nice ring to it. "Mrs. Townsman." She laughed.

From her open window, a multitude of trotting horses could be heard beating its way up the gravel path. Darla's heart quickened. She revered the sound of her man's approaching carriage. Each and every day since little Michael's birth, Blake would rush upstairs as soon as he returned from town and smash his luscious lips against hers, this before hoisting their son into his arms.

My loving family. What a difference a single week made. Looking down at her son's full head of hair, she smiled. *How could something this small make such a profound difference in my life?*

"I love you, Michael," she whispered. "You saved your mother's life. You... You gave me life as much as I gave you."

Darla was so taken by the moment that she pulled her still-feeding infant from her bosom and kissed his still-puckered lips. Her greedy baby gave an irate squeal, imploring Darla to return him to her nipple.

Nearly twenty minutes had come and gone, but Blake had yet to come upstairs. Darla smiled. He must be heating her up some of the barbecue she told him she was craving the other day. She forgot he promised he'd slide over to the hotel and whip her something up.

Darla's mouth watered at the thought. She could almost taste the thick tangy sauce as she sat anticipating the coming meal.

Looking down, little Michael had fallen asleep at her tit. Laying him down briefly, she pulled up the straps on her sleeveless gown, slid into her house shoes, and found a robe to throw on. With her son in tow, she exited the room on her way down to the kitchen.

Just as predicted, her nose caught the sweet whiff of an aroma coming from the kitchen. She couldn't tell if it was barbecue, but something was definitely brewing.

Darla came off the steps gliding slowly through the hall. The potential of the could-be trademarked Loner's barbecue ribs almost quickened her pace, but the ordinance was when carrying little Michael, she was to step quaintly.

Once, only days after the baby's birth, Darla stubbed her toe on the leg of an ill-placed chair while holding him. To her detriment, his uncle was there to witness the blotched carry. Darla's foot sustained no injury, but the small misstep earned her a severe scolding from the overbearing uncle. Darla didn't mind too much. She actually thought the way Michael worried after her son was cute. Ever since then, little Michael was to be treated as precious cargo.

Everyone was so delicate with little Michael. It was like the boy was charmed. Only the gentler of hands altered his royal posture. All persons were instructed to walk extremely sure-footed when carrying him.

Instead of taking the long hallway to the kitchen, Darla rerouted. Taking a shortcut, she crossed through the living-room area to the dining room on into the grossly spacious, windowless den. A vibrating shimmer from single-lit candles stationed in all four corners always gave this underutilized room an ominous feel. Muddled sunlight leaking in from the two adjoining doorways did little to curb the room's gloomy feel.

Midway through the sparsely decorated, normally empty open den, Darla was scared stiff. To her left, shrouded in the room's ghostly shadows, sat a large unshaven stranger sitting up on one of the rooms two-seated leather sofas.

"Oh, hello," Darla said, addressing the large man who stood as soon as he realized a woman had stepped into the room.

"Hi, I'm Ridley," he informed. "Nice to meet you, Ms.?"

"Waverly," Darla answered.

Stepping forward, Ridley extended a huge callus-toughened hand. "I'm a friend of the family."

Darla nodded and took his hand. "Nice to meet you as well," she conveyed confidently while looking up into the large man's face. However, preoccupied, Ridley's eyes were not set right to meet hers. Looking down past her chin and across her chest, his dark beady peepers were fixed on the small bundle of brown baby boy in her arms.

Noticing his point of focus, Darla reared back. Suddenly panicked, she threw the blanket over baby Michael's face and took a couple of evasive steps away. Protectively she pulled him closer to her heart, spinning a shoulder to the man.

Recognizing her discomfort, Ridley straightened his three-day-worn shirt with a wipe of the hand. "Oh… I'm sorry. Did I frighten you?"

'Where's Blake?" Darla inquired, now suspicious of his presence and, more importantly, weary of the information he was now privy.

"I hope this apple brandy is all right. It seems my sons have—" Mrs. Townsman began as she entered the room holding a bottle in one hand and two glasses in the other, but she was halted midsentence seeing Darla there holding a baby.

Mrs. Townsman's seasoned old legs seemed to absorb an additional ten years as her stability lost a bit of its immediate luster. As if pulled by an invisible force field, her shoes dragged her forward. Absent words clogged her throat as she pulled her grandchild from Darla's protective grasp. Snatching the thin veil from his face, she instantly teared up at the sight of his perfect being. Tenderly Mrs. Townsman clutched him to her chest. She was near out on her feet with blissful yet lethargic cheer.

A long kiss brought the sleeping child's eyes to life. "My baby," Mrs. Townsman cried. "You are just as I imagined you." Thick salty tears slid down her recently traveled suntanned cheeks. "My baby." She kissed him again.

Baby Michael was a quiet child. In his short span of life, he was used to being overly molested. His mother, on the other hand, was gratifyingly shaken with amazement. Happy tears accompanied a relieved smile as she watched the proud grandmother gush over her son.

"You are so beautiful," Mrs. Townsman accurately declared. "My grandbaby." She kissed him again before turning to find her way to the nearest sofa. Baby talk, rocking back and forth, kisses and hugs—Mrs. Townsman was in her own world. It seemed like forever before she realized Ridley was also in the room.

"Good-looking kid," Ridley admitted, snapping the hysterically happy woman out of her secluded muse. His wide six-foot-four frame eclipsed the candlelight on the left side of the room.

He had seen too much. Mrs. Townsman knew there was no way to spin this. This blue-eyed, blonde-haired white woman had had a black baby, and her treasured son was obviously the father.

The room had gone quiet as the three adults looked back and forth between one another, each trying not to appear to be thinking what the other knew they were. Ridley was a dear friend, but there was a limit to loyalty. And for most white men, Blake had just crossed that gun line.

Following a last heartfelt kiss, Mrs. Townsman stood and walked over to where Darla was standing. "He's perfect," she said, handing her the child.

"Thank you," Darla returned before appropriately exiting the room. There was a most important discussion Mrs. Townsman needed to have with Ridley, and the content could do without an audience.

CHAPTER 31

Like every day since he'd first laid eyes on his son, Blake managed to make it home before the stars set out. However, to his surprise, riding into the plantation this evening, his heart swelled when he saw his mother's stagecoach in the stable. Hopping down from his wagon without tying it still, he rushed into the house like his hair was on fire.

The reunion between him and his mother was monumental. Record-settingly overcame with emotion, the two shared an embrace that needed no words to convey the love and relief they each felt at that moment. With the separation from her boys being so abrupt and situationally rooted, the uncertainty of the others' well-being had no doubt taken its toll on everyone involved.

Mrs. Townsman was only gone two short months, but for Blake, it felt like an eternity. Woeful of the torment that motivated this trip, he was glad her return could be softened by the induction of her first grandchild. And in the spirit of introduction, Blake was surprised when his mother explained that she had brought home with her someone she wanted them to meet.

Barry, whom Mrs. Townsman earlier dropped off in town, was instructed to purchase a room at Loner's Hotel. Mrs. Townsman explained that he was to lie low until she had been given the chance to address the reason for his presence to her sons.

Ridley, who elected to spend the night before leaving in the morning, made it his duty to take Blake aside and have a not-so-friendly heart-to-heart with him. In a vacuum, Ridley had seemingly taken the news of Blake's indiscretions relatively well. He had known Blake since before he could walk. A fatherly scolding and a please-be-careful, more or less, summed up the gist of the conversation.

Ridley's warning, suffice to say, really put Blake's situation in perspective—or, rather, reiterated the harsh reality. The world was not ready for such behavior. And in the court of public opinion, his son was considered an abomination. Blake knew that from now—until, scrupulous steps were to be his best friend.

Outside the fear of Ridley and the man his mother was yet to introduce him to knowing about the skeletons that lay in his closet, the night was rather gleeful. His mother was home and safe, and there wasn't much that could ruin that reality for him.

The following evening, Blake stopped by the hotel to notify Michael of his mother's return. Within an hour, dropping everything, the handsome young hotel owner and his pretty brown assistant mounted a horse and were riding back to the plantation.

Outside of Ridley's absence, the night pretty much replayed itself. Blake, not yet prepared to leave his mother, made it back to the house less than an hour after his sibling. Both brothers were happy, basking in their mom's presence. Michael was especially thrilled, hovering around his normally vexatious mother. Though she often served to work his nerves, he truly missed his troublesome mom. He knew she was his rock—their family's anchoring foundation.

As the night stiffened and the excitement of her long-awaited return had settled some, Mrs. Townsman pulled her two sons to the side and caught them up to speed. She told them about the money their father had accumulated, the wide array of business ventures he was invested in, and his business partner Sylvester's request of Michael. The only topic that caught some resistance was when she explained how she planned to relocate Blake, Darla, and little Michael to Connecticut.

"But we already have a nice piece of property over in Sylvania," Blake complained.

Mrs. Townsman shook her head and declined that solution. "The South is no place for a threesome as complex as yours."

"Mom," Blake tried to rebuttal.

But Mrs. Townsman continued, "A black man living with a white woman who had just conceived his child is dangerous no matter where you live. But in this state, with such talk already swirling around..." She paused to temper her rising frustration. "You three will be safe up North."

"Mom," Michael cut in, "the property we found is in a quiet, secluded area miles away from anything remotely residential. He and—"

"Michael," his mother stopped him.

"They will be safe," he continued.

"They will be safer in Connecticut," Mrs. Townsman insisted.

"Mom." Blake sighed with pleading eyes. "Please just—"

Mrs. Townsman interrupted him before he could finish, "I will take no chances with the rest of you. I already lost my husband behind this blasted controversy. I will not lose a son. And my grandson..." She affirmed, rising to her feet, "My grandson will not be put in harm's way."

"Mom," Blake called, but Mrs. Townsman held up a hand.

"Mom," Michael said, putting a hand on her arm, "Connecticut is very far."

Mrs. Townsman stopped a second and looked into his eyes. Then she looked over at Blake. She realized they hadn't been apart their entire lives. The prospect of being split up worried them.

"Look," Mrs. Townsman began with a mellowness in her tone, "next month we are all going to take a trip up to Connecticut. Sylvester needs you to show your face at a few meetings. We'll see the property he has in mind, and if you don't like it..." She said with a nod, "Fine, Sylvania it is."

Several minutes later, after a few more what-if objections were debated, both Michael and Blake ultimately agreed to at least see the property; and for Mrs. Townsman, that alone was a win.

CHAPTER 32

In their illustrious travels back and forth across Georgia and its bordering states, Amanda Snyder and Charlotte White, two white members of Debra's all-female band, were always crowd favorites and often not only for their musical talents alone. A couple of free spirits, these two very attractive starlets' post-performance antics had become infamous among Georgian talking circles.

After hours of teasing and flirting onstage, it was becoming a common theme for them to find a couple of strapping studs to take with them to bed at night. From city to city, after each and every show, Amanda and Charlotte were consistently mobbed by a slew of horny drunks vying for the opportunity to make a memory with one or both of the two performers. With their skintight dresses squeezing their cleavage out the top of their blouses, these two women always had the pick of the litter. However, this time, at this hotel, things were different.

Drenched with half-naked woman of all colors, the competition competing for the company of the hotel's male callers were mind-blowing. It was like one minute Amanda and Charlotte were talking to a couple of potential winners, and the next they were watching those same fellows being led into a room by any variety of elite women.

Debra and her band had been staying at Loner's for nearly a week with Amanda and Charlotte consistently being overlooked by men who would rather pay a toll to make love to a professional fantasy rather than to take the time to woo an iffy performer. Though they were very nice-looking women in their own right, walking around the hotel in last year's clothing, Amanda and Charlotte were nowhere as sexy or glamorous as the world-class whores being employed at Loner's.

Celebrities for less than a day, the intrepid morale of these women had sunk to an all-time low. It wasn't until Saturday evening before they were able to secure an interested party. And digging into him with four grubby painted fingernail claws, the now well-satisfied bandmates felt the delay was well worth the wait.

Engaged in a hot, ever-moving, sweat-nasty threesome for several hours, Amanda and Charlotte sucked, fucked, and swallowed Mr. Loner's rock-hard tool until they could absolutely take no more. Exhausted and all smiles, the two women came stumbling out of Michael's room right past an irate Meissa who had spent the foremost part of the last couple of hours hovering by his closed door. With her eyebrows narrowed, Meissa's face held a hate-filled scowl as she stared after the drunken white women who had just serviced her man. Pushing into Michael's room without the courtesy of a knock, Meissa quickly turned, locking the door behind her.

Michael was just pulling into his underclothes. "Meissa, um," he started, "can I help you?"

The scorned pretty black girl just stared at him, infuriated.

"Meissa!" Michael repeated.

Dropping her gaze, she kicked off her expensive custom-designed hard bottoms, which were crafted more for look rather than comfort, and walked over to his liquor cabinet. Still without a word, she grabbed a bottle, ripped out the cork, and poured herself a drink.

Michael, standing in his undershorts and looking at her strangely, allowed her a moment. He thought Meissa was becoming more and more unruly as the days progressed. "Meissa, is there a problem?" he asked after the awkward silence.

Meissa had her back to him. Finishing her drink without answering him, she poured herself another.

"Meissa! Did you not hear me?"

"I don't want you having sex with other women in this room." Her bluntness caught him off guard.

"This is my room," Michael answered.

"Yes, but I sleep here as well."

"Yes, but you have your own room."

"Yes, but I sleep here as well," she repeated.

Michael pinched the bridge of his nose in frustration. He didn't want to be having this conversation with her right now. "Meissa, I think you may be getting a little beside yourself."

"Am I? When every time I turn my back for five minutes, my man has his penis in some other woman?"

Michael smirked. "Jealous?"

"Of course. I don't like sharing you as much as you don't like sharing me."

"Meissa, you are not my wife. You are my slave."

"No, I am your Negro concubine, just as…" She lowered her voice. "Darla is Blake's," she finished.

"No, you are my slave."

"Am I? I don't feel much like a slave."

"Well, you are."

"I don't believe too many slaves spend their morning sitting on their master's face."

Michael shook his head with a smile. "Meissa, make no mistake, you mean a lot to me. Your sex is unmatched in my determination. But just because the insides of your thighs are entertaining to me, that doesn't make you a free woman. You suck a magnificent cock, and yes, I like the way you taste. You are my favorite whore, but you're still just property."

Meissa stood silent for a minute, her eyes burning a hole in Michael's face. Then killing the last of her drink, she sat the empty glass on the countertop, walked to Michael, and *smack*. She hit him in the face with the back of her hand.

Michael was shocked. His hand reached forward in a procrastinated motion and grabbed Meissa's face. He had her head sandwiched between his reddening hands. "Are you out of your mind, woman?"

Meissa licked her lips seductively, and with no fear, she probed, "What makes me a slave?"

"You were bought and paid for. I own you."

"So why don't you whip me for striking you?" she asked, grabbing at his crotch.

"You're mad," Michal professed, shoving her away.

"Admit it. I am your woman, not your slave."

"You are my slave, woman."

"Must I slap your face again?"

"You would be wise not to test me, Meissa "

"Do not call me your slave again."

"You are."

"I am what?" she said, walking toward him.

Michael hesitated. "You are my…"

Meissa's eyes widened. "Say it," she dared.

"You lay a hand to me again, and I will be forced to discipline you."

"How?" she attested doubtfully. "Are you going to hit me?"

"Yes, I will."

"Prove it," she said before *slap!* She gave him another, but this time she was quickly repaid for her actions.

Meissa grabbed her face, smiling. "You hit like a woman," she teased before charging at him, arms flaring in a fiery rage. Michael held her with one hand and balled the other. "You would hit me with a closed fist?" Meissa asked, looking up at him.

"Do not force me."

"I'll tell your mother."

"You are my sla—property. My mother gave you to me long ago."

"I'm aware. But do you suppose she would appreciate you mistreating me?"

"You struck me."

"Let go of me." She pulled away from him and went and sat on his bed.

"What is the meaning of all this?" Michael queried, flustered.

Meissa turned her head away from him. "Why do you treat me like this?" she screamed.

Michael realized she was crying. 'What is going on, Meissa? Why are you acting so...so strange?"

"You treat me so bad," she complained.

"What am I doing?"

"I am your woman, yet you constantly lay with other women."

Michael was flabbergasted. *Women,* he mused, *such emotional creatures.* He could never figure them out. "What do you want from me?"

"I want you to stop sleeping with whores."

"Those were not whores." Michael smiled.

Meissa was not amused.

Michael let out a deep breath. Then walking over to her, he pulled her to her feet. Sitting down, he then pulled her onto his lap.

Meissa was warm with emotion, and her heavy breathing was warming his heart. "Look, Meissa, you knew me your entire life. I took your maidenhood. You know it is going to be hard for men to... I like having sex, and I need different...something... I would much rather lay with you, but sometimes..." He continually paused, searching for the perfect phrasing. "I am a man—a very freaky man," he said, tickling her.

She gave a small chuckle. "Stop, Michael. Why can't I be enough for you?"

"Someday, Meissa, but right now I'm working in a whorehouse. I'm...you and..." He couldn't find the correct statement to convey his thoughts, then giving up, he finally asked, "Meissa, what is bringing all this on? I mean, would you rather stay at the plantation?"

"No, I love working with you."

"So what is it?"

"I don't know. I…" She wiped her eyes. "I love you, Michael," she said, grabbing his face between her hands. "I… I guess… I just let my jealousy get the best of me today."

'Well, don't. It hurts." Michael rubbed his cheek.

Meissa smiled and kissed his reddened face. "I'm sorry, Michael. How can I make it up to you?"

"You can act like my supportive woman and not let these recreational whores get to you."

"They weren't whores," she mocked. Michael smiled; she smiled back. "I really am sorry," she confessed before seductively biting her bottom lip. "You said I'm your woman?"

"You know you're my woman," he confessed, kissing her lips. "We've been together for our entire lives. You were never my slave. You are my Negro wife."

Meissa hugged him tight. "And are you going to let me have your Negro children?"

"I knew that was what this was about."

Meissa smiled guiltily.

"We'll discuss this another time," Michael declared.

"What is there to discuss?"

"Meissa."

"Your mother loves little Michael."

"Yes, but—"

"She is going to love our child as well."

"Meissa."

"So," she said, cutting him off, "the next time you try to pull out of me, I'm going to stop you."

"I will have to talk this over with Mom."

"Good. Get dressed. I want to leave tonight."

"It's almost midnight."

"Come on, Michael, please."

"Tomorrow, I promise."

Meissa gave him a sad face. "All right, Michael," she conceded with a small voice. "Tomorrow morning."

"Tomorrow morning," Michael agreed.

"Now did those white whores leave any left for me?" She smiled.

"Meissa, you know you can always get me hard."

Meissa giggled and slid down to her knees.

CHAPTER 33

Early hours, Friday morning

And I thought this Georgia assignment was going to be a total bore.
Gritting his teeth under the fluctuating glow of five strategically placed scented candles, Barry McCoy was naked with his hands bound behind his back. Pleasantly he swirled above a distinctly designed pillow-top sex chair as well as two busty long-legged blonde delights taking turns riding and mouthing him like he was the last man on earth.

Barry processed this had to be the happiest place on earth. Loner's was like nothing he'd ever encountered. Sure, among his frequent New York Island visits, he definitely witnessed his fair share of elaborately constructed hotel extravaganzas. Nonetheless, Loner's was a different level of fancy. It was an entire hotel designed to enrich the lure of its beautiful assortment of women; the ideal was unprecedented.

Stone statues of goddess-like half-naked women signified the elected themes of that specific section of the hotel. The different cliques of elaborately dressed whores patrolled their designated territory, swaying their best lethargic customers this way and that. There were marble and ivory countertops, huge hanging chandeliers, and a half-dozen giant marble-encased fireplace that cornered the ground floor; and every inch of the lobby was laced with tiled flooring.

On the top floor of the hotel, where Barry was so graciously stationed, there were three large glass-enclosed washrooms where valued customers were permitted to watch the hotel's nude commodities bathe themselves in between clients. The beds were soft, the liquor was strong, and the food was absolutely delicious. For Barry, Loner's Hotel epitomized blissfulness. He determined the two months in which he was contracted wasn't going to be long enough.

Thinking back to when Sylvester first approached him with the task of traveling to Georgia to serve as an interracial family's live-in security guard, Barry, for the first time in his life, nearly denied the large black man's request. Two months in Georgia sounded like a social death sentence. He had become too accustomed to the bounteous Northeastern atmosphere, and from what he knew from his patchy travels, the whole South, as a collective, was a draggingly slow ride. Until recently, a sixty-day stay in any state on the Southern region of the country sounded like torture to him. But honoring his commitment to Sylvester, here he was.

Barry McCoy was born the son of a Mexican woman who had been savagely gang-raped by a platoon of white American servicemen during the Spanish-American War. Growing up, Barry was constantly tormented. His strong chiseled features and frosty-white skin made him a constant patsy for his war-wary young brown Mexican colleagues.

When Sylvester and his men began visiting his small town, Barry, then only a preteen, instantly caught the ambitious Negro man's opportunist eyes. One hundred American dollars was paid to Barry's mother. In return, her son was entrusted to Sylvester to be raised and schooled under his stringent tutelage. Sylvester assured Barry and his struggling mom that he would provide the young man with smarts and talents best suited for a successful life in the US.

From the age of twelve to his twenty-five, Barry had become an intricate member of Sylvester's ever-expanding merchant enterprise. From small Army training to hand-to-hand combat and deceptive espionage, Sylvester taught Barry everything he learned from his time in the US Army, along with all he required from his hard-walked life as a former slave.

Utilizing the privileges of his fair skin, Sylvester placed Barry in positions that a less-Caucasian soldier could not gain access. From breaking in to military weapons stockpiles to staking out white-only banks, Barry had become one of Sylvester's greatest weapons. By the mature age of seventeen, he was a seasoned outlaw who had already killed several men—all of whom Sylvester deemed an opposition to his company's success. Sylvester had a goal; he wanted his name to be the most recognizable name in firearms since Samuel Colt, and no man—black, white, or other—was going to stand in his way.

At his mother's behest, Michael found Barry two days after he had checked in to the hotel. By this time, Barry had already sampled a number of women. Still, Michael, being grateful for him helping to deliver his mother home safe, moved him to one of the larger rooms on the third floor and treated him to an endless supply of feminine merchandise. Black, white, Asian, Mexican, Indian—the selection was extensive. All the women in Loner's were always so very elaborately dressed. He indulged his sexual appetite every couple of hours, with every encounter being better than the last. Barry bankrupted his sexual healing with the last three-way.

The erotic evening began with the one heavy-breasted blonde dressed in a military nurse's uniform. During a whole examination spill, the impersonating medic came in the room already in character. Not much for theatrics, Barry was quickly into her six and a half inches when a second lustrous blonde burst in the room dressed as a sexy sheriff. Taking control of the room, the would-be law woman threw a pair of cloth handcuffs on his wrist and shoved Barry into an isolated sex chair.

What a life. Barry thought of Michael, who was only a few years younger than he was. *He is king of a top-rate luxury whorehouse!*

The highly active women double-teaming him left him little wiggle room to deceptively prolong his orgasm.

"I'm ready to release my..." Barry breathlessly sounded. But before he could finish his statement, the sheriff woman riding him jumped off his lap—only to have the awaiting nurse dive in face-first under his spray. Not bothering to open her mouth, she used her hand to help Barry's seed to continue to properly spill while she caught every drop onto her angelic face. A second later, the sheriff was right on top of her. The two kissed long and hard before the law women began licking Barry's would-be children off the nurse's face. This was a practiced maneuver that always drove their clients wild. Barry was not immune. *What a life,* again he marveled.

Friday, before noon

It wasn't the most esteemed cross-family relationship, but at least the association was civil. It had been two weeks since her endearing return, but Mrs. Townsman, though she loved her some little Michael, still had trouble trying to remain mannerly with the mother of her Negro son's child. The woman was just so tainted and wrong for her family. Plus far too much had happened in the wake of her intrusive acquisition.

Mrs. Townsman was at her boiling point. She had so much pent-up resentment that if she didn't mentally prepare herself for the interaction, Darla's mere presence would be enough to make her skin crawl.

Darla, in Mrs. Townsman's estimation, was a scum, a female demon, a vampire leech, and a bloodsucking, opportunist harlot who had duped her innocent, naive young Blake into impregnating her. Because of this vile woman, her husband was dead, and soon one of her sons and new grandchild would have to be relocated across the country in order to ensure their immediate safety. The woman was practically worthless in Mrs. Townsman's assessment. Still, looking down at her perfect grandbaby, Mrs. Townsman reminded herself that if not for Darla's deception, little Michael would not have come to be. This was one reason, the only reason, she continually rejected her inclination to shoot Darla in the head and bury her vile body in the yard.

Mrs. Townsman's low-held admiration for her was blissfully obvious, and Darla was nothing, if not gainfully, perceptive. For fifteen days, Mrs. Townsman's icy demeanor and silent, dismissive attitude eventually compelled Darla to try to avoid the woman altogether. Still, as the quiet, lonely days in her room grew long, Blake in town all day and her newborn son always down on the first floor with his scornful grandmother, Darla felt a constrained obligation to try and close the hardened communication gap with her lover's mom.

It was early, not yet noon but not far-off; Darla had just fed her son an hour earlier. It was like Mrs. Townsman had mapped out a timeline, or maybe she had a secret peephole hidden in her room somewhere. However the case, every time, almost up to the minute, no soon as she pulled her son from her tit did Mrs. Townsman come up or send Mary up to collect him.

Darla had been doing a lot of thinking as of late. She had the whole scenario charted in her head. She needed to confront this old woman head-on. This was her son, she reasoned; and if his grandmother was going to be allowed to enjoy him, Darla planned to demand that she at least be shown the proper respect.

Being a working woman for so many years, it didn't take her long to get washed and dressed before she took to the stairs.

Articulating cryptic cut cutesy talk, Mrs. Townsman had little Michael laid out on a small table changing his wrappings when Darla came walking into the room. Instantly perturbed but trying not to show it, Mrs. Townsman greeted Darla politely. "Hello, dear. Are you coming to steal my grandson from me so soon?" she asked, forcing an insincere smile.

"No," Darla retorted politely. "I just wanted to...talk. We never get to talk."

Eyeing her over, Mrs. Townsman could tell by her distant mannerism that the girl had something of consequence on her mind. And though she could have done without the intrusive conversation, curiosity implored her to indulge the woman.

"Well, come sit." Mrs. Townsman gestured Darla over to a chair at the table. "What's on your mind, child?"

"Well, I just wanted to impart... I just wanted to..." And suddenly Darla's confidence had begun to seep out from under her dress onto the floor. "I wanted to...thank you for inviting me into your family. I know that my…ingression was a bit…turbulent, but I just wanted to say that… I am very grateful for your gracious hospitality. And I will do my best to raise little Michael as you did Blake."

The last part of her statement seemed to rub Mrs. Townsman the wrong way. Darla noticed the subtle yet unmistakable shift in her face as soon as she said it.

"I mean, I will do my best to be a good mother and an obliging wife to your son."

This seemed to enrage Mrs. Townsman even more.

Watching Mrs. Townsman defensively posture up, Darla realized the seemingly innocent conversation she thought she was having was apparently not being received in the same light. "I'm sorry if I caused you any ill fortune," Darla tried saving her rhetoric. "I know how much you used to hate me when—"

"Darla, let me first say," Mrs. Townsman cut her off, "you weren't invited into this family. You deceitfully whored your way in."

"I—"

"Let me finish," Mrs. Townsman stopped her again. "You're not my son's wife, and you will never be able to raise my grandchild as I raised his father. And that is not to say you won't do a good job. I'm sure you will. In fact, I'm going to make certain of it." The intent behind her words was more threat than suggestion. With piercing eyes, Mrs. Townsman continued, "But you will have to be careful your whole life. Outside this house, little Michael is not your biological son. And Blake, he is not your lover. From now until the end of time, you will tell all who inquires that this baby is your brother's child you are raising. And Blake, he is little Michael's uncle—brother of the sister your brother impregnated."

Mrs. Townsman had it all thought out. "Blake will be known as nothing but hired help. This is until the world seems fit to allow a white woman to deal with a black any sort of physical capacity, and that doesn't ever seem likely. You are in a dangerous position." Staring Darla over from her standing position, she allowed for her words to penetrate. Then she said, "I never liked you—since the first time I laid eyes on you."

232

Darla's throat clamped tight as the words she had already known to be true were spoken. Instantly realizing without reserve, her large ocean-blue eyes glazed quickly over.

Mrs. Townsman continued, "But I don't hate you. Not anymore. You are my grandson's mother. Meaning you are the mother of one of the most important black men ever to grace this world. This child here," she emphatically pointed down at little Michael's naked body, "will someday influence this changing world. He will do great things, and being his mother, you will assist in his endeavors. Or..." Mrs. Townsman pulled her chrome pistol out of the hidden pocket on her dress and placed it on the table by little Michael's blanket.

Darla's eyes widened at the implication.

Mrs. Townsman continued, "Or you will not be allowed to participate in his upbringing at all." She paused to gauge the temperature of Darla's reaction. "Because of this child," she went on, "you are an important woman. A son will do well to know his biological mother." She paused again. "Do you understand me?"

Darla's head jerked up and down with exaggerated bop. This subtle movement was enough to shade free the building liquid that had been threatening to surf her emotion-flushed rose-colored cheeks.

"You are a beautiful woman, Darla. But, of course, you already know this. Those pretty eyes are what got you to this point. Nonetheless, you have arrived. With my son, you will never have to want for anything. I will make sure you have a league of obedient Negroes to tend to your every need."

Darla's face was drenched with salty tears at this point, but the mention of her being a slave master brightened her spirits a bit.

"Do not do anything to jeopardize my son or his son."

"I won't. I promise."

"Then you and I are square. Welcome to the family, Darla," she said with a smile.

Lifting her head, Darla tried to reciprocate the gesture.

"Come give me a hug," Mrs. Townsman said, attempting to repair the young woman's wounded self-esteem."

Darla stood and fell into Mrs. Townsman's open arms.

"I'm depending on you, child. Don't let me down."

"I won't. I promise. And thank you," Darla declared while fixing her ruffled blouse. "Do you mind if I take…" She gestured toward her son.

"No, you can come get him after his nap. I have him now." Mrs. Townsman affirmed. "Go upstairs. I'll send for you when he's ready to feed."

Darla shook her head hesitantly boking back and forth between Mrs. Townsman and the small chrome pistol on the table. Then with a huff, she turned to exit the room.

Mrs. Townsman bent over and kissed her grandson on the top of his head. "And Darla," Mrs. Townsman called.

"Yes?"

"I may want another one."

Shaken, Darla quickly hustled out the door and through the hall before Mrs. Townsman could elaborate further. *What the hell?* Darla cringed.

Friday, between 3:00 and 6:00 p.m.

Ever since the night she held baby Michael in her arms, all Messia could think about was having a precious bundle of joy of her own.

"Baby Michael is going to need a companion," she resolved. "How come Darla gets to have a baby and not me?"

Michael bringing her home to discuss the dangers of this premise with his mother only served to heighten her incentive.

Mrs. Townsman was more than supportive of this proposal; she was obtrusively in favor of it. This ringing endorsement of yet another child born out of wedlock got Michael to wondering if this sudden aggressive baby push was actually Meissa's true longing or a formula of his mother's meddling. Michael knew how creatively crafty she was and how it was really her own ideal.

No matter the initial impulse, with his mother officially on board, Meissa had begun to imperiously pursue her objective. Sex with her had become a battle. Fighting her off, it was getting harder and harder to pull out when the time came. She'd been active with him for so long that she knew the precise moment his soldiers were climbing the tube. And in attempt to restrain him, she would lock her arms around him, digging in while at the same time contracting her walls in a tight gripping suction. She almost had him a half-dozen times. Missionary and doggy style were his easiest escapes, though she had her tricks to keep him locked in those as well.

And in spite of how much he wanted to see his nephew, he didn't dare go home. Michael held no reservation about Meissa diming him out to his mother, whom he was sure would be hitting her up demanding an active progress report. Meissa, being the obedient stooge she was, would no doubt inform her that he was still spilling his seed on her stomach. And this would, of course, garner him a stringent earful. *No, thank you.*

What they couldn't understand was he just wasn't ready. He had a lot more living to do before he could prepare for a child. He had hundreds of thousands of women to meet before he would choose a womb to saturate. Maybe he wanted a white baby first. Maybe he'd choose to be married. In any case, he definitely wanted to be as hands-on with his child as his father was with him and Blake. Spending multiple consecutive nights at Loner's only to see his child on the weekends was not his ideal of being a good parent.

Meissa could never understand, and he could never fully explain his reasoning. He did love her, but a child was a lot of work and compromise—and a black child! He definitely needed to have a white son first. He couldn't imagine how Blake could have got by on his own. And who would he choose to carry his Caucasian child? All he knew were whores. No, he wasn't ready. Nothing was ready. Little Michael was all the adolescent responsibility he was willing to take on at that juncture in his life.

To women, the concept of procreation was simple. He thought as Meissa's soft flopping breasts bounced up and down above him, *You fuck, there's a nine-month wait until you have a child.* But for men, especially a man in his position, there were so many important variables that needed to be considered:

1. In that nine months, she would get fat. Fat would be a problem for someone who liked his women slim and trim. And with so many beautiful women roaming around, who was to say he wouldn't fall for another? He couldn't do that to Meissa.

2. When the baby would come plowing through her body, there would be no predicting how much damage it might do to Meissa's tight, moist, delicious-tasting, and pretty young flower. Some women never bounced back from that experience. He'd totally resent her for taking that away from him.

3. If she had a child, she'd be stuck raising him on the plantation. There was no way he'd consent to her bringing his child to the hotel, and he needed her by his side. Loner's was no place for children—not his children anyway.

There were a host of reasons not to allow her to have his child. Lying under Meissa as she bucked and bounced, all these issues ran amok inside his head. However, watching the determined woman work her goods, Michael knew that his concerns were really just carefully thought-out excuses. When it came right down to it, he was positive that no matter what, he'd never love another woman as much as he loved the one on top of him at that moment. She'd be in his life forever, through thick and thin, to death do them part.

He could feel his sensitivity prepping for a release. *Why not?* he spoke to himself. Damn, he wasn't ready for this; but finally conceding, he allowed Meissa to ride him into ejaculation.

Feeling the familiar shift to his business, Meissa clamped down onto Michael's shoulders and began riding him hard, thinking he was going to throw her off at any moment. But grabbing her soft ample bottom, he gave her all of him, allowing her to scrape the back of her inner realm on his stick until he was empty.

Meissa felt it immediately and began laughing a giddy sexy little giggle. Her delight was so innocent and teasing, it made him laugh as well. Kissing down on him, she was still pumping her hips. She wanted to make sure to get all of it. Michael was content. It felt so good. He was going to be emptying into her from now on.

That evening, Michael loaded up his wagon, heading to the plantation. Having littered Meissa's womb with his seed, he figured he might as well go home and see his nephew. Meissa was sure to inform his mother of the good news. And having done his part, he felt he deserved the praises for his unselfish sacrifice.

Riding home, the realization of his actions began to settle on him. Quietly he tried to think positive. Meissa felt the uncomfortable tension, but she didn't care. In her mind, she was already pregnant. Smiling silently while leaning up against Michael's arm, she was thinking what to name her son. She already knew it was a boy. Baby Michael already lay claim to his name, and for some reason, she always hated the name Blake. It didn't matter; she smiled. Picking a name was trivial—a dilemma, a beautiful problem to have.

Friday night

The Townsman gun store had become extremely popular as of late. Unfortunately for Blake, this unanticipated boom in market revenue was causing him to abandon his unofficial curfew. Rousing interest was the large shipment of nickel-plated revolvers that arrived three days hence, and it had the whole town in a feeding frenzy. Every gun enthusiast and would-be cowboy in the region had come to make a purchase. Plus it seemed just to annoy him, a whole cluster of I'm-just-looking-for-right-now hagglers were pouring in every other minute.

The new-fashioned chrome pistols came in three distinctive makes: five cylinder, six cylinder, and a small model five-cylinder handgun that required smaller bullets. The miniature pistol was the same model Blake had seen his mother with. These dainty-looking weapons were, to Blake's surprise, being purchased just as frequently as their large counterparts.

Constantly fiddling with this small pistol, Blake took a shine to the size of the weapon. The pistol he normally wore, concealed at the small of his back, was so bulky that even when tucked beneath his jacket tail, it sometimes got noticed. Although he preferred his custom seven-shot .45, he took to carrying the less revealing weapon out of convenience.

Many of the men who came to spend money actually purchased both a large and a small pistol. Most, too masculine for such a petite-looking firearm, insisted the smaller weapon was for their women friends, wives, or daughters. *Women and guns,* Blake mused. And he fancied his mother an anomaly.

The adored chrome guns were flying off the shelf. When the four boxes first came in, twenty-five pistols to a box, Blake gasped at the pricing associated with each weapon. Ready to write Sylvester to apprise him of what he figured must had been a mistake, the pistols started moving—each sale generating more and more momentum.

The new weapons were more than twice as much as he charged for any of his other pistols. Even the small model was pricey. At first, he thought for sure he'd be stuck with the guns for a year, but the beauty and Intrigue surrounding the guns made them a must-have. Shiny silver-looking handheld firearms, the pistols were the summer's must-have for the well-off.

Every night since their arrival, Blake, Billy, and Lowel were stuck entertaining fickle customers until after sundown. The amount of money being generated on a daily basis made Blake uneasy. Though he had a secure lockbox in the store, he often chose to ride over and store large quantities of money in the hotel safe every now and then.

The gun shop's dragging days had become an irritant. The enthusiasm surrounding the guns was unprecedented. Billy and Lowel loved the lively atmosphere. The more people who came to the store and saw them working, the more prominent they felt.

It had to be after 7:00, maybe even closer to 8:00 p.m., by the time Blake closed the doors. He had sold a record of seventeen firearms that evening. The place was so busy, he didn't even get a chance to stop by Loner's and drop the money off.

The sky had darkened early this night. Standing back to crunch numbers, Blake had already sent both the boys home. He was down to sixty pistols in a little over three days. Now he was ready to write Sylvester and demand he send twice the order this coming month.

It took him twenty minutes to count and recount the day's take. Blake was very particular when it came to numbers, learning to balance the books from his dad. Blake took great pride in staying on top of inventory. The shop had been closed a half hour by the time he packaged all the cash in his black suitcase. Locking the rifle case, he was ready to go when there was a loud thump on the door.

The shades on the window were shut, and the sign on the door clearly read closed. But Blake's wagon was still outside, so he figured a brash customer had it in their mind that it was okay for them to catch him before he left. "If they're not spending at least $500, I'm sending them away," Blake whispered to himself.

Pulling the shade on the door's barred window, Blake smiled. "Ridley." Unlatching the lock, Blake opened the door. "I was just about to go," Blake admitted, moving out of Ridley's path.

"Well, I'm glad I caught you. .45 chrome, two of them," he requested enthusiastically.

"These new nickel-plated pistols are a gold mine. Nearly every person in town has been through here looking for these. I may only have a handful by the week's end. You're lucky you caught me tonight," Blake embellished, turning to run into the back, where he had packaged the hardware.

"Grab me a box of shells while you're at it," Ridley hollered after him.

The pistols were in a large solid metal box that was built into the ground. Blake had to use a special key to unlock all four sides of the near-impregnable structure in order to open it. The floor safe was designed so that whoever decided to break in at night would have to suffer through hours of pounding in order to get it open. And in such a residential area, their actions were likely to be discovered.

The bullets, rifles, and knives were kept in the back behind a steel-gated cage on the wall. Everything was super secure. There was nothing like a room full of pretty guns to inspire an all-night-would-be thief to try his hand. Luckily, there hadn't been an incident as of yet.

Two nickel-plated .45s and a box of shells were enough to reassure Blake that staying that extra hour was a worthwhile sacrifice.

And since it was Ridley, Blake decided to throw in a couple of brand-new leather holsters free of charge.

"You're going to love these pistols!" Blake yelled from the back room. "I took a couple out for a spin the other day—fires smooth as a wagon ride. And they're surprisingly light for the—" Blake's words got caught in his throat as he stepped back into the lobby. "What is this? Ridley?"

"Shut up, nigger," Ridley spat harshly as he and two other men stood in the foyer with weapons drawn. Ridley had a large black revolver, and the two men with him were both carrying rifles.

"Rid-Ridley, what are you doing?"

"I said shut up, nigger," Ridley insisted harshly. Lowering his pistol, he took a step forward, pulling out a pair of metal handcuffs.

Blake instinctively took a measured step backward.

"Don't even think about it, nigger," the man to Ridley's right threatened. "Keep your hands where I can see them," he said, leveling his weapon at Blake's head.

Ridley pulled behind Blake and grabbed him by the back of his neck, forcing him to his knees. Blake was at a loss for words. He knew Ridley all his life. This couldn't be about money. From what Blake knew, Ridley was very well-off.

"My brother is going to kill you," Blake said through clenched teeth as Ridley cuffed his hands behind his back.

"No. Your brother's killing days are gone. I lost a cousin under-estimating you two. My sister lost a husband."

"You sent those men to my house?"

"I put up with your mouth because of your father. He's dead. Shut up!" he said, smacking Blake across the face with his revolver. The blow opened up a large gash over Blake's right cheekbone, but it didn't put him out. "You got cocky impregnating that whore. Your kind is designed to be slaves, and before I kill your brother, I'm going to have him sign over the deed to all your father's ranches—and that hotel. I'll think about taking your nigger baby as my slave."

Blake was so mad he couldn't even speak. His hands were in tight fists; he was sitting up against the small five-shot pistol on his back tucked beneath his jacket. He hoped Ridley didn't see the imprint on his back because when he'd get the chance, he'd pull this chain under his feet, grab his pistol, and send Ridley to hell himself. Michael wouldn't have to save him this time. This time, he promised himself, he would be the gunman.

"Give me something to gag him with."

One of the other white men asked the third member of their team. Looking around, the man walked into the back. Minutes later, he came back carrying the black briefcase. "Look what I've found," he said, sticking his hand in Blake's briefcase and pulling out a handful of bills.

"You three are nothing more than a pack of crooks," Blake snarled.

The man holding the case threw Ridley a shirt he pulled out of Blake's personal dresser. Ridley ripped a sleeve off and tied it between Blake's open mouth.

Blake gave resistance as they pulled him to his feet. He was stronger than the men holding him, and even with his hands bound, the three struggled to control him. He had just about freed himself enough to make a run for the door when the bunt of a double-barrel shotgun caught him in the face. Losing consciousness, the floor racing up to meet him was the last thing he remembered.

CHAPTER 34

It had been two whole days since the last time anyone had laid eyes on Blake. Certainly not the one to play the disappearing game, Blake's unexplained absence had his family and friends fearing the worst. No stone was to be left unturned as Michael had everyone he could gather scouring the town for leads to where he might be.

As evidence mounted, there were no misconceptions about whether foul play had taken place. Blake's wagon was found still tied up outside the gun store, and the front door had been discovered to have been left unlocked. The black case where he often kept the store's daily profit was also missing.

Standing behind the glass counter of the gun store, Michael assumed the motive was robbery turned kidnaping or kidnapping to convenient robbery. However it happened, all indications pointed to abduction for ransom. Michael would pay the toll gratefully in order to get his brother back—this before employing all his resources to find and destroy the perpetrator.

Jumping ahead of the investigation, Michael put out a $4,000 reward. This was four times as much as the state of Georgia ever offered for any one outlaw, dead or alive. He had the sheriff and his deputies on paid skirmish, going door-to-door in search of any information concerning his brother's whereabouts. Michael had personal sit-downs with every one of his whores and instructed them to interrogate all their customers before and after taking their clothes off. His bluff was he'd shut down the hotel if Blake was not found soon. Oddly enough, with all resources deployed in this always-vibrant city, it seemed no one knew or saw anything. This made Michael suspicious of everyone.

The brothers Billy and Lowell (the last one to see Blake) explained all was well when they left him. They remembered the day had been particularly profitable, and from what they could see, there were no signs that someone was plotting anything nefarious. The two swore that leaving the store that night, they heard Blake lock the door behind them. The brothers were questioned together and then apart for over an hour. Michael was exceptionally thorough in his inquiry, but in the end, he believed their story wholeheartedly. He knew firsthand how much Billy and Lowel looked up to Blake, and Michael was certain they'd wish him no harm.

At the gun store, Michael saw no sign of a struggle. And if Billy and Lowel's said account was accurate, Blake would have had to unlock the door for his attackers. And either he was quite familiar with these men or he walked in the back and one opened the door for the others because Michael couldn't see Blake being taken by only one man. Without Billy and Lowel around to watch his rear, Blake was comfortable enough with whoever it was to let his guard down.

Keeping optimistic, Michael hypothesized. Already in possession of the money case, there was no need for them to take Blake out of the store. If the shop's purse was the endgame, the robbers could have easily just left Blake bleeding inside. Kidnapping him from the gun store was a very dangerous, risky procedure. Hopefully, Michael considered, this meant they were holding him in anticipation of some sort of payday. This was, of course, the best-case scenario. This was what he sold his mother, who had flipped at the news.

Returning home after the first night he noticed Blake was missing, Michael was forced to suffer through a bevy of cleverly assembled curses—his mother exasperatedly declaring she told them he'd be safer in Connecticut. Unable to stomach an entire night of her badgering, Michael was headed back to his hotel only hours after arriving, insisting Barry remained at the plantation. Michael needed someone there to protect his family. However, at this time, Mrs. Townsman was experiencing a cluster of emotions. She was angry, sad, apprehensive, and scared. Her pistol close at hand twenty-four hours a day, she didn't want to be bothered by anyone outside her grandson. Barry, whom she didn't fully trust, was prohibited from roaming the rear portion of the second floor. Only little Michael, she, and Mary were permitted to occupy this restricted space.

Darla, if not for the usefulness of her suckle frontal area, would have been sent to stay in the back of the house. Mrs. Townsman didn't trust her either. Mrs. Townsman knew something about this was her fault; she just didn't have any proof. Still, taking no chances, Darla's mommy privileges were reduced to feeding, burping, and occasionally changing. She was not to be alone with little Michael at any time. When he was hungry, she was called on to remedy his craving, and right there to hover over her naked titties was his overprotective pistol-wielding grandmother.

CHAPTER 35

Navigating the winding maze-like roadway, Ridley felt the thick tension on the Townsman Plantation. Ridley could feel the anxiety as he came riding onto the property. Greeted at the door, he was brought into the den by a long-face Mary. Mrs. Townsman was sitting on the sofa, her right hand rubbing the back of the baby lying beside her. Even in the bantam lighting of the room, Ridley easily noticed the dark sleep-deprived rings circling her eyes. He could tell she was desperate, and he had expected as much.

Over the last couple of days, Ridley had practiced this performance twenty-some-odd times. Sitting both Mrs. Townsman and Barry down, his face remained solid as he told his tale of how several men ambushed him at his ranch. Flaunting a nasty red scratch on his left forearm and a bloody scrape on the right side of his forehead, he explained how they claim to have Blake and how they were going to kill him if they didn't receive $50,000 and the deed to the hotel. Visually distraught, Ridley went on to say that they told him that they were kin to the men Michael killed the night her husband was shot.

Allowing her eyes to water, Mrs. Townsman politely asked Barry, who didn't believe a word Ridley was spewing, "Can you excuse us? Just wait in the kitchen."

Barry could tell that Ridley's awkwardly delivered news didn't register well with her either. He didn't want to leave Mrs. Townsman alone with him, but looking into her eyes, he saw that she had her own design on dealing with the treacherous turnout. Plus, knowing what she carried in her dress pocket, after a split second of hesitation, Barry turned and stalked off without a fuss.

She knew Ridley was a masterful wordsmith and an equally skilled liar from her late husband's many stories. Ridley was said to, after only a short sitting, be able to talk most landowners into selling their property for half of what it was worth. Nevertheless, today his lies were falling on deaf ears. Within the first five minutes, he had already said enough for her to call him on it; but biding time, she had to play it cool. Her son's life ultimately relied on her passive discretion.

Ridley's posture showed no sign of deceit, and only his voice held a shrouded hint of urgency. In Mrs. Townsman's opinion, his performance was expert. He told his tale like a recent experience being relived. Unfortunately for him, there was no way anyone could have known that Michael and Michael alone was the one who chased down and killed the gunmen that night. The only way anyone could have discovered that bit of info was hearing it from Blake's own tongue.

"Tell me exactly what happened. Please, Ridley," Mrs. Townsman begged. "And spare me no details."

Employing a precise amount of anger and sadness, Ridley spoke of how four masked outlaws carrying pistols and shotguns converged on his ranch and, after wrestling him to the ground, told him how they dragged Blake from the store and threw him in an awaiting carriage. He explained that he was sure he didn't recognize any of them by voice or physical makeup, but he was very certain about their demands.

In Ridley's annotation, the riders forcefully enjoined him the task of brokering the deal for Blake's life. They wanted $50,000 by sundown the next day, or Blake was going to hang for the crime of soiling a white woman.

Mrs. Townsman listened intently, gasping appropriately when the moment called for it. When asked why they chose him, Ridley said he guessed they must had been watching them for a while, waiting and plotting.

Testing the waters, Mrs. Townsman pretended to take the bait. "There is no way I can come up with that kind of money by tomorrow. There's got to be another way… I need at least a couple weeks."

Ridley put a worrisome hand to his hairy chin and rocked back and forth. Until standing to his feet, he began pacing the floor. Eyes concocted in a distant muse, he appeared to be in deep thought. Looking back and forth between Mrs. Townsman, the baby on the couch, and the floor, shaking his head in a negative manner, he began, "I've known Blake his entire life. He's a good kid." Mrs. Townsman nodded. Ridley continued, "I…if Michael were alive… You know how much your husband meant to me. We go all the way back to before the Army." Mrs. Townsman continued to nod silently. "I… I could never forgive myself if anything happened to one of your boys." Sincerity was in his eyes. "That child needs a father. But $50,000…"

"I can get the money," Mrs. Townsman assured. "I just need to get a letter to my bank up in Connecticut."

"That will take weeks, and the bastards were adamant about tomorrow evening."

"What should we do? Do you think the sheriff could help?" The look on Ridley's face answered her question.

"Mary, I… I may be able to scrape together the money."

"Oh, Ridley, please." Mrs. Townsman sighed. "I'll have it back to you just as soon as I get in contact with my lawyer. Thank you." She went over to hug him, but he held her by the shoulders.

"Hold on, Mary. Now you know I trust you. And I'm sure your husband has left you in a secure position."

"Yes, I promise."

"$50,000 is no small sum."

"I can pay. I promise. I'll give you $60,000 in return," she assured.

"That won't be necessary. Getting Blake back safely is what's important. However, and I'm not trying to encumber you, it's still $50,000." He pondered visually. "I may need a little collateral. In fact...yes," he said. "I have a perfect solution."

"Anything," Mrs. Townsman pleaded.

Walking over to the liquor cabinet, Ridley began as he poured two nice glasses of whiskey. "Before your husband passed, we were actually in discussion about me buying his share of the horse ranches."

Mrs. Townsman's face showed no sign of distrust, but her mind registered aha!

Ridley continued, "I'm sure you aren't going to have time to manage the horse ranches yourself."

Mrs. Townsman nodded. "You can have them. All of them."

Ridley nodded.

Mrs. Townsman went on, "Just as soon as we get Blake back, I'll have the lawyers draw up the papers."

"Well, like I said, your husband and I have been in discussions for some time now. The papers have already been drawn. When we go to the ranch to grab the money, we can handle the paperwork."

"Perfect. When can we leave?"

"I'm ready right now."

"Great. Just let me grab a few things," Mrs. Townsman said before she reached over and picked little Michael up off the couch. Wrapping him gently on his blanket, she held him against her breast as she scurried out of the den.

Ridley shook his head with an unbelieving grin, and in one swallow, he threw back the drink he had designated for himself. A second later, he had begun sipping the one he poured for his gracious hostess.

"What are we drinking?" Barry asked walking into the room.

With the hand that held the whiskey, Ridley pointed to the open liquor bottle on the counter.

"Can I refill your cup?" Barry asked, sliding over to where Ridley was standing.

As Barry was taking the glass from Ridley's hand, Mrs. Townsman crept in. Ridley's eyes went wide when he saw the shotgun cradled in her hand. He nearly defecated when she swung the mouth of the weapon in his direction.

"What are you—" *Smack!* Ridley was cut short when Barry smacked him over the head with his heavy revolver.

CHAPTER 36

A cold bucket of water woke Ridley from his trauma-induced slumber. Disoriented and gasping, he sluggishly realized he was naked from the waist down and tied to a chair. Shaking water off his face, he saw Mrs. Townsman was sitting in an identical chair not even a yard across from him. Fluttering, his heart rate jumped instantly as he noticed the large knife she had cuffed in her hand. Trying not to appear too frantic, he said, "What is the meaning of this, Mary? I—"

Ridley was interrupted. "You have ten fingers, ten toes, and one..." She used the tip of the knife to point to the small pink prick sitting between his legs.

"Mary, I don't know what you think this is, but—"

Mrs. Townsman stuck a silent finger to her lips while sliding the sharp end of the knife up the inside of Ridley's thigh.

"Mary!" Ridley yelled as she neared his penis.

From a towering side angle, Barry swung a solid right hook, catching him hard in the jaw, quieting the man. "She said be silent," Barry reiterated.

"Thank you, Barry." Mrs. Townsman smiled. "I'll start with your fingers two at a time. Then your toes. Then..." She again pointed the blade at his shriveled sausage. "I don't know how long it'll take, but in the end, you will tell me where you've hidden my son."

"I don't know. No!" Ridley screamed as Mrs. Townsman grabbed the pinky and ring fingers on his left hand. The sharp knife cut deep into his flesh, but it took her unfamiliar hands a moment to saw all the way through the bone.

Holding up his two fingers, she again asked, "Where's my boy?"

CHAPTER 37

There was a nagging queasiness bubbling Blake's unsettled stomach—not butterflies, not fear. It was more like a physical hate had knotted up inside him. Blake's trouble-prone ass had been taken for a second go-around, and this time the circumstances surrounding his rescue were exponentially more complicated.

This wasn't riding down a group of lone wolves who hadn't made it off the property. Blake had been held captive for days now, and he was in an undisclosed location probably guarded by a number of very alert and capable killers.

Ridley Booker was one of his father's oldest friends. At one point, Ridley was considered family in Michael's eyes. With this unspeakable violation, he was making this situation very personal. Not only did he have firsthand knowledge of little Michael's origin but he was also decades intertwined in their family's history.

Michael, emotionally compromised, listened to Barry detail the encounter with a heavy heart. By specifying that Michael was the one who killed the three men, Ridley inadvertently confessed to orchestrating the raid on the Townsman Plantation. This boiled Michael's blood.

This entire time, Michael steamed, this was the same man who accompanied his mother to Connecticut to bury his father—all the while knowing that he was the architect behind his murder. Ridley was already dead in Michael's rendering. All the cowardly man was waiting for was the bullet between the eyes or maybe the Townswell blast to tear his head all the way off.

The ramifications of Ridley's involvement were not to be taken lightly. Ridley was no small fish by any means. Michael thought back to the dismissive cold shoulder he had received from one of the sheriff's deputies. Michael shuddered to think just how many people were actually made privy to the specifics of Ridley's betrayal. The Booker family had ties all through the state of Georgia. Ridley's uncle Warren was serving as an alderman in town. Many of the folks in Atlanta owed their jobs to the man. Getting rid of Ridley would not go as easy as the three riders before him.

Ever since the horrid night, he had blackened his soul with the deaths of those men; Michael kept his Townswell with him at the hotel. Wrapped snugly in a custom-fitted smoke-gray duffel bag hidden in the bottom drawer of his dresser, Michael's five-shot equalizer remained submissive. Sowed into the pockets of the duffel bag were a case of shotgun shell, some .45 rounds, and five sticks of dynamite (the wicks cut short for a speedy detonation). Slinging the bag across his back, Michael mounted his horse prepared to wage a small war. He was going to get his brother back by any means. And with Barry by his side, he was confident they could meet any challenge.

They both rode horseback, but with the weight of the duffel bag tearing at Michael's shoulders, he struggled to keep pace with Barry's unrestricted stride. Michael surmised Barry rode like a gunman. There was something about his presence that Michael admired.

On two separate occasions, Michael had been out shooting with Barry; and though he could more than adequately match his accuracy, Barry's smooth target-to-target transition was impressive. Barry was a shooter, no doubt. He was a man who could handle himself in the heat of battle. Michael thought back to the outlaw stories he and Blake would read when they were young. Now he was riding across town with the same type of person portrayed as the villain in those books. Michael noticed the man's unperturbed mannerism.

At the hotel, Barry explained that he had Ridley securely tied up in a chair downstairs in the den. Probing him for information, he admitted that Ridley wouldn't budge. As if talking about the weather, Barry said that Ridley was relieved of two fingers on both hands—a total of four to go along with the four toes he had lost. Michael was taken aback at first, but rethinking his apprehension, he was just glad Barry was on their side. Torturing a man—he wasn't sure he had the stomach for it. Nonetheless, someone had to make him talk; and if chopping off fingers and toes got his brother back, then so be it.

The suffocating temperature of the dry afternoon had cooled significantly as they pulled into the plantation. Greeted by bright teeth and dark faces, the slaves in the fields waved, welcoming him home. The happy-go -lucky blacks on the property were totally oblivious to the intense atmosphere surrounding the plantation.

Riding right up to the steps, Michael jumped down from his horse; and without bothering to hitch it to the post, he dismounted and urgently took the porch stairs three at a time. Half-delirious, he charged into the house.

"Mom," he called as he sped across the ground floor.

Angry, scared, and passionately disturbed, Michael's heart was pounding four times its original speed, forcing him to take quick heavy breaths to keep up with the demand. His forehead beaded with perspiration; he appeared to have run a great distance by the time he reached the den.

Eyeing the back of Ridley's head, Michael took out his eleven-inch black-steel six-shot revolver and gripped it tight. With murderous intent, he took long refined strides toward his target. He could see his mother was on the couch sitting in front of Ridley, who was leaning slouched down in a chair, his back to Michael.

The obscurely candlelit room held a soiled smell that hit Michael all at once. He was slowing a step; a spooky ambience lifted the hairs on his arm. Still raising his pistol high, he was ready to smack Ridley across the face when the energy surging his emotional charge instantly wane.

What in God's name? he silently cursed. The image before him was sickening—really sickening. Immediately nauseous, he nearly dropped his pistol as he was forced to look away. It took Michael a moment for him to regain his composure. Then looking back and forth between Ridley and his mother, he said, "Ma?"

"He's at the ranch," Mrs. Townsman opened. Her mouth kept moving, but Michael couldn't hear it. He was too busy processing the visual that was in front of him.

Ridley was covered in blood, pantless with two blood-soaked clothes wrapped around his fingerless hands. Pinning his bloody feet to the ground were three knives; two dug into his right foot, and another was sticking kitty-corner up out of his left. Thick gashes and protruding knots decorated his entire face above the beard. The skin on the left side of his face, from his chin to his eye, was blistered and burned to a bubbling scar—apparently having been cooked over an open flame.

Ridley's shirt had been cut open, and blanketing his partially burned chest was thick streaks of blood running down from shallow stabs and cuts all over. His stomach had a large rip, and looking further down, Michael cringed when he saw the man's genitals stuck to the chair by a large fork that was grotesquely bent out of shape—obviously from being repeatedly stabbed into the man.

"Are you sure he was telling the truth?" Barry calmly asked from behind Michael. His demeanor was so tranquil, one would've imagined seeing such brutality was a common occurrence for him.

"Yes, he wasn't lying," Mrs. Townsman said assuredly. "But be careful. He has several men working the ranch, and three of them are assigned to watch over Blake." Pausing for a long second, she said, "His wife and son are in the house. Kill everyone else."

Michael was still partially in shock. His mother was talking about killing people like it was regular around-the-table dinner conversation.

"Go now," Mrs. Townsman continued. "He isn't expected back until tomorrow night, so if you leave now, you can catch them unaware."

"Yes, ma'am," Barry conceded. Pushing past Michael, he reached over Ridley and snatched the large hunting knife out of his left foot. Ridley gave a soft vocal response then passed back out. This exchange shook Michael to a visual shiver. Opening his mouth to say something, he looked at his mother, but the words wouldn't come out.

Mrs. Townsman couldn't look her son in the eyes. She could only imagine what he was thinking of her.

"I'll ready the horses," Barry volunteered before hustling out of the room.

"So you're just going to leave him like this?" Michael amplified.

"Shh." Mrs. Townsman put a finger over her mouth. "I just got him to sleep," she said, gesturing over to little Michael, balled up in a dark blanket at the end of the sofa.

This did it for him—torturing a man while his nephew was in the room. "Get… Get… Get him out of here. And…" Michael was half-hyperventilating. "And get one of the men to put him in the ground."

"Your brother deserves to put the final bullet in him," Mrs. Townsman declared.

"Get someone to put him in the ground," Michael repeated himself. Then turning, he adjusted the heavy bags on his back and walked out the room.

Walking up with two fresh horses already saddled, "Your mother is an intense woman," Barry said, talking to Michael who finally found his way out front. "You do know where the ranch is, yes?"

Michael just nodded. Then killing the last of the brandy in his glass, he tossed the cup into the flower garden. "One second. Let me go grab this for Blake," Michael said, jogging around the side of the house.

*****

The Sword

The Sword let his pistol fall as the woman walked off with her life and the life of the baby boy she held. The Sword turned and, with a heavy heart, walked out of the murderous valley for the last time.

Michael "the Sword" Townsman found his trusty steed where he left it, tied to a tree branch in the thick of the woods almost a quarter mile out. With sharp pains shooting up through his arm, mounting his horse was difficult, but he managed.

The woods were near pitch-black, but even in such murky conditions, Michael navigated easily. He knew these woods like the back of his hand. Cutting, pushing, and maneuvering through the green brush, his shoulder burned with every twist of direction. He suspected he was losing a dangerous amount of blood. The loss of blood accompanied his throbbing wound, and soon he found himself riding blind at times—his consciousness wavering with every mile past.

It took forever to get back home. And by the time he pulled within a few miles of his property, his horse had become the foreman of the voyage. His body bobbed back and forth atop the saddle.

"Grandma," he called with less effort than a squeak. "Grandma!" he tried again; this time his voice was almost inaudible.

Yards from his front porch, Michael dropped from his saddle onto the unforgiving dry dirt. He had made it all the way home only to fall out in the front yard.

"Grand… Grandma…help…" His words were only whispers at this point.

Lying on the hard, parched Northern turf, he heard a rooster crow, signifying the first light of day. The Sword deliberated he should have died on the battlefield. Then at least his grandmother wouldn't have to find him like this—dead, covered in blood, and dressed in what she might speculate to be clothes stolen from a vagabond. The very sight of him in this condition was enough to stop her old heart.

On the ground he lay looking up with blurry vision at the slowly color-shifting sky. His body was almost unresponsive, but for some reason outside his sense of touch, his other vitals seemed magnified. His eyes were facing the rising sun; it was beautiful, the prettiest sunrise ever. He was astonished. The clouds moved to part at just the right angle to augment the dazzle of the rising sun. The sky appeared an orange-red color, just about the perimeter of the glowing circle of life. The rays didn't even hurt his eyes, and he was looking directly at it.

The North country air was fresher than normal this morning. Michael could smell the withered soil beneath his nonmoving position. The scent of his grandmother's flower garden tickled his nose. The smell was sweet and strong. So much so that it thankfully drowned out the smell of the fresh horse shit that his inconsiderate ride had taken only a few feet from where he lay.

It was beautiful this morning. Smiling gently, still beneath his mask, the feeling of peace washed over him. If only he could have told his grandmother how much he loved and appreciated her and all she had done for him. If only he could have spent a little more time with his uncle. This was not how his life was supposed to conclude. His family would be disappointed in him. That was what hurt the most. He knew the big dreams they had for him. But they could never understand. He had to do it. This was for his people, his father and mother, and his race. And no matter how sympathetic his grandmother was, she was not black; he was. He couldn't sit idly by and watch his people being slaughtered like cattle. He had the power, the know-how, and the will. He had to fight.

His uncle had been training him his entire life to use his guns. Wielding a piece of iron was what made him feel alive. His uncle Michael told him he got his ability to shoot with both hands from his father and his grandfather before him. He only wished he could have met them, at least his father. Rather, he wished he could remember him or his mother, both of whom died by the hands of riders when he was a baby.

His grandmother would say, "Us Townsmans are in the business of firearms. That's what we do."

With every ounce of life left in him, Li'l Michael reached for his sidearm. He wanted to die with his weapon in his hand. The cold steel felt right. It felt like his arm was made complete by the extension—his Negro-designed pistol built and handcrafted by his slain father.

He took one last look at the sun, then he raised his revolver to the sky. *Boom, boom, boom, boom, boom, boom, boom.* He squeezed every last round out of his revolver before his arm dropped to his chest lifelessly. The repercussions of a wild evening came to collect.

CHAPTER 38

Blake could hear Harold was coming. Slowly, while whistling his signature brassy melody, Harold took his time. The choppy whistling was procedural—an old Jim Crow practice. He wanted Blake to hear him coming. He needed him to cerebrally cower on his anticipated approach. An effective master's impending presence should always provoke the fear of God into his slaves. One dragging deliberate foot after the other, Harold took his sweet time. Stepping sure-footed and proudly, he could only imagine what mental terror Blake was experiencing at the sound of his lip-pucker music.

This was the tenth or eleventh time in the last two days. Torturing Blake was like making love; there was nothing more enjoyable. Harold had broken the spoiled, delusional young Negro; he was sure of it.

Raised by an enabling family, Blake had spent his entire life living in an alternative reality. Walking around with a pocket full of cash, fancy threads, and freedom papers, he essentially thought he was an actual white man—but no more. Harold (by any means) intended to make sure that Blake's remaining days (no matter how limited) were spent getting accustomed to that of a groveling slave.

Blake could hear him coming, closer with every rhythmic breath. Blake's stomach flared and released a small involuntary spill. He pinched shut his bladder; the front part of his thighs burned from the filth. Blake was a natural clean freak. The sordid liquid staining his trousers actually hurt him. This was hell for sure, and the blue-eyed, pale-complexioned, fire-red-haired turnkey was the devil.

Exhausted and broken, Blake had been on his feet for the last two and a half days. His arms were hoisted above his head; the twelve-inch chain linking his wrist was pulled up and through a circular metal hold that was attached to the thick-wooded post running parallel over his head. Battered and bleeding, Blake was consistently subjected to Harold's creative aggression in the indefensible position.

Harold worked Blake ragged with unimpeded punches, kicks, and demoralizing backhand bitching slaps. Powerful whip-cracking strikes ripped through Blake's thin-woven suit jacket, leaving him scraped and scarred from the front to the back. Swinging high and often, Harold even put the leather across Blake's handsome beige face, breaking skin and opening slices that bled freely.

Once, in the middle of the night, Blake, half out on his feet, was startled vigilant when the barn doors were flung wide open. Out of the opening came an onslaught stone. This aerial assault of large clumsy-shaped rocks was being hurled across the barn at breakneck speeds. Harold and another man were taking Blake through a biblical chastisement historically reserved for adulteresses, thieves, and murderers. Fortunately, the sharp piercing rocks peppering his stationary body only lasted a short stint with the visiting unknown contributor reminding Harold that he was to be kept alive and in reasonably good health.

How could this be happening to me? Blake cried. What could he have done to deserve such dreadful treatment? To be punished for his lustful sins was one thing, but even death was more merciful than what he was being subjected to. *Inhuman,* Blake mentally cursed.

Cruelty of this proportion was worse than even a rabid dog deserved. Violence of magnitude was a foreign concept to him. Only through discussions with slaves purchased from other plantations did

Blake ever hear of such treatment. Even then, he thought the tales of evil, unadulterated, were being embellished. But here he was.

Dry blood that had drizzled down from a cut on his forehead itched the corner of his right eye, while the wound itself moistened as his heart rate accelerated. He couldn't take much more of this. Blake knew he was no slave. He was not accustomed to abuse. His pampered body was ill-equipped to sustain such abuse. He had to escape; he had to be free of these chains.

Harold was coming. The red-haired devil's whistling grew more and more pronounced, spiking Blake's nervous system and stirring him to action. Pulling and twisting, Blake commenced to loosen himself of his wooden dungeon. The rusted metal semicircle that held his shackles was worn to a dull brown. Blake had to rip it apart somehow. Grabbing the chain right above his wrist, he began jumping up and down, working his weight against the rusted metal. He yanked five, ten, fifteen times and pulled and fell against the metal with all his size, but his efforts were useless. His confines were solid.

Closer by the millisecond, his evil captor approached. Crushing dry dirt and hard grass beneath him, Harold's crisp footsteps, once drowned out by his piercing whistle, now scheduled his appending arrival.

Furiously Blake pulled at his shackles. His eyes swelled with sorrowful tears. He'd kill the fire-headed bastard. All he needed was to free one hand. He could feel the small five-shot revolver still hidden at the small of his back. This immensely made his loathsome predicament even worse. Knowing in his possession, on his immediate person, was the instrument required to quell his abuse. "Ugh!" he fussed; it was so close yet so far.

Shoving the barn door open, Harold briefly stood in the entrance. The sun at his back, he towered in situational stature over his helpless capture. Harold was quiet as a wolf in hunting; he remained patient, waiting for his signaled cue.

Blake had his head down at this time. His first glimpse of Harold this evening was of his long streaking shadow blanketing the ground, reaching all the way across to Blake's bare feet. Even Harold's shadow seemed sinister. Blake, coiling, quickly altered his feet so as not to step in the man's dark reflection.

Fighting the regrettable inclination, he didn't want to look, but somehow Blake's prying eyes managed to drag his face forward involuntarily. No soon as Blake's line of sight positioned in Harold's direction did he push into the barn.

The return of his whistling and his casual strides did something to Blake's fragile psyche. Harold's even-tempered, placid demeanor was that of a man about to sit down for supper. It was like his torturous practice was second nature for him. And to heighten the terror, Blake noticed that in his right hand, Harold was holding a dual-handle metal pail. With eyes locked on its shape, Blake recognized the pail right away. He'd recently purchased an identical bucket for Bessy after she mistakenly crushed her tomato basket during his last visit in the garden.

Blake's body shook with skittish misgivings, wondering what horrors awaited him within that pail. Maybe it was brimful of large rocks. Maybe it had oil in which he planned to douse him with in order to set him ablaze. Maybe... Blake grabbed at the chain with two clenched fists. Maybe he planned to have him sit the bucket like Bessy. Pulling on the ungiving metal, Blake cringed. Blake silently vowed he'd bite it off before he'd pleasure him.

Harold was amused at Blake's attempts to break the chain. He processed that niggers were naturally dull species. "Try as you might, you are never escaping this barn."

"Kill me. Kill me. Why won't you just kill me?" Blake cried for mercy.

"All in due time," Harold began, tranquility in his tone. "Your nigger-loving kinfolk should be here tomorrow. Ridley has big plans for them. You will remain alive. Boss's orders."

"Why is Ridley doing this?"

"Ridley... Ridley's motivations are always financial. Me, I'm more of a simple man. You represent the newfangled moldering in this country. You big, strong niggers are designed to be slaves, not free men. And you—you are a perfect example of why we cannot allow your kind to roam around unchained. If we start allowing you to impregnate white women, where would that leave us? You'd breed us right out of the country. And don't you worry. By noon on Sunday, we'll be to your plantation to collect that little nigger of yours."

"No!" Blake cried.

"Yes!" Harold mocked. "He and his whore of a mother will hang."

"Please! He's only a child."

"And my bonus." Harold laughed. "I get the plantation when this is done." His laugh was extensive yet barely audible.

"No!" Blake screamed as he pulled at the chain.

Laughing still, Harold put his free hand under the bucket. "Here. Ridley said it was to keep you fed."

In one swift motion, Harold hurled the insides of the pail onto Blake. The slimy mess splashed across the entire upper portion of his body, from head to groin.

"Ah! Ah!" Blake animated as blood guts and feces dripped down his torso.

On the other side of the ranch, several Booker faithfuls had gathered in celebration of tomorrow's payday. Over an open flame, they roasted a pig. Cutting the animal open, Harold collected its insides in the bucket. On his way over, he had Tobey scoop a few pounds of horse shit into the pail just to top it off. It was a perfect meal for his new pet nigger.

The horrid mixture was like venom to Blake's prudish physique. This was the straw that broke the camel's back.

"Ah!" Blake screamed. "Ah!" He grabbed the chain on his wrist—pulling, yanking, and jumping. The smell and texture swimming his person were so nasty, Blake went temporarily insane. "Ah! I'll kill you."

Harold was amused.

"Ah!" Blake continued. Pulling himself up, he held on to the chain and leaned back. Swinging his legs above his head, he kicked from an upside-down position at the rusted metal loop.

Harold was bent over laughing. His nigger monkey was upside down swinging like an actual monkey. The irony was hilarious to him. Retrieving the long leather whip he had dangled around his neck, he gave Blake a bone-chilling crack across the back.

"Aн!" Blake's feet fell to the ground, but still he jumped up and grabbed a hold of the metal circle. Again flipping himself upside down, he pulled his legs through the chain of his arm shackles, then he locked his legs around the wooden beam. *How did I not think of doing this before?* Now Blake's hands were behind him right at the hidden pistol on his back.

"Damn monkey," Harold hollered as he gave Blake another swat.

"Aн!" Blake screamed as he again grabbed ahold of the ring, and one by one, he pulled his legs back through his chain. Letting his feet fall to the ground, his large hand inadvertently concealed the small gun in his grasp. With a newfound strength, Blake put the barrel of the weapon in the base point where chain met cuff and pulled the trigger.

Harold's chest jumped a foot in front of his body when he heard the weapon sound. Suddenly his capture was free and somehow armed. Frozen stiff, Harold stared wide-eyed at the large blood-and-shit soaked black man holding the small revolver down by his side. What a shift of position. He was instantly thrust into the submissive party in the equation. Harold dropped the whip and held up two pleading hands. Taking a measured step back, "Please" was all he could manage before Blake lifted his weapon, sending a speeding bullet barreling into his cold blue eye.

The inconsistent evening's smoldering temperature had returned with gusto. Baking in his saddle, Michael, for like the hundredth time, was compelled to swipe his already soggy sleeve across the sweat-beaded forehead. Drowsy from the heat, he forced himself to straighten up as he snapped the reins, needling his horse to quicken its pace. Barry, seemingly unaffected by the temperature, was almost twenty yards ahead, and coming up on the right was the break in the road that would lead them to the ranch.

The three-hour ride through the blistering tropic was several times as rough for Michael as opposed to his detached travel mate.

With the weight of the Townswell duffel bag slung across his back, Michael's shoulders ached with every buck and bounce.

The two rode hard in order to make it to the ranch in good time. All business, this rough-and-tumble trip was a relatively quiet ride, with the only dialogue between the men consisting of Michael conveying directions and Barry nodding in comprehension. Nonetheless, pulling onto the final road leading up to the gated ranch, Michael assertively guided them to a provisional stall.

Looking over into Barry's calm, ungiving eyes, Michael briefly lost his train of thought. Stagnant, sitting for that short uncomfortable silent moment, Michael began to feel every ounce of the bag on his shoulders. Impelling him to redress, the heavy war bag felt as if it was astonishingly gaining an additional pound every few seconds.

"I need a moment," Michael, said climbing down from his slightly shimmering vehicle. Placing the Townswell bag on the ground, Michael gave his overtaxed torso a gentle spin. His back, neck, and shoulders all cracked with relief as he continually turned from side to side, trying to loosen his knotted extremities. "So what's…the plan?" Michael spoke through a massaging bend. "How do we approach this?" He was deferring to the seasoned professional.

"We kill everyone—man, woman, and child," Barry spat without a pause.

Michael didn't have an immediate response. Barry's surprising comment took his conservative colleague aback. *Man, woman, and child?* Michael mentally echoed.

Barry's posture after such a statement was uncanny. Barry's harsh wording was spoken so nonchalantly that Michael's innocent processor figured the message behind his ludicrous statement must have been meant to be heard in terms of more of a riddle rather than an actual statement. *Man, woman, and child.* Looking up with an inquisitive eye, Michael searched for an explanation.

However, failing to return Michael's study, Barry was beyond the moment. Preoccupied, he looked across the plain toward the gate surrounding the ranch. Obviously not cognizant of the deprecation in his partner, Barry's mannerism held no sign of exaggeration as Michael continued to glare up at him.

"We…can't kill everyone. There's—" Michael began before Barry cut him off.

"There can be no witnesses. If even so much as a single slave is left to tell his narrative, you, your brother, your mother—none will be safe."

"There are women…children…babies…"

"There are women and children on your plantation as well," Barry said before pausing for effect. "No, we kill everyone." He dismissed Michael's arrant grievances. Looking back to the long picket gate, Barry's eyes narrowed as he caught something in the distance. Placing his hand on his pistol, he focused on the blurred movement that, for some reason, looked awkwardly out of place.

Shaking out of his jolted funk, Michael, too, reached for his trusty six-shooter. Turning in the direction that Barry was looking, Michael began, now leaping over to grab the duffel bag, "What?" Swinging it across his back, he nervously asked before sticking a foot onto the toehold and climbing onto his horse, "You see something?"

"I think… Hell, that's him!" Barry animated before giving the reins a spirited snap, goading the horse to action.

CHAPTER 39

Sneaking off the gigantic six-sided multisectioned horse ranch, Blake employed a crouched run. Staying low, he used the property's kindly infrastructure (barns, staples, and gates) to conceal his agile escape.

Already malnourished and starved for strength, the unrelenting sun gave Blake no clemency as he ran bare chest across the dirt field. Virtually smothered by his own stench, Blake peeled off his blood- and shit-stained shirt once he reached the property's end. Notwithstanding, the stink of the impromptu shit shower was seemingly fused onto his person.

Sickened to the point of feeling faint, Blake was practically running blind. Exhausted and haplessly plagued with signs of dehydration, the smell of the warm sewage on his skin seemed to be burning a hole in his fragile unconscious—half-driving him insane.

Life, through this experience, had instantly changed for Blake. The concept of living a normal life was now a distant thought. All he saw now were death, hurt, and blood. Revenge was to be his only foreseeable occupation.

Blake was no longer yearning to make it home. His son had already lost his father; his mother, a son. Vengefully centered, Blake was heading to the gun store. He needed his pistols. The tiny chrome shooter in his fist was insufficient for the job he needed to do. Every man on the ranch would be held accountable for his treatment. Ridley would die last. *Ridley.* Blake allowed himself a small grin. *Ridley would die slow.*

Jogging slack-legged down the jagged roadway, the sound of drumming hooves spent Blake on his heels. Two riders immediately made him grip his chrome in a tight fist. He had three shots left. He assured himself he only needed two.

"Blake!" Michael called. "Blake!" he screamed with set relief.

Coming into view, Michael saw his brother's arm fall to his side. With relief, he climbed down from his horse as soon as it pulled to a stop. Dropping the bag to the ground, Michael took two animated steps forward before the smell halted his advancing embrace. Blake's battered face and chest were glazed over with all manners of filth. *What have they done to him?* Michael cringed.

Blake and Michael both stood unmoved for an awkward moment. Then dropping his gaze, Blake whispered, "Water."

Michael, snapping out of his muse, jerked awake. "Yes," he said, reaching over to grab a container from his saddle bag.

Barry, not surprised by Blake's condition, reached into his saddle and pulled out a meat-heavy sandwich he had packaged in a dark napkin. "Here," he said, tossing Blake the wrapped sandwich.

Ripping into the breading with savagery, Blake's throat was sore from dehydration, but he managed to muscle the meal down in less than a minute. Sipping the water, Blake walked over and untied the duffel bag Michael had dropped. "I need a bigger gun," he said, dropping his chrome pistol into the bag.

"We have to get out of here," Michael said, almost to himself.

"No one on the property can be left alive," Barry shrewdly reminded him.

"No, we have Blake. That's all that matters."

"The men on this ranch will not allow this to end so…delicately. Eventually this will make it back to your mother's house."

"Then we'll deal with it then."

Pulling out of his bag his two seven-shot pistols, which Michael had so conveniently thought to pack for him, Blake smiled. "No one on this ranch lives."

CHAPTER 40

Mrs. Townsman had little Michael propped up on her lap, holding him under her arms to allow his feet to stretch down as if he was standing under his own weight.

"That's my baby. You are so strong, Michael." She smiled as her grandson extended and contracted his leg muscles in a jerking bounce.

After allowing Darla an hour to feed and burp him, Mrs. Townsman was again back down in the den with Ridley, who was still strapped to the chair. For hours, Ridley remained nonresponsive, yet he was breathing audibly. He was still a credible threat in her determination. Thus she insisted he not be left alone for an extended amount of time. Accordingly, with firearms close at hand, she insisted on standing watch.

Lifting little Michael up and down in a fluent playful jump, the baby happily let out a loud excited giggle. At that moment, flinching in his chair, Ridley coughed a violent gagging breath—this before letting out a dragging moan.

Startled, Mrs. Townsman looked up at him and saw that he was slightly flexing his bound limbs—his body moving in a somewhat coherent fashion. Eyes closed in a way that suggested he was in a hellish nightmare, Ridley continued to moan and mumble under his breath.

Grabbing the handle of the pistol in her dress, Mrs. Townsman gave him a suspicious once-over. The ropes knotting him to the sturdy oakwood chair were sufficiently secure, but Mrs. Townsman was nonetheless apprehensive. *Blake will just have to suffice with seeing his dead body,* she rationed because she couldn't take the chance of him getting free—not with her grandson in the house. Readying herself to stand, about to take her grandson out of the room so he wouldn't have to witness her killing Ridley, from the corner of her eye, she spotted Darla standing in the doorway.

Darla, Mary, and Meissa were instructed to stay out of the den all this day. Nonetheless, standing in the door, Darla watched the struggling man tied to the chair wide-eyed.

Shaking her head in frustration, Mrs. Townsman laid little Michael on the couch. Grabbing her rifle from behind the cushion, she stood to her feet and walked over to where Ridley was stationed. Holding the stalk of the weapon, Mrs. Townsman swung the rifle hard, striking Ridley in the forehead with the bunt of the gun. Ridley's head snapped back like a can being kicked then instantly fell to his chest. Satisfied, Mrs. Townsman walked back over to the couch, picked up her grandbaby, and continued his leg exercises. Without even looking up at Darla, she said in a sharp not-so-kind tone, "Get out!"

Darla, tripping, spent into an expeditious about-face, backing up into a legs-wide run. "What the hell?" she muttered as she turned up the staircase, speeding back to her room. "What the hell?"

CHAPTER 41

For an elongated span, Michael remained stock-still, trapped in a catatonic state. He was sweating profusely with a screaming toddler cuffed in one arm and a smoking black six-cylinder death bringer steaming in the other. He stood on the second floor of Ridley's newly remodeled ranch house, staring from an open window down at Barry who had just laid an empty rifle across the chest of a dead slave.

Every barn, chicken coop, and horse stable was already engulfed in flames. The all-out assault on the ranch was a complete and merciless slaughter—bullets, screams, and deaths. And in the end, Barry began setting the scene of a murderous slave revolt.

The pale horse for the deplorable came as swift and as vicious as a desert snake. Locked and loaded, the head-hunting party of three rode full-on toward the open-field pig roast, catching the drunken picnic participants unarmed and unaware.

Blake, taking the lead, was the first to open fire. Setting the tone, full speed without breaking to aim, he loosen a roaring shot that caught a standing full-bearded Caucasian man high in the chest.

The ghastly screams of flowing horror were short-lived as one, two, three, four more shells parted the flesh of the unprepared. Utilizing both pistols simultaneously, Blake fired with accuracy—

every bullet seeming to crease its victim in just the right location for maximum devastation.

Not to be outdone, Barry was next to take aim. Slowing his horse at the base of the gathering with mortal exactness, he squeezed off at the decamping orgy, idly trying to escape their lives.

After clearing the area, pulling wooden torches from beneath the planking swine, Barry and Blake went out in search of the hidden. Weeding through every barn and stable, unadulterated death accosted each individual found. Then setting ablaze the wooden structures, Blake and Barry left the bodies inside to cook.

Blistering gun cackle over the roar of multiple uncontainable fires could be heard as Barry and Blake circled the ranch scouting for persons they might have missed. After several turns around the property, they finally set their sights on the slave quarters.

Barry and Blake were like peas in a pod. They were all smiles as Blake kicked in the door of the one-room shack. Straightaway, Barry bent the corner firing into the room to the chorus of tormented voices. Murder was fun for Barry, and Blake, who had all but set aside his Christian values, was evidently enjoying himself as well. Michael was significantly less enthusiastic about the hunt. In accordance, he was the duly appointed reaper of the only ranch house yet to be torched. *Man, woman, and child.*

This is not right, Michael reflected. This was hell's work if he ever saw it. It was an appalling, sacrilegious, and abbreviated ethnic cleaning; and unfortunately, while left with little choice, he was smack-dab in the middle of it. Pulling shut his eyes, Michael gave the child in his arms a tender squeeze, trying to ease his nervous spirit and, in effect, hoping to quiet his own as well.

After long laying the baby to his chest with blood puddled around his leather boots, Michael carefully spent around, high-stepping over the child's mother on his way out the door. Pushing through the short hall, down the stairs, and into the front foyer, Michael found Blake sitting in a cushioned chair, nibbling from a large slab of freshly cooked pork. Blake, who had spent the better part of the last half hour soaking in a tub of hot water, was dressed in an ill-fitting three-piece suit—complete with hat and tie.

"What are you doing…with the kid?" Blake asked without looking up from his piece of pig.

Michael looked over at his brother with a contemptuous eye. Something was different—not right—about his little brother. He was changed, darker. His whole persona was off—foreign.

"I'm taking him with us," Michael informed.

"No one lives."

"What! He's just a child."

"No one…lives," Blake repeated, looking up from his seated position. His eyes were distant and even more bloodshot than when Michael saw him only a half hour earlier.

"I'm not killing a baby," Michael declared.

"No, I'm going to kill him."

"You're not going to kill him either," Michael challenged. The pistol in his fist was now weighing its relevance.

"He's Ridley's kid."

"You're. Not. Killing. This. Baby," Michael announced hesitantly.

"You think he'd show my son the same mercy?" Blake animated, now standing to his feet. "What do you think were they going to do when they made it back to the plantation and found my son lying in his crib?"

Michael's eyes were narrow slits as he stared across at his brother who was also holding a pistol tightly in his hand. The baby in his arms had stopped sobbing, as if to pay better attention to the debate that would determine his fate.

Michael never saw Blake like this. His timid little brother was now a vicious, bloodthirsty killer. *Man, woman, child. No, he can't have this one.* Michael snuggled the child protectively to his chest. "Burn the house," Michael growled through clenched teeth. "I'm keeping him." And without a second look back, he turned, holstered his weapon, and stormed out.

On the porch, Barry was dragging a thin barefoot white man up the stairs by his ankles. The slave he had planted the rifle on was twenty yards ahead, pooled in blood. Barry was attempting to make it appear that the two had shot it out, with neither man surviving the exchange. Digging in his pocket, Barry dropped a fistful of rifle shells at the man's feet. Then running back down the steps and retrieving the rifle that was laying at the base of the stairs, he trotted back up the stairs. He was breathing heavily as he dropped the rifle across the man's chest. Finally touching a hand to his hip, he stopped to suck in a deep breath. Smirking over his shoulder at Michael who had the child tucked securely against his chest, he teased, "You couldn't do it, could you?"

Michael shook his head. "No, I'm going to take him back with us."

Barry's face registered a look of concern; Michael shrugged away. "My nephew is going to need a big brother" was Michael's excuse. Barry smiled and nodded in accordance.

Seconds later, thick black smoke began pouring out of the broken window to their left. Blake, in no hurry, came waltzing out of the dark clouding, still chewing his pork slab. "He's not my son's brother," he said, tossing Michael a hard glare.

Ignoring him, Michael turned and walked off the porch.

"Letting this kid live is a bad idea," Blake complained to Barry.

"Maybe. Still… I'm thinking your mother will appreciate it. She did tell us to allow the child and his mom to live. One out of two isn't bad."

"That's Ridley's kid."

"He's only a baby. He'll have forgotten all about his parents in no time. Come on. Your mother has a surprise for you at the house."

Annoyed, Blake stood stationary, holding his pistol at his side as Barry descended the steps. Then shaking his head, Blake pulled a handful of bullets out of his pocket and pushed off the porch as well.

Barry had the horses tied to the gate thirty yards ahead. Walking slowly, still visually groveling about the survivor, Blake began reloading his pistols.

Barry, signaling to Michael that he'd handle it, courtly slung the duffel bag across his back, giving Michael a break so he could more comfortably ride with the baby.

Spinning the cylinder, Blake was reloading his second pistol, walking as if lost in a daydream. Watching steel meet flesh over and over in his head, there was no way he was going to allow Ridley's son reach maturity. He and his father were going to feel all fourteen rounds; he smiled. Amused at his sadistic imagination, Blake snapped the last bullet into his pistol. Holstering his weapon, he looked up just in time to see Michael's eyes widen. Reaching with both hands, Blake turned around, pistols drawn and ready. *Boom!* The piercing shot echoed across the whole ranch. Immediately Blake let his guns fall to his sides as he looked across at the burning house ahead.

The moment was surreal, a cruel act of God. The moment sounded like church bells ringing on a Sunday evening—slow, blaring, and repetitive. It was like one's mother calling him in for dinner right when he was having fun outside. No, it wasn't like any of that. To Michael, the moment felt like déjà vu—like months back, like the night he lost his father.

The shot exploded, catching Blake square in the chest. Rocking back a stumble yet astonishingly still on his feet, Blake saw the man on the porch (previously thought dead) holding the rifle Barry had given him. With lumber-like hands, the man tried to work another round into the chamber of the single-shot rifle.

Blake, leaking from the chest, was out on his feet. Stumbling around dazed, he dropped to a knee. The rifle man's second shot whizzed right by Blake's face. He could feel the heat from the errant bullet burning with inaccurate disappointment. Blake could tell he was already mortally wounded. Another shot would do nothing to expedite the forecasting; still, with blurred vision, Blake zeroed in on his assailant. With both pistols pointed, he began to squeeze, punching sizable holes in the front of the shimmering smoke-shrouded house. Round after round his weapons released until eventually, by artistry or just blind luck, a bullet found the top of the man's face, taking his whole hairline into the open doorway behind him.

Everything seemed to be happening in slow motion. Michael felt as if he'd been riding for five minutes by the time he pulled to a stop. Climbing down from his horse, he placed the screaming baby on the ground beside his dying brother.

Eyes rolling to the back of his head, Blake appeared to be drowning. His chest was heaving in and out violently as if he was choking on his own blood. With arms flailing aimlessly, he reached and searched until Michael grabbed and held both hands in his own.

This was the moment he missed the night his father passed—his last moments. Reaching down, Michael lifted Blake's back off the ground, scooping him into his arms. At that second, Blake's body became very still as a tranquil peace came over him. "My son…son. Son" were Blake's last words before he fell still.

The whole event had come and gone in the span of a minute, minute and a half maybe, but for Michael, it seemed much, much longer. Lying on the ground holding Blake on his lap, Michael looked down into Blake's light-brown eyes. His brother's still peepers were cold and unforgiving as they stared back up at him, judging and accusing. The accusation in his brother's eyes would forever haunt him, but he couldn't bring himself to manually close them. After a time, he just looked away, ashamed.

Michael had been sitting for a good moment by the time Barry came over with the horses. "Come on. He's gone," Barry informed. "We have to go. We'll bring his body back to your mother."

Emotionally drained, it took Michael another minute to find the strength to stand. His brother was dead—murdered and killed right in front of him—yet Michael hadn't shed a tear. It was odd. He loved his brother with all he had; still, leaning over to kiss his forehead, he realized that he wouldn't miss him. He couldn't. Michael rationed he was his biggest burden. And helping Barry to lift him onto the horse, he reasoned that he had served his purpose: little Michael.

Leaving the baby sitting on the ground alone, Michael climbed atop his horse. *He's not my nephew's brother,* he asserted. Looking after little Michael was his job, his new burden. Michael smiled. And by God and everything holy, he'd make sure little Michael wouldn't end up like his father—no drama, no violence, and by God, no white women. He was going to raise his nephew to be a great young Negro. No harm would ever come to him. He'd stake his life on that.

CHAPTER 42

Of course, this was the worst possible ending to the most tumultuous year of her life. Rocking back and forth under the dim lighting of a sorrow-filled den room, Mrs. Townsman sat completely dejected. Holding her ever-lighthearted grandbaby across her lap, she sat on the sofa only ten short paces from where her darling son Blake lay eyes forever shut. Curtly and without favor, Mrs. Townsman kept quiet all the sympathetic well-wishing rhetoric while, at the same time, perpetually waving away any and every suggestion to remove her son's bloody body.

Occupied by eight, the room was sectionally split into grieving cliques of two. Mary and Meissa were in the corner by the bar hugging, swaying, and crying their eyes out. Michael and Barry, who both felt responsible for Blake's death in their own way, were on the wall leaning quietly by the door. Ridley, while still out cold, looked relatively peaceful, bleeding silently in his designated execution chair, three feet in front of where Blake was lying. Both their blood were slowly soaking into the texture of the hardwood flooring.

On the couch, locked in a tug-of-war of emotions, sat Mrs. Townsman and her grandbaby. Little Michael, who loved being rocked by his grandmother, stared up with playful, attentive eyes.

Reaching with small active hands, he grabbed and pulled at her salty-tear-moistened blouse, totally oblivious to the anguish saturating the room.

When Michael and Barry first carried Blake's body into the house, Mrs. Townsman's reaction was so detached it was as if she had already known. "Don't put him on my couch," she snapped, halting the high-strung pallbearers midstride. "Where are you taking him?" she again complained when they attempted to usher him from the room. "Put him down."

She spoke and gestured in a temper, cutting the men off as they nervously expounded their individual narration. Mrs. Townsman only wanted to hear the relevant information regarding her son's blotched rescue. (The entire ranch, save the one-year-old child, was mortally punished. Blake conducted himself admirably, and every precaution was taken to ensure the deadly confrontation could not be traced back to the family.)

Essentially mourning quietly, the gathering collectively allowed for a much-deserved extended moment of silence.

Rocking back and forth, the tears racing down Mrs. Townsman's cheeks wouldn't seem to cease. *Michael,* Mrs. Townsman silently called to her dear late husband, *I tried to keep safe your boy. I always treated them as equals.* She stared at her only biological offspring. He was her only blood heir. He and her grandson were all she had left to love.

A kiss on the lips invoked a big smile from the baby boy as he reached little hands up to grab at his grandmother's face. She loved this little boy. He was his father's son. He was her dear late husband's grandson, and he possessed his strength and ability to make her feel like everything was going to be okay.

"My grandson," Mrs. Townsman whispered with a smile.

Besides the bae in her lap, this was the first smile to grace the room since the guys returned carrying her son's corpse. A welcomed sight, her small shift in disposition was missed by no one.

Capitalizing on the tiny break in momentum, Michael offered for what felt like the hundredth time, "We have to get him buried."

Letting out a deflating breath, without lifting her eyes to meet his, Mrs. Townsman hesitantly nodded. Receiving confirmation, Michael slightly nudged Barry; and impelled, the two pushed off the wall.

"But first," Mrs. Townsman said, lifting little Michael from her lap, "Meissa, take this baby upstairs. Mary, go with her."

"I'm so sorry," Meissa said, lifting little Michael from his grandmother's outstretched arms. Mary, on her way by, mumbled something similar as her weak, emotionally distraught knees carried her out of the room.

Her face promptly turning from mourning mom to vengeful mother as soon as Meissa and Mary cleared the door frame, Mrs. Townsman decreed, referring to the man bound and bleeding in the chair, "Kill this piece of filth."

Ridley, with his chin tucked in his chest, seemed to be taking in a little more air as his heavy breathing became the only audio in the room. Michael, standing to his side and looking down at him, couldn't help but feel a bit sorry for him.

Ridley was torn to pieces and beat to a pulp, and the blood dripping from his forehead down into his beard seemed fresh as if the woman ordering his execution had recently busted him upside his head. No matter, he had brought this all on himself.

Unholstering his pistol, Michael looked down at Ridley then back over at his mother. Feeling uneasy about doing this in front of his mother, with a squint in his eye, Michael asked, perturbed, "Here?"

"Yes," Mrs. Townsman answered with ice in her tone. "Here and now."

"Are you sure?" Michael again questioned hesitantly. "I can take him out back and—"

"No. Put your gun to his head and pull the trigger. I want to see his head explode."

At first, Ridley's groggy moan bubbled blood from his slightly parted lips as his chest rose and fell with frequency. This was followed by heavy coughing, then as his head went back, they realized he wasn't moaning; he was giggling. Then opening his eyes, Ridley looked ahead at Mrs. Townsman, who was standing only a few feet in front of him, and he began flat-out laughing.

Playing possum for who knew how long, Ridley was now making himself vibrantly accessible. "Your pri-prized...," he began before falling into a coughing spell. "Your prized nigger...dead!" he animated, laughing loud and hard.

Michael, taking a step forward, forcefully jammed the barrel of his pistol into the back of Ridley's head.

Briefly cringing, Ridley again began to laugh. His enjoyment was boisterous, sinister, and unfortunately for him, revenge-provoking. His eyes were trained on Mrs. Townsman, taunting, begging her to react.

Michael could not take the idea of his delight another second. He was thumbing the hammer into position; he was stalled only when, raising a hand, Mrs. Townsman gestured for him to stop.

Her demeanor was unruffled; her face was imperturbable. Pulling out her chrome hand pistol, she said, "Everyone at the ranch, including your wife," she paused to gauge the impact of her words, "is dead. And tomorrow, after your one-year-old son has spent the entire night alone, scared and crying under the pale moonlight, I'm personally going to ride out there, find your little bastard, and hang him from the tallest tree I can find. Your sniveling weasel of a son will be shot, burned, and left in the woods to be eaten by coyotes."

Ridley fixed his lips, about to respond, but crashing the bunt of his pistol across his mouth, Michael kept silent the soon-to-be-dead man.

Mrs. Townsman continued, "My prized nigger's son will live a full and healthy life, while yours will die a slow and painful death."

Thick blood dribbled from Ridley's lips. Moving his mouth in a chewing motion, he worked loose and spit a tooth onto his lap. "I'll meet you in hell," Ridley promised as Mrs. Townsman lifted her weapon.

Two to the stomach, one to the chest, and the fourth hit Ridley in the face, catching him right below the left cheekbone.

"Darla," Mrs. Townsman startled. Then she shot Ridley a last time, the fifth bullet creasing the top of his head. "Get out of here,"

Mrs. Townsman cautioned Darla. But falling on deaf ears, her idle threat was completely ignored.

Darla was shocked stiff. Numb from head to shoe, she tiptoed across the hardwood to where Blake lay face up. Darla's traditionally flawless face was, at this moment, contorted into the ugliest sad face Mrs. Townsman thought she'd ever seen. The tears pouring from Darla's big blue eyes were coming down like rainwater. Light-headed, she knelt down beside her negro lover.

Blake was lying flat on his back with his chin slightly tilted upward. His chiseled face, also normally flawless, was battered and bruised in a way Darla never imagined it would be.

Totally undone, Darla reached out and laid a gentle hand on his soft curly head. "Why?" she cried. "Blake, no, please." She screamed at the top of her lungs.

Michael and Barry stood behind Darla not knowing what to do. Darla had completely lost it. Out of all reason, she climbed on top of Blake, straddling him. With a fist full of soggy jacket, she laid her head on his blood=soaked chest.

Michael, making eye contact with his mother, gestured as if to ask, "What should I do?" Mrs. Townsman gave him a wait-a-minute finger. This was surprising to Mrs. Townsman. The performance Darla was putting on could not be faked. Mrs. Townsman finally realized she was really in love with her son, and the premise of it warmed her heart. And to think, just hours prior, she was absolutely certain that Darla was just in it for the money.

Walking around the hysteric blonde, Michael went over to his mother. Leaning in to be heard over Darla's loud wailing, he said, "We have to leave tomorrow."

Mrs. Townsman shook her head. "We're leaving tonight," she corrected. "Right after you bury your brother."

Michael nodded. Wandering over to the bar to fix himself a drink, he grabbed a glass off the counter and held it up to Barry. From across the room, with a raised hand, Barry accepted.

Smiling at her grandson's mother with pride, Mrs. Townsman then glimpsed over at Ridley, and her face instantly turned to a frown. This man, whom she had known for over twenty years, had turned her life upside down. Putting away her pistol, she walked over to the couch and picked up her rifle. Her life in Georgia was over. Mary and the rest of her slaves were free as far as she was concerned. She'd have the papers drawn up as soon as she got settled up North—only her, her son, and her grandson, she reasoned, as she checked to see if there was a shell in the chamber. Taking aim, Mrs. Townsman smiled a proud smile.

The explosion from her rifle was much louder than that of her pistol. She heard the boom of that rifle break a thousand times, but hearing it echo indoors was an entirely different animal. Ear-popping, the impact of the power drummed. And when the proverbial smoke cleared, all she could hear was the sound of her grandchild crying all the way from the second floor. He hadn't cried the whole night—the entire day. Now that she thought about it, Mrs. Townsman couldn't remember the last time she ever heard him crying like he was at that moment. But now his voice rang through the halls, bullying the house as his mother fell facedown over his father's body; the hole in her chest was the size of a ripe plum.

Shaken to the core, Michael dropped his glass, shocked as he watched Darla's shivering body twitch before ultimately falling still. It was like something out of a bad dream. Staring over at his mother in amazement, he had no words.

Barry, also stunned, stood wide-eyed; but recovering quickly, he raised a hand reminding Michael about the drink he had offered.

Michael, though shaken up, wiped his hand across his eyes, trying to pull it together. The lack of moral restraint being exercised today had broken him. First was Blake's murderous tirade—now this. Grabbing another glass with unsteady hands, Michael filled it halfway and threw it back. Nothing was ever going to be the same. Nothing was sacred, he reasoned. Only him, his mother, and his nephew, Michael deducted—his mental coinciding with his mother's rational. And Meissa, he added.

*****

The Sword

Nearly two months had come and gone since a single drop of rain had sprinkled Connecticut's hapless agriculture. It was almost as if for seven and a half weeks, the Lord totally forgot to water his Northern plants. In accordance, he was now, with a heavy hand, emptying the well in attempt to make up for the neglect.

The storm seemed to come out of nowhere. One minute, the night's sky was completely clear; and the next, there were long dark thunder clouds spread across the heavens as far as the eye could see. Utilizing the turbulent language of a strident drum, the storm cursed angrily down at the planet, brightening the sky with streaky bolts of static electricity and battering the open land with savage hurricane-like winds. Heavy rain, falling at a lively clip, soaked the placid area, flooding dirt road and muddying valued farm land into a matted slush.

All travel was stalled due to this storm. The persistent bullying winds were strong enough to kick over an adult man, and the lightning scorching the air was a fixed deterrent.

It was the crash of a ground-shattering thunder blast, booming like two mountains colliding, that finally rocked the Sword out of his pained, exhausted, and blood-deprived slumber. Remote blackness greeted by decrepit gray streaks now replaced his trauma-induced suspension of consciousness.

There was nothing for a while—only darkness and a faint lingered humming to confirm his ridged mortality. For an undetermined amount of time, the Sword lay motionless, suspended in naught.

Idly drifting in a feeble void, it felt like days, weeks, months, or longer. Then without warning, he felt a shudder—something physical. This was the first time he'd felt anything since he'd waken. It was like the nerves in his body suddenly blinked to life. Fighting, he could feel his five senses pulsating, trying not to come back online. His hearing was the first to make the jump.

Slowly, as his vitals continued to flicker, the bleary humming that first accompanied him from the abyss was now replaced by a constant dribbling of plush raindrops beating against the surface of the earth. Dramatically and way too often, loud blasts of irate thunder eruptions would break, causing the Sword's fragile tenor to jolt.

Ever so seldom, when the crashing of the wind eased and the falling cloud water calmed a bit, Michael "the Sword" Townsman could faintly hear a shy rhythmic song or some kind of melody being played in the background. Concentrating, he desperately tried to place an authorship to the familiar song; but then interrupting, the noisy storm would kick up, and he'd lose his train of thought.

The next ability to return to him was his sense of touch. This potent capacity frightened him, as it just seemed to snap. Panicked, he suddenly could feel something prickling or nibbling his face, neck, and on down to his chest. With immediacy, Michael called for his body to mount a defense; but unresponsive, he lay desolate, unable to resist whatever assault the unfamed creature had in store.

It took him a nice long hysteric second, but eventually he realized that it wasn't something nibbling at him at all. There was no pain, scrapes, or tears—just a soothing caress. Something was being dragged against him—a cloth of some kind.

Someone was wiping something off him or smearing something on. Then just as suddenly as it began, the smearing ended. Without warning, he felt his body rock from the difference in weight distribution as whoever it was picked up.

He realized he was on a bed or a sofa of sort. This brightened his spirits. He'd been found. He reasoned his grandmother had saved him as the memory of his last conscious moments played in his head. This reflection brought back the realization that he had been shot, and now a stinging pain was rippling through his upper body.

Wow. The stinging in his shoulder was bringing him back. The more he thought about it, the more it hurt. He would have screamed out, but he hadn't yet regained that ability.

Suppressing the pain, the Sword told his mind to order his torso to lift up off the bed. However, either he didn't have the strength to perform such a task or his base was simply ignoring his commands, because lying unmoved, he didn't feel like his body even made the attempt. Maybe he was paralyzed or in some kind of shock-imposed coma. Nothing was working at the moment. He couldn't move, talk, or even open his eyes. All he could do was wait and wait, and eventually he waited himself back to sleep.

Coming to, the Sword was quickly reminded of his predicament by his shoulder. This was no coma, the pain assured. And though he was still not fully roused, he could tell he was less drowsy.

Now not-so-little Michael assumed he was home, but where exactly, and how much time had passed? What was his grandmother thinking? What if she contacted the sheriff? Surely his aberrant wounds would be traced back to the valley. There were too many unanswered questions. The Sword was beginning to stew.

Suffering in the dark wasn't cutting it. He noticed there was no movement in the shadow behind his eyelids. Concentrating his facial muscles, he pried them apart. At first, everything was still dark, but then shapes began to form, and eventually colors were added. He was lying on his back; with his head propped up, he could see straight ahead. There was a bright flickering in the room. The fireplace was ablaze. The yellow flames were mesmerizing. He realized he was in his bedroom—his bed!

He was becoming more and more aware of the shadowy figures in the room. Focusing, he made out Lady (the maid) and his dearest grandmother, sitting at the table in his room. The sight of the old woman brought tears to his eyes. His grandmother—she had saved him. She was his guardian angel.

It took him a minute to get a handle on his unstable emotions. His grandmother was sitting at the table eating from a large platter that was filled from edge to edge. Eyeing her plate, Michael was suddenly aware of how hungry he was. His sense of smell had arisen apparently, accompanied by his ability to taste—the way his mouth was watering.

His eyes were perfectly focused now, and he could feel himself breathing—the air dragging in and out of his nose. He watched Lady fill his grandmother's glass before walking out the room. Michael was glad she was gone. He only wanted his grandmother in the room when he made himself available.

Mrs. Townsman was humming. This was the familiar melody he was helplessly deliberating. She was staring right at him, but he hadn't yet moved, and his eyes were so low that he was sure they still appeared to be shut.

Experimenting, he felt his lips move. Then opening his mouth, he exercised his jaw. He was sure he was ready; he could speak. Still testing his abilities, he opened and closed his hands and wiggled his toes. He wasn't paralyzed, just stiff.

Michael watched his grandmother for a bit longer. Knife in one hand, fork in the other, she ate slowly but steadily. Michael was certain she'd spit her wine when he surprised her with his voice. The thought was enough to bring a weak smile to his detached face.

His first attempt came out with less effectiveness than a hard breath. Then letting the momentum build in his chest, he squealed, "Grandma!"

Looking up from her plate, his grandmother shot him an annoyed glare. Then ignoring, she went back to her meal.

Did she even hear me? Michael pondered. "Grandma," Michael tried again.

And again, his grandmother looked up at him; but this time, she held her glare for a long menacing moment, looking as if she was about to say something. But turning away, she picked up her glass and took a small sip.

"Grandma!"

"I hear you, Michael," she dismissively spat. And for nearly a minute, the two just stared back and forth at each other.

Damn, Michael processed, *she is mad.* Looking down around his grandmother's plate, he noticed she had all four of his father's black handguns laid out on the table. How could he have missed them before? The large pistols were so thick they towered above her platter like adults surrounding a small child. *Guns on the dining table. She is so dramatic,* Michael mused.

Michael, "the Sword," did not feel like having this out with her right now. But, of course, she'd have the evidence laid out before him with no chance of him avoiding it. She was probably sitting in that chair the whole time he was out, waiting to confront him. Why couldn't he have a regular grandmother? One who would simply be glad he was alive. No, she was going to begin her scolding immediately.

Fresh out of a coma, Michael prepared himself for another battle. Closing his eyes, the Sword took a deep breath. Letting it out slowly, exhaling from his mouth, he began, "I'm hungry."

"I bet you are," his grandmother shot back. "What were you doing out there, Michael?"

The Sword, so bold in battle, fearfully held his tongue.

Mrs. Townsman continued, "Dressed like a homeless drunk. Wearing your father's guns—four guns, Michael. What…how did you get yourself shot?"

"Grandma, I… My arm hurts."

"Boy, you better tell me what happened before I come over there and punch you in that bandage."

This got a smile out of Michael. It was just like his grandmother to still be threatening him on his deathbed. *She is so rapscallion,* he joked to himself.

"Michael, did you hear me?"

"Yes, Grandma. Can I tell you after I eat?"

"No. You can tell me now."

"Can I at least have something for the pain?"

"Dr. Usly is in the back room, stranded here by the storm. I will let him know you're awake after you tell me what happened."

Dr. Usly was a good friend of his uncle Michael. He was one of the only doctors who treated both black and white patients. His uncle Michael set him up with a nice two-story building for his practice.

Michael, "the Sword," was in a lot of discomfort, and he needed something to alleviate the pain real bad. But he was sure his grandmother would let him pass out, wake up, and pass out again before she'd allow him to avoid this interrogation.

"Michael!" she animated.

"They were burning him, Grandma. I just couldn't just walk away this time."

Mrs. Townsman gave him a hard look, but weirdly, he could see a slight hint of intrigue behind her youthful blue eyes.

"They were burning who?" Mrs. Townsman further inquired.

"I don't know. He was black, and he was not the first. I've personally witnessed them doing this a half-dozen times before," Michael embellished.

Mrs. Townsman began shaking her head. "No, Michael, this... This is not the path we set for you. We've sacrificed too much. Your uncle, your father...your mother, me—we've all sacrificed too much for you to be risking your life out here," Mrs. Townsman implored. She had an idea of what had happened, but hearing him admit it was demoralizing to her. Her grandbaby was not supposed to be following in his uncle's footsteps. This was not his war to fight.

"They had him strung up, firing shotgun shells into his burning body."

"You were supposed to be a teacher, a minister, a lawyer even, a doctor—anything. You are not a freedom fighter!" she screamed in frustration. Then quelling her emotions, she walked over to the door and locked it. "Where, Michael?" she asked as she turned around.

"In a field."

"What field?"

"It's this big hole in the ground in the middle of the forest."

Michael told his grandmother the entire story—from when he found the dead man whose pants he stole to him letting the one woman and child go.

"I killed them," Michael admitted. "I killed them all." The fallout of his immoral deeds was now weighing heavily on his heart.

His grandmother's face did not waver.

"I could not let that... I could not let this continue," Michael, choking on his words, emotionally admitted.

"No, you could not," Mrs. Townsman agreed. This caught the Sword off guard. Mrs. Townsman pushed on, "You're a Townsman. It's in your blood to fight. You are a strong black man, and what you did took courage. I think you're exaggerating your number a bit." Mrs. Townsman smiled. "You couldn't shoot twenty cans off a fence."

"Grandma, you know I let you win."

"Boy, you didn't let me do nothing."

Michael smiled. "I won't stop."

"I know. That's in your blood also. But if this is to be your path, there's someone I want you to meet."

Book 2, *A Bad Black Man*, is coming soon.

ABOUT THE AUTHOR

Not married but not single, open-minded yet traditionally grounded, God-fearing but still not overly religious, Michael Massey is an eighties baby humbly raised in the city of New Haven, Connecticut. A true patriot and father of two, he began writing because he felt strongly that the world shouldn't be deprived the chance to share in the vivid movie-like dreams that he had reverberating inside his head. A Good White Woman is his first publication—but far from his last.

CPSIA information can be obtained
at www.ICGtesting.com
Printed in the USA
FSHW010615120321
79363FS